MARKED IN SECRET

This is a work of fiction. While some places, historical references, and traditions are based on fact, characters and other events in the story are created entirely from the author's imagination.

MARKED IN SECRET

Copyright © 2013 by Cynthia H. Paul

All rights reserved. This book or any portion thereof may not be reproduced or used in any manner whatsoever without the express written permission of the author except for the use of brief quotations in a book review.

Published by CreateSpace

First printing, 2015

ISBN 13 978 1515161523

ISBN 10 1515161528

MARKED IN SECRET

Anna's Journey

A Novel

Cynthia Paul

A Note of Acknowledgement & Appreciation…

For my mother's wonderful and interesting Mennonite relatives, from whom grew my strong roots and sense of place…

To Ed, Theresa, and Steve, for time spent editing, for insights, and encouragement…

To all the willing readers who graciously encouraged and critiqued the novel in its infancy; and Lori, who would not allow this book to become a dusty memory.

~

Dedication

Carole, Paul, and John ... with love

"...most men lead lives of quiet desperation and go to the grave with the song still in them."

Henry David Thoreau, Civil Disobedience

~

Journal Entry of Anna M. Moyer

October 1, 2013

The way I see it, only a few of us are born for greatness. The rest of us live ordinary lives harboring extraordinary dreams. I guess I have been one of those dreamers whose life appears so ordinary, but, oh the dreams and the secrets I have kept protected in the deepest part of me. Since I love fancy words, I will say I categorize myself as an enigma, or in plain language, a baffling person. My life has raised a lot of eyebrows as well as questions.

Regarding my mortal parts, well, they have been functioning for sixty-five years, and that is somewhat astounding. How did it come about that I now have fewer years ahead than behind? My heart has been beating a long time and has not let me down. My mind sees fit to have some closure on certain things in my *past.* *I've led what seemed a rather commonplace life, a disguise concealing the true one, which has been far from ordinary. My earthly commencement is quite a story, I truthfully admit, and it's a handful to swallow and digest. In a hazy memory, I hear Great Grandmother Moyer with her strong Pennsylvania German dialect spouting an adage for every occasion. She was a great one for "letting sleeping dogs lie" which I did not understand until I was older. Now I think back on my life more often and I wonder… do I have the nerve to awaken the hidden beast? I hesitate.*

My teenage years through early twenties were devoted to an obsessive search to uncover who I was, and this was often a confusing and fearful quest, driven by the need for answers, which, by the way, finally erupted like a boiling pot, spewing everywhere. It took time but eventually the hurt that followed brought on a strengthening inside me; I know that now. Still, we Moyers guarded our secrets. Let the sleeping dog lie or rouse the beast? Could my singular life have any good thing to offer a reader? Will I invoke scorn from my church community?

So, my choices are before me: dust off my story and place it front and center in the guest parlor for all to see, or let it remain my unsung song. For the most part my life was not a page-turning thriller, but it carried its thread of mystery. It evolved mostly around the lives of two women, my mother and me. We were the central characters and, of course, our loved ones were our supporting cast. The family secrets, decades' worth, have never been brought to light either by voice or pen, not even to extended family outside my little brick farmhouse.

Is it time to share my story or leave it untold? Door A or Door B? It is time to make a choice. Behind Door A is the never before shared version of my life, kept locked in the far recesses of memory. Door B opens to the airing of the house, windows and doors wide, inviting all to enter in and view the contents. It is a gutsy move, a vulnerable choice. Closed, Door A shields its contents to anonymity, the mediocre safe road. Door B throws itself wide. It prompts me to give it a try, write it all out come what may, whether to rejection, disappointment, or the chance that someone may benefit from the telling.

The audience in my mind chants in support of Door B. At this point our legendary gameshow host would have said, "Anna Mae Moyer! Come on down! You're a contestant on The Time is Right!" Okay, Anna, up and out of your seat. Make the choice or forever hold your peace.

At my age what do I have to lose? Door B it is. I do not want to go to my grave with the song of who I am trapped within me. It's time.

~

ONE

My mother cried. She cried as she loved me and rocked me at night. Her tears fell into my dark tightly curled hair. No one had arms like my mother, so soft and so white. After a while I thought less and less of her tears, so often they flowed. Some mothers are yellers, mine was a crier and I would choose the second over the first any day.

"Anna, my little girl, my precious child…"

There was nothing but love in her sadness. She would rock me with her body, often.

Once I saw my mother's hair when she removed the pins. It was wondrous, a soft brown with gentle, pretty waves. She brushed it over and over as I watched, mesmerized, while my skin goose-bumped and tingling chills radiated from my scalp down my arms. Before that, I'd only seen the soft smooth waves braided down her back at night or wound tightly under her white starched prayer cap.

"Anna, my child, what will come of us?" or "Anna, how did this happen?" or "Oh my poor dear Anna." The repetition became etched in my mind, so often I heard it. I did not even wonder at her words, let alone her tears which fell on my arms and left wet stains on my shoulders. Those tears were a part of our life. I was very alone in my mother's sorrow, as alone as she was herself. Her sadness never turned to meanness but it turned us both inward, two souls clinging to the vine of mutual need.

~

We were a quiet, peaceful family surrounded by community, family, and friends of like-minded Believers who chose to live pure lives following the Holy Book. Men who chose sturdy wives to raise large families, who worked the rich land since their emigration from the German Rhineland hundreds of years past, these people were my people. Pennsylvania *Deutsch* Mennonites clustered in valleys coursing like veins through the state of Ohio. The first Moyers settled in Hemlock Creek, so named for obvious reasons, though we boast of three unrelated creeks that ramble through our surrounding acreage. Daily our eyes viewed a vista created for a painter, with softly undulating hills and a greenish gold palette of fields bordered in a patchwork of ancient hedgerows and rambling old oaks.

Some two hundred years have passed since my ancestors retired their Conestoga wagons into their German Bank Barns and ceased their westward push. Now Hemlock Creek is a good-sized town surrounded by meticulously tilled rows of deep rich brown soil. We were a God-favored group of people, or so Great Grandma Moyer used to say. This was the world into which I was born in the year 1948.

The land was set geographically so as to have every advantage of the seasons, a perfect balance between all four. Year upon year nature graciously yielded its strength into our soil creating abundant crops. My father and uncles were straight and strong while their women were rosy and plump. People were recovering from the world's second war that came on the heels of its predecessor. From every little burg across this land, folks put new tombstones on fresh mounds next to the ancestors and retired empty kitchen chairs to the attic. Then the tears of grief and anger were dried and faces turned upward to stare a bright new future squarely in its industrial face. As hard working farm families we were frugal and self-contained. There was limited involvement with outside worldly influences. Little was needed since our church community was our social world. Oh, there were the down-and-outers, society's peripheral men wandering here and there, belongings in a sack, asking only for a bite to eat or a place to sleep in the outbuildings. After all, we lived near a major rail line. But for the most part, by choice, our community was secure and closed off from the ways and people of the world. The living of a life was centered in family and faith, land and work.

My family, the family of Jacob Moyer, had a modest six room brick two-story, a no frills abode as was becoming a humble Mennonite family. The barn and the lands were my father's domain over which he presided with the authority of a baron. My extended family was a large one with many aunts, uncles, greats, grands, and, of course, the cousins numbered as firsts, seconds, and thirds. But no brother or sister for me, as if I broke my mother with my birth.

Often I played with my cousins, many of which were close to my own age. We lived in adjoining acres, the cornrows our playground, the hedgerows our boundaries, the creeks our pastime. After hours of summer play we would run to an auntie's house for a cold drink and a breather under the shade of a massive tree with its billowing canopy that reached over the house. Then my cousins and I would plop down, smooth out our cotton skirts, and settle in for one of our favorite pastimes, clapping rhymes. We knew at least fifteen rhymes to go with the hand clapping. There were crisscross claps, lap, chest, and thigh claps and every combination imaginable. Fair, blond Cousin Esther and I became quite adroit. Palms, clap, crisscross palms, clap…thigh slap, clap…Miss Mary Mack…black…our palms clap, palms that match, fair and red from the slapping which always grew in intensity. We fed off each other's laughter as silliness overtook and our hands flew randomly. There was something mesmerizing about watching Esther's face, her mouth a mirror image of mine as we chanted in tandem.

Summertime dusk ushered in our favorite thriller, running to find hiding places in the semi-darkness while Cousin Abram counted. Our unrelenting seeker would open the creaking wooden door to find my dark eyes peering out from the cold springhouse, my heart pounding. Maybe he heard my teeth chattering, so chilled was my burrow. He'd laugh and then he'd always say, *Anna, you're the hardest to find.* How easily we laughed when we were children. There was no frantic chasing of time as the warm days sped by; summer lasted ever so long in our childish perception.

I knew the year Cousin Abram was too old to play. He laughed us off as we chided him for becoming so serious. "I have things to do and I only have so much time," he stated with the voice of an old man. We knew then. Things would change somehow. And sorry we were, for Abram was such fun. He always made me laugh, being older and yet still of an age to enjoy games, especially our evening hide 'n seeks. I must have been very good at hiding in the same place. It was a cool, moist spot, our springhouse, with crocks of butter and brown eggs in storage. It smelled like the cave we found in a rock outcropping on Abram's farm. When embraced in its moist darkness, I became a little wild rabbit hiding in the cool hole of a fallen tree trunk, the exposed roots shielding me from predators. Then, as my cousin inevitably stepped aside inviting my escape, I'd bolt, initiating the chase, and run like fury back to the safety of home base, the porch, without feeling the touch that meant I was now *the chaser.* Panting and laughing, with sweaty hair plastered on grimy faces that drew mosquitoes, we'd claim the porch swing, if no adults did first. There my cousins and I would lull in its rhythm as we listened to the creak of the chains and the summer night sounds of the crickets, the adults inside chuckling over some story they had probably heard before, while cups clanked on saucers, and spoons scraped clean the last of the pie.

~

Anna, my poor little daughter, Mama would cry as the moon filtered through the white muslin curtains, her soft face illumined as she would hug me to herself before I'd scoot under the quilt. By the compassionate age of seven I wished to say, "Mama, my poor little Mama," and hold her in my pudgy strong arms. To protect her was a role reversal that emerged around this time, whereas I felt the need to shelter her fragileness and to chase away the ever current tears. Even at this age in my young life, I saw a marked difference between my aunts, grandmas and this bird-like woman who brought me into this world. No one spoke ill of her that I ever heard, but she was treated as a fine china cup, held daintily, and stored in dark places with care. She never entered the barn and did not perform the usual outdoor chores, other than hanging wash from the rope between the two oak trees. She was clean, so very clean, her aprons like fresh snow. I instinctively grasped a vague notion that my purpose in life was to help and care for her, and I took that mantle of responsibility in childlike earnest. Life would have been far too quiet for a healthy, imaginative little girl like me if not for my cousins. The closest playful side Mama ever showed me was swinging on the porch swing as she discerned animal shapes in the cottony clouds.

~

"Anna Mae, see to your mother while I do business in town."

Of course, Papa, I always do. He took one last look at the two of us and headed out the door. Mama continued to work on her hand-stitching, which was the one thing she loved and could do by the hour. She would ask me to sing.

"What would you like to hear, Mama?" although I already had an idea. Mama did not have a large selection of favorites. She would think a moment before replying, her blue eyes never wandering from her stitches.

"*Nothing but the Blood of Jesus,*" she replied.

It was her inevitable choice. I humored her as her hands danced to a rhythm with needle and thread over her fabric, singing the old gospel hymn because any song was better than none. *What can wash away my sin? Nothing but the blood of Jesus...* I would watch and sing until inactivity made my legs twitch. Still Mama sat and stitched. Me, I was ready to run over to Cousin Esther's, but Papa's admonition kept me glued to the kitchen chair.

Childhood passed in a rather ordinary way with ordinary milestones such as chicken pox, mumps and measles, all lumped in with learning to ride a bike and advancing from board books to picture books to chapter books. My May birthdays were celebrated by the increase of a candle on my favorite applesauce cake, but little else. Every summer the Moyers or Lapps met from as far away as southern Pennsylvania to reunite in a bond of bloodline unity. How we all looked forward to those reunions. I loved the natural way we all joined in singing favorite old time ditties and hymns, since singing was not given much attention at home or in church.

With a sigh of remorse, summer would transition into the inevitability of autumn. A new teacher would start strong and enthusiastic, but after our cherished seventy-five day mental hiatus we were hard pressed to stop looking out the classroom windows, our minds wandering back to carefree days of unshackled freedom.

~

The farm carried on as usual, following the seasons and meshing into my school years. Quickly they passed, like infancy, those innocent endless hours of childhood. Cousin Abram, now tall and lanky with a handsome appearance, was five years my senior and a close second cousin. He now had the lean face and supple build of a man and Papa hired him as his second-in-command on the farm. Inside our plain brick farmhouse Mama made my dresses, skirts, and jumpers of floral print in the summer and wool in the winter. There must have been a well-hidden flamboyant side to my mother which sneaked out through her fingers as she sewed. She embellished my collars with tatted lace and taught me to double the thread as I secured pretty buttons and outlined button holes. In stark contrast her clothes had no such thing. She fastened her plain floral print Mennonite dresses with the most inconspicuous of "hooks and eyes". Cousin Esther dressed plainly from childhood into her adult years, a prayer cap restraining her beautiful hair the color of sunflower petals. Sweet Cousin Esther. How she loved to finger my buttons. When I sported white ankle socks with a lacey trim edging the cuffs, she let slip a gasp of admirable envy. I was one of the family, but strangely different. By the time I was ten I was still a bit short for my age but showed evidence of a good healthy appetite. Mama no longer wore a prayer cap, her long graying hair a figure eight on the back of her head. My own hair, well, it defied description.

~

I loved the distant sound of the train as it passed through our little town. At night while lying awake staring at the moonlight threading its way through my white muslin curtains, I would hear the whistle, far away, as a muffled mournful sound. With each passing second it became louder and louder, the rising and diminishing rhythm of the pistons and the wheels on the rails heralding our connection with the rest of the world. I think Hemlock Creek was a desired jump-off stop for traveling men, the ones without roots. After all, Mennonites were populous in the area and a very caring group. Our mothers and grandmothers had the distinction of being excellent cooks and bakers. Combine compassion and a good meal and how could a hungry man pass up such an opportunity? Besides, one never knew if a stranger was an angel in disguise.

Once, Esther and Abram showed me the hobo markings on our barn door. These scratches were a language all their own. They just looked like marks carved by a child with a new pocket knife, or sign language fashioned with care by a native tribe on a cave wall. Abram knew these things and shared his knowledge continually, sometimes to my frustration. I liked to think I knew just as much as the next person, but these markings were a curiosity which clearly showed my lack of worldly education. He seemed to think that the one which resembled a sleeping face with a line slashed through the mouth meant "no food here but can sleep in barn". Well, anyone could figure that just by looking at it, I thought. Yet, curious to know the truth, I asked how he knew for sure and he said he learned it from one grizzled boxcar jumper who made frequent stops at their place.

"Ma always gives them a piece of bread since it's the Christian thing to do," he stated matter-of-factly.

It is? Here was something new, something to mull over. Hobos had never stopped at our place, not that I could recall. Yet, they *must* have. Here was the proof, clear before our eyes, right there on the fence. I looked inquisitively at the carved symbols and wondered what the four clusters meant. They spanned intermittently from barn door to nearby fence post. I ran a timorous finger across the gouged surface, wondering if Papa knew about these, but of *co*urse he must, so visible they were. Why hadn't he sanded them out? He was very particular about his buildings.

~

The car slowed down as I walked home from school. I never minded the walk home, about two miles. It was a spring day and I had stayed after closing bell to finish my seventh grade home economics project. I swung my books, held tightly together by a strap, and softly sang a tune from our chorus program that had stuck in my head all afternoon. There seemed to be some ruckus down the road. A loud car vibrated behind me, the volume increasing and I listened as I walked, aware of its rather slow approach. Thumping music and laughter grew louder and louder, assaulting my quiet little world inside my imagination. A glance over my shoulder registered a red and white shiny-chromed '57 Chevy. I only knew it was a Chevy because Cousin Abram was fixated with them and showed me the identifying emblem on the hood. But such things had no place in my twelve-year-old world and I quickly dismissed the noise, turning back into myself, earnestly trying not to step on any cracks in the sidewalk as I headed for the outskirts of town toward home. I gave no further thought to the loud car until it was keeping pace beside me.

"Hey there, pretty little black Jemina!" yelled a slurred male voice. He drew out each syllable so it sounded like Jah-my-ma.

Who was he yelling at?? I swiveled my head to see the pretty black Jemima. No one. I looked behind me following their line of vision and looked back, crinkling my forehead in wonder. The faces registered no familiarity, all distorted in raucous laughter, and heads hanging out the open windows like dogs. It would have been more of a surprise had I recognized or known them. Only cousins and church friends made up my small world. School acquaintances were left behind when the 3:30 departure bell rang. These boys looked to be about seventeen, and that was pretty old to me. What were they staring at me for?

"Hey! *Nigger Girl!*"

I flinched, recoiling at the vulgarity. Even a *goot Mennischt maedel* knew the degradation that word held, young as she might be, and I was a good Mennonite girl. My eyes connected with the jeering face in the passenger side front seat, dark hair blowing back from an angular face with a hint of beard just on the chin. He was doing something with his finger that felt like an insult, a violation. His arrogance frightened me, causing my insides to churn. It was so personal…directed at *me*. We are a peaceful people, as I had thought most humans were. The dark haired boy continued to find great humor in his strange gestures. *Dear Gott! He ... they ... just called ... me ... a what??* Suddenly, I felt sickly, like my head lost its balance. *Someone help me!*

I would not look back at them. My eyes stung and I blinked quickly, looking straight ahead. My heartbeat threatened to burst my veins.

I may as well have been punched hard in my stomach or shot with a pellet gun. *Don't look back, Anna, keep walking. Gott! Don't let them follow me. I can't stand hearing and seeing any more. Please don't let him say that to me again.* I broke into a run. *Don't go down, Anna. Run like you run so you don't get tagged.* Past Elm and Maple streets, keenly aware of the sound of that engine as it roared to life before tires squealed down Maple, off to my left. The sound of their laughter grew increasingly muffled. I had to slow down a bit to keep my chest from bursting open. Over and over I whipped my head to look behind.

Were they really yelling at me? What if they follow and see where I live? Oh, Jesus! Help Me! Unlike my dreams of running and not moving, I now seemed to defy gravity. This new and unjustifiable label repeated itself over and over with each pounding of my sneakers on the pavement. A million implications were becoming clear in a matter of seconds, baring my body for the world to see. A confusing piece of anatomical incongruities: nose, skin, mouth, hair. But, how could this be? I am Anna Mae Moyer!

I hafta get home. Are they coming? Keep running, running... Please, Gott, help me get home. Papa, I need you, Papa...

Houses got fewer and fewer as I raced down the road toward home, stumbling but fighting to stay upright, my strapped books whacking my leg, my mouth wide and lips dry as I gasped for every available lung-full of oxygen. My legs felt as jiggly as Mama's molded gelatin, so limp and useless. I thought I would explode, yet on I ran propelled by fear.

My skin, so much more tanned than my cousins. *Run, Anna.* And my hair, it certainly felt different than theirs. *Keep running, Anna.* Mama and Cousin Esther with hair the color of silk in the sweet butter corn. I knew mine was not at all like theirs. *Keep going!* Mirrors were a vanity, yet my reflection in the teapot never gave me cause to think myself so different. *I don't know if I can run anymore, but I must!*

It was at least a mile from town to home. I had yet to cover the half. Every car I heard coming from behind rendered a new strength within me to keep going as a crazy painful side cramp hindered my breathing. My arm clutched around my waist. I stumbled over a stone, but did not fall. There was no sound of a motor behind me, but I dared not stop or even look over my shoulder for fear. Our pasture fence came into view, the hay field, thank God. Past the lilac tree. Home appeared like a vision of heaven. I did not stop until I threw open the screen door and sidled away from the opening. I listened for the car, for voices yelling as my heart pounded out of control and my lungs hungrily drew in great gulps of air.

Sweat poured down my face, and I couldn't even see for the burning in my eyes. I flung aside my books, still intact in their strap, before collapsing into a heap on the braided rug. My world had fallen in on itself. As with a single drop of brown dye in a large container of clear water, my life became marbleized and the sudden clarity of the truth about myself left me dazed and weakened ... the world around me was light. I was dark. Gone in a moment's time was the illusion that we were all the same. I felt as if I had run right out of my old life and now faced something new and threatening. So much for being all one, all the same in Christ, and all being sons and daughters of *Gott* through our faith. That was a truth I had to re-learn as later years healed me.

"Anna!" My mother yelled my name, her face ghostly white as she rushed toward me. "What's happened?" Could I ever tell her? "What's happened?" she frantically repeated, throwing her sewing behind her. She must have heard my feet charging up the porch steps and into the house. I guess I hadn't needed to say a thing. She got right down on the floor with me, her lovely face distorted with my pain. Every day her blue eyes searched my dark ones as I returned from school. She was just waiting, biding time. For what I did not know, until now.

If I hadn't had to complete that *schtupid* sewing project I would not have been alone for the long walk. Now that I think back on it, cooking and sewing were inbred in every Mennonite girl. Why did the school hire someone to teach what our mothers already taught us? We should have all received perfect grades, every Alderfer, Yoder, Lapp, Detwiler, or Moyer girl. Then I would not have been walking home alone. I would have been spared the verbal attack that pierced through my perceived reality, my very identity.

Those "should haves and would haves" came to me in moments of retrospection, such as right now, and believe me, they never do a body any good.

~

Out of the blue you are living life, minding your own business, when you inadvertently bump into something breakable, and suddenly the loud speaker announces a call for clean-up in your aisle. This call came through without any loud speaker. A silent communication. My heaving sobs betrayed me. Mama, the fragile one, was there to help with the clean-up of my emotional mess. The inevitable had finally happened. She held me at arm's length, assessing the damage as her fearful blue eyes bore into mine. Then, with still no words exchanged, she wrapped me within herself, her thin white arms encasing me. She rocked me there on the floor. We rocked. And rocked.

"*Mei little maedel…*" I didn't care that to her I was still "her little girl." If not for my size I would have curled up right there in her boney little lap, protected and loved while I cried my eyes dry. The wound was very deep but not a mortal one. The scar would be jagged and nasty but I would live, even with this rather large chunk of my innocence cut right out of me.

TWO

We Mennonites, *Mennischt* in our own tongue, are a cookie cutter bunch. Every year at the family reunions, I was surrounded by blue, black and white clothing, with the occasional splash of print from worldly relatives in standard non-Mennonite attire. The women's and girls' heads were covered with white mesh prayer caps, all identical, or the wrinkled faces were minimally seen behind large-rimmed cotton bonnets. We believe we are all the same in the sight of God and one must not make oneself stand out in any way. Sameness promotes humility and this is the basis of our relationship with God and with others. We are not as strict in our dress as the *Amisch*, but still, we share the similar patterns. Frills like lace, buttons, zippers and the like were conspicuous in their absence. If you happened to be in a different order, the expectations varied. My cousins Eva, Mariah, and Molly, of the Brethren order, had lovely dresses and lacy collars and cuffs. Cousin Abram was allowed to wear buttons, whereas my aunts and uncles dressed in the plain order. Mama was plain but I was not. A confusing anomaly, for sure. It seemed as if, here in 1961, we stood at a crossroads as to what was outwardly considered acceptable. The Mennonites were changing ever so slightly with the times.

~

"Well, look who it is!" a girlish voice said as a finger tapped my shoulder. Amidst the rumble of greetings and laughter, I recognized that voice. I smiled as I turned toward my first cousin, Lydia, and we embraced, an awkward arm around shoulder, head to head, but not touching much else since we were not little girls anymore. Lydia's side of the family lived in the next county over and we visited maybe twice in a year's time. Though all related through a singular ancestry, there were so many unfamiliar faces, but the garb and the female prayer caps were a commonality. Well, mostly.

We had arrived at the large picnic grove across from the meeting house. I had been standing by my parents, very unsure of myself. Who was I really? Were people staring at me? I watched the ground as my shoe teased a stone. Was I really so different? I had looked for cousins, but not very hard. Shame felt like an uncomfortable garment. I did not wear my button-up blouse but opted for a pull-over that hung like a sack over my simple A-line skirt. Many around me were barefooted, but the Moyer family did not consider this an option.

Lydia had spotted me first and her warm welcome, added to the fact she singled me out, allayed my fears of not fitting in. She had come across the grassy knoll, bare feet churning up a cloud of dandelion seeds that had pasted to her sturdy sweaty arms and legs. Lydia was not what anyone would call pretty but she was healthy and strong looking, her sunburnt cheeks glowing under laughing blue eyes. Her smile and sincere joy sent any insecurity from my mind and I heard myself laughing as she commented on how I'd grown. Lydia and I were of the same age, just entering our teen years, she being taller by a few inches. We linked arms and walked away from the picnic pavilion, chattering simultaneously as girls do. She was prattling on about winning a prize for her jams and something about her calf placing at the county fair. As I let her go on, my focus wandered.

Our arms. Our side-by-side arms. Why hadn't I noticed before? The difference was a stark reality to me now that my innocence had been wrenched from me. It caused a raw feeling. I slid my arm out of her crooked elbow, acting like a bug was pestering me. Lydia was too astute for my feigned nonchalance.

"What's wrong, Anna-kin?" she stopped to question, confused by my abrupt action. Anna-kin was her nickname for me. With Lydia, every cousin's name ended in –kin: Esther-kin, Jonah-kin, Katie-kin. I did not want to cry. Mama's tears wore me out and my own offered no relief. I shook my head, signifying there were no words to be said. *Just allow me time to snap out of my mood.* She had stopped her chatter and had taken me by the arms, bending her blond head slightly to catch my eyes. I blinked rapidly.

Too soon, four other cousins, whom we only saw at reunions, ran up to us, and Lydia dropped my arms to receive them. I had quelled the tide of my tears and no one noticed. After warm greetings we headed toward the pond, the six of us engrossed with one another. I held back for a moment, taking in the scene. Each was draped in a dress of blue or small calico print, light hair, most with the tight rolls on either side from a center part and then pulled severely back into two hanging braids or under a pure white mesh prayer cap. Only a dab of vegetable oil enabled me to force mine into a plait. It was easier to just let it go and keep it shorter. *Why?* The question buzzed like a swarm of honeybees inside my head. *Why am I different?*

We rejoined the large gathering of Moyers who seemed an ever-expanding network of marriage alliances. Did it just seem as if some aunts treated me with less familiarity? Mama looked miserable, but then that seemed to define who she was. Papa, whose family we were re-uniting with, was engulfed among a large group of men having a grand time. My cousins and I joined our respective family units as massive containers of food were being uncovered, filling two entire picnic tables. The bell had rung, summoning us to gather around. All stood clustered as an elder, great uncle so and so, offered up an extensive prayer to the Almighty. His deep voice quivered and shivered as he summoned the Good Lord for a blessing. Directly after the *A-men* left his lips, the boys were swarming around those laden picnic tables like flies in a barnyard. I forgot about myself as I was caught up in the feeding frenzy. No one can cook and bake better than *Mennischt* women. As a family of only three, we seated ourselves with my uncle's brood of seven, our red gingham tablecloth marking our territory. Out from large wicker baskets came plates wrapped in linen napkins, silverware, and cups for the many refills of lemonade and iced tea. My cousins, flanking both sides of the surrounding tables, were younger and it seemed they saw in their Cousin Anna no difference compared to anyone else, though an inquisitive little hand kept fingering my hair as it curled in abandonment at the nape of my neck. Conversation centered on crops and the year's milk production with the grunt of satisfaction over some tasty mouthful as a fork pointed to the exceptional fare. After gorging myself sufficiently and that sleepy relaxed sensation crept over me, I could tune out my surroundings, my mind rehashing the conversation, using that word loosely, that occurred between my parents and me about a month ago. Wounded I was, with no antidote to relieve my pain.

~

"Mama, am I adopted? Maybe I should not have been so abrupt, but I had been bursting to ask. Mama and I were folding our sun-dried clothing and linens, making piles on her bed with its bright rose and blue wedding ring quilt. The towels smelled fresh like her rose soap and I could not resist burying my face in the softest one. *Now or never, Anna.* The question was eating away in me, and it was the only deduction a thirteen year old mind could conceive. I hated making her cry so I had to be strong and brace against the inevitable tears. She surprised me by remaining quite level-headed about it. Had she expected the question to arise at some time?

Instead of the rush of emotion I had expected, she shook her head adamantly, shaking Papa's poor socks to every inch of their threads. "No, Anna. I gave birth to you. You belong to us." How could that be? I don't know much, but I knew that Jacob and Elizabeth did not add up to Anna Mae Moyer!

"But... Mama! *Look at me, Mama!*" I grabbed her arm and held mine next to it. "Mama! *How*...tell me *how*?"

It took only a second for my mother to crumble like a crushed bird. Oh, what had I done! She melted down onto the quilt, hands covering her face as she cried out, "I don't know, I don't know!" It was then I saw how quickly my mother was aging. Her hands were crisscrossed with protruding purple veins, her forehead no longer smooth. How could I get any answers from this fragile parchment?

"It's okay, Mama, don't cry," I patted her arm, unsure of what to do or say as I reverted into my old pattern of peacemaker and consoler. She straightened, breathed deeply, and swiped her fingers under her eyes. One last ragged breath and she turned to me, her gaze like a wounded animal. She began shaking her head as if palsied, a vehement *no*, or a *please, no more*. A graying brown tendril, so baby-fine, took on a life of its own as it sashayed back and forth.

"I don't know, Anna," she conceded one last time, her frenzy mode having sapped her energy. Thin veined hands fluttered in despair as I removed my handhold on her arm. The face I loved surrendered to her pain as it scrunched in agitation. "I was never with another man, Anna, you must believe that. Only your father. *Never another man!*" Her pale face looked savage in its rebuttal. Such a confession, stated that way with such force, blew wind right out of my sails. At thirteen I did not know much about the ways of men and women, but I knew enough.

"I never meant that, Mama, honest...." What *had* I meant then? Oh, I didn't know anything anymore. But I did, with growing apprehension, believe I understood why my mother cried. Did I affect her so? Was I the reason she cried? Without meaning to, had I made life hellish for her? I was a most somber girl that afternoon. We finished gathering the piles of clothing and towels and without conversation went about our chores. The silence lasted all evening until Mama went to bed early that night. Oddly, that silence fed my determination and bolstered up my need to address Papa.

I had no litmus test to show me the right time to approach my *vadder*, so distant was he, so I plunged right in shortly after. I knew Mama would have told him about my school incident. He was a good man, a hard worker, but not as much a part of my life. We ate together without conversation and he wished me a good night's sleep every evening. I assumed every father was more caught up in the farm than in the life of a child.

"Papa, I know Mama told you about, well, about what happened to me after school last spring." He stopped for a minute to think before affirming with a slight nod. His dark tanned skin was a welcomed sight to me and I pushed aside the temptation to do to his arm what I had done to my mother's. Was I so terribly different after all? No turning back now. There were unanswered questions.

"Well, Mama does not know why I am not like either of you, and I want to know if you know why I am not." What did I just say? It sounded *schtupid*. I sighed in agitation over my verbal fumbling. I was never one for eloquence, but neither were my parents. "Do you know what I am asking?" I pressed, tempted to hunch down on the floor to make eye contact with the man, seeing as I was talking to the top of his head.

I was met with silence. Was he going to answer? I felt I had never known such exasperation in one I loved.

"Please, Papa!" He jumped, ever so slightly, like his mind had wandered in a split second. "Please! I *need* to know." He sat up and looked at me then, cocked his head, his big work-worn hands on his thighs as he sat, trapped by my questions into an uncomfortable confrontation. His brown hair waved at the crown and, like a little boy's, fell slightly over his left eye. He looked away, patting his muscular thighs with wide-spread thick hands. Would he say anything?

His answer came haltingly. "You may *need* to know," he replied as he studied the view out the window, "but I have no answer for you, Anna." With a terse shake of his wooly head, his eyes scrunched shut, and his mouth formed a tight line. A cry of exasperation flew past his lips before he blurted out, "What do you want me to say?" He flung his arms up, hands out in a gesture of surrender. "You were just born the way you are. You are our daughter." He shook his head, once more, still avoiding my eyes, as his arms came to rest with both big hands slapping his knees. He was as frustrated as I was, but things could not end there.

"Are you my father?" I blurted out savagely. He jolted back in his chair. I may as well have hit him. Now he looked at me.

"*Goot Gott,* Anna Mae! Never, *never* ask such a thing *ever* again. *You hear me?*" While only a loud breathy whisper it roared with passion. His eyes pierced mine. He changed like weather in July. His eyes became like dark thunder clouds. Two beet red stains flushed the skin on each cheek and burnt his ears. The permeation of color was a little frightening, like watching a cork about to pop under great pressure. "You are our daughter, you are Anna Mae Moyer!" He stood suddenly, catching the chair as it started to fall backwards, and righting it, he lumbered past me, escaping to his open fields, his barn or the workshop. I sensed a rip in my heart, as if I did not mean that much to him. As if he desired his peace of mind over a daughter's need for truth. I fought tears by gritting my teeth.

I knew I would never ask that question of my father again, but it could not be erased from inside my brain. His back spoke volumes as I watched him through the muslin curtains which waved with the slight breeze like a call to surrender to a mightier force. With long purposeful strides, he made a beeline toward the small work shed attached to the right front of the barn. That stride made a statement so obvious to me: my papa had to get himself away. He had to get away from me, or maybe…away from himself.

~

Lydia once again sought me out as my aunts were placing dirty plates and silverware in their baskets and tidying up after the feast. The sun was setting on our reunion. I jumped when she plopped down on the picnic bench recently deserted by an antsy toddler. Mother looked over at us and smiled a very tired smile.

"Penny for yer thoughts," my cousin joked. "You looked very far away from us." She could never know how right she was about that.

~

Life went on uninterrupted. No more vicious slurs from passing cars, no more discoveries in my attempts to uncover the truth behind my dark self. But I felt a veil had lifted from my consciousness and I saw things more clearly. I saw how shop keepers looked at mother and me as we paid our infrequent visits into town. We walked together like silent friends, commenting every so often about a bird, or Deacon Gehman's flower garden. We would enter the village by way of the west end, head for the main street by going down Elm and crossing over. There were three stores Mother frequented, only three: Miss Arlene's fabric and notions shop, Mr. Widrig's hardware store, and Canady's butcher shop and food market. We purchased needed items without much conversation, carefully following her list. I carried the basket which held our purchases. It was hard going when Mama needed flour and sugar the same day.

Was I crazy or was there a decided reserve toward us? Other customers came and bantered in friendly terms like neighbors do. Not so with Mother. And there were little to no greetings for me personally from the town residents. Yet we had lived near the town of Hemlock Creek all my life. An unfamiliar emotion emerged inside me and I could feel it raising its ugly tentacles right through my head. How dare people judge us! How dare they think they know something about us! I could have sworn people had been friendlier toward us until that Chevy incident changed my entire outlook. Blissful ignorance may actually have some merit.

In the summer of '61, I was old enough to ride my bike into town, by myself, to visit the library, a two-story landmark solidly constructed of brick with colonial white paneled shutters and four front colonnades. The distinctive smell of boxwood rose from overgrown shrubbery as I settled my bike in the metal rack next to three others. I had come on a mission, searching for something I could not yet put into words.

Earlier that spring I had asked Mrs. Ledbeder, another solid town landmark with the distinction of having been librarian over thirty years, if I could have a library card. With that surge of independence, I became the only person in my family to have one. It was my key, that card. A key to unlock the world, maybe even unlock the mystery about myself. Certainly it was my key to adventures and knowledge far beyond what my 7th grade classroom could offer. There were several fascinating Civil War books, and some about slave and owner relationships. On my third visit I found a book about Sally Heming and her love affair with Thomas Jefferson. I checked it out, my cheeks on fire as I felt the scrutiny of good old Mrs. Ledbeder, who was a study in outfitting oneself with gusto. Today she looked cool and Polynesian in a huge floral print tent dress, her bare upper arms a tribute to youthful years long gone. She always smiled innocently enough but her memory was known to be like a bulging filing cabinet, chockfull of information she readily shared in the interest of our community. My library card went into my pocket, the book I hid in my satchel.

Later, hunkered alone in my little room, I devoured that fascinating biography late into the hot nights when sleeping was near impossible anyway. Could I have been the product of some way-back relationship like Thomas Jefferson and Sally had? That meant at least one parent would have carried the traits, and that looked highly unlikely. Both my parents were decidedly NOT like me. Nor did either set of my grandparents have the slightest hint of anything other than *"goot Deutsch"* blood. The more I studied books and the illustrations about slaves in America, the more I knew I resembled that group of people, from my wide nose to my full lips. In the 60s it was acceptable to be called "black people". The shocking word hurled at me on that pivotal October day had become a crass, insulting slang term. As much as a thirteen-year-old could seethe with anger, I did, and more so as I studied about injustices toward people of color, and how oppressed and brutalized they had been. As unaccustomed as I was to the emotion of anger, I was powerless to stave it off.

I had blown dust from a book by Mennonite historian, John Ruth, and had also checked it out to study at home. I learned of the Mennonite stance on slavery and how my pacifistic ancestors were the first to stand for abolition and the rights of all humanity. So that shot my theory of a past generation of slave holding Mennonites becoming too free with the females and raising the little indiscretion as their own. Besides, that would not have produced the likes of me through either parent. I just couldn't make it work. Who was I? Why was I? I *must* be adopted - it was the only rationale that worked.

By August I was into the 500s of Dewey's system of topical arrangement, specifically the shelves where the scientific books were placed. Genetics. That might help me. I studied pictures and the workings of the gene pool. I thought I came to the only feasible conclusion. Having studied myself clearly, I surmised I was a first generation *mulatto*, meaning my mother, if she *was* my biological mother, had relations with a black man. The word was new to me and sounded so foreign. Mulatto. Yet, how could that be? A whole new Pandora's Box of vipers and demons opened and infiltrated my mind: a Mennonite wife in an adulterous relationship with a man of color? How was it our church did not boot her *and* me right out its doors? Mother with another man. The very thought made me feel sick. No, please, God, show me another scenario! This just cannot be. Peaceable or not - there was such a thing as maintaining the right fellowship. Mennonites were so strong on that. Oh Mama! Would she ever open up to me? Mama? Not my delicate frail Mama! She must have known what was going on. Simple math placed her age at twenty-two and already married when I was conceived.

What of Papa? He knew something and was not telling me. An adult would have figured this out much sooner than

I was able. The whole thing consumed me. I decided what I needed to do. I had to make my mother confess about what happened. I would not give up until I knew about myself. Be hanged if we were all ostracized by church and family. It needed to come out. That day I did not take any books out. I just wanted to stomp through the ornate double doors, ignore Mrs. Ledbeder with her red fingernails and Hollywood smile, get on my bike and ride into the sunset, opposite from home.

~

I wasn't all about self-discovery that summer of 1961. I would tire of my mysterious birth and head over to Eva, Mariah, and Molly's place, about a mile away, where I could be a girl again, nothing more and nothing less. Just Cousin Anna. The Clemmens family was related somehow because the three girls were my cousins, but I guess they were seconds or thirds. They occupied a very old stone farmhouse with a wonderful summer kitchen attached to the right side of the main quarters. It was a large structure dating back to George Washington's day, and it was large enough to divide so grandparents could inhabit the other half. Those girls made me forget all about me and my miserable life. Their lives were fun and without worry or much responsibility. They were not allowed near the horses, or up in the trees, but could go for long walks and wade around the edges of the duck pond, providing the leeches were not too hungry. There was a remarkably pretty little brother, my youngest cousin David, who toddled after us babbling unintelligibly. Eva, the eldest, was in charge of his welfare but we all helped her in this responsibility. In age, I was between Mariah, the second oldest, and Molly, the youngest of the sisters, so I figure Eva was fifteen, Mariah fourteen and Molly twelve. My aunt was very proud of her beautiful girls, which alone caused a stir in the church fellowship. They were somewhat pampered, to use a phrase I heard from another aunt. As the family entered their meeting house on the Lord's Day morning, one would see plain-clothed Grandmother Clemmens and my Aunt Mariette, then the fancy dressed girls. Even little David wore little vests and shorts with cuffs. *Quite unconventional.*

Mennonite women accepted hard work or chores around the farm as a part of life. At four years of age I had been given chores which I carried out on a daily basis with nary a thought of neglecting them even just once. I worked the vegetable garden, and grew prize tomatoes and melons. My three pampered cousins were not to do any work the farm hands were hired to do and only had minimal chores inside the house. What a strange family! Pride was definitely a sinful trait, but they seemed oblivious to any such humility. The girls, especially Molly, were delectably vain without being obnoxious. Their recently purchased bedroom dressers had large mirrors attached, an oddity in my world. I found it was not easy to look at my reflection and I averted my eyes. If my cousins saw any differences in me, it was never mentioned. Maybe they did not notice any.

Maybe they did not care one way or the other. I was just Cousin Anna, plain and simple.

I became quite close to Molly the year I was thirteen. Being only twelve, she was like a sister to me. She was what the aunts called olive-complected. With her dark hair, though soft and baby fine, and her marble blue eyes, I thought her oh, so beautiful. I often found myself doing the "test" and would casually place my arm near hers to see the contrast. Though I was still darker, Molly and I weren't too many shades apart, causing me to feel a strange bond of commonality with her.

One hazy hot late August day as I was shoring myself for the return to school, Molly and I were enjoying a lazy hot afternoon together, mostly talking. We had finally discovered where the new litter of kittens had nested near the summer kitchen. A dusty haze filtered through the air as the hired workers were harvesting the corn. Eva and Mariah were indoors doing whatever older girls did. Little David must have been napping. The gray and white kitten, still so tiny, claimed my heart. I named it Perry. We had a mysterious great uncle by that name but mostly I liked the sound vibrating from its warm soft little body, like the purr of a far-off tractor motor. Molly and I were just chit-chatting about any and everything. A small engine airplane with its unique sound flew overhead and we watched as it dipped and turned. The kittens were cuddly but Molly was afraid hers would wet on her. We laughed thinking about such a thing before lapsing into a quiet mode.

Dare I? Was this a *goot* time? I would be venturing into uncharted waters. Oh, what had I to lose? After all, she was my cousin and bound by family and church to be honest with me.

"Molly, I am not the same as you and all our cousins, am I?"

Perry's nails stuck into my blouse right through to the skin on my neck. I squealed as I eased him off, aware of the burn of scratches. Molly glanced at my neck, screwed up her nose, then resumed her far-away look. She yawned and flicked a bug from her face.

"You are not so different, Cousin Anna. If anyone is different, I'd say it's Cousin Stella." She gave me a knowing look. It just figured she would bring up the family's poor little black sheep, the young girl who constantly bucked against our Fellowship's norms by running away with a train man. I refused to let Molly turn the subject to another, yet what was left unsaid spoke volumes.

She hadn't said, "How so?" or "What do you mean?" Her nonchalance in face of the question raised even more questions. She had tried to divert the conversation by fiddling with the blond kitten and bringing up Stella. Was she avoiding me?

"Do you think I am a ...." No, better not use that new word, that foreign one I had never heard before. "Do you think I may not be like a German Mennonite?" She sighed, like I was wearing on her.

"You are our Cousin Anna. That's what I know and all I need to know."

The kitten, tired of so much pampering, swiped a paw toward Molly's face, its bared talons razor sharp. She quickly dropped it and watched it scurry under the porch. My cousin sat upright and smoothed her light summer skirt with a delicate slender hand. I would not let her off so easy.

"Do people ... talk about me?"

"No." she replied in a clipped tone. "I never heard anyone talk about you." Her blue eyes held a defensive look. "They talk about Stella. Did you know she is..." On she went repeating things I did not need to hear. Once again she had changed the course. Boy, was she good.

I did not like this Molly so much. She had put me off, and sounded like an overly protective cousin. One thing was clear - she was not being forthright with me. I could tell by her eyes.

Perry jumped down and scampered to join his siblings. I was aware of my loneliness even though I was not alone. Molly unbent herself and stood, stretching her arms to the sky. "Your scratches are bleeding," she mentioned, pointing to my blouse collar. "We'd better wash them off." Our moment ended. Oh, I loved my cousins all right, but that did not change my inner turmoil much. They were pure-blooded *goot Deutsch* girls, pride factors and all.

I had made little progress finding answers to my questions this summer. School would resume soon and I was losing sleep. My body was also changing in annoyingly bothersome ways. Now the passing months became a sort of calendar only understood by another female.

My hardest challenge of all was still looming like Mt. Olympus before me. I had yet to face my goal of winning Mother into my confidence. *Good Luck, Anna.*

THREE

I was in the dry goods store waiting on Mama's order of cotton. Our household had been in the throes of one of Mama's complete cleaning frenzies. It did not even need to be spring when the mood came upon her, indiscriminate and all-encompassing. She attacked every corner, every crevice in every room with an untypical energy. Last week she had been determined to make new bed sheets. To ensure her desire she stripped her and Papa's bed and cut the white cloth into squares for, and this she whispered in my ear, "female monthlys". As I reflect back on my mother's drastic mood swings, I see with clarity the label she would now have on her medical chart. But then, in the 1960s, this was just part of my life and doctors were not. Papa did not scold or chastise Mama for these energetic outbursts and the unforeseen changes it brought into our home, such was the great patience he showed regarding his fine "china cup". Yet, he was not in the home much, eking out our existence in the fields with no sons to work by his side. Just me, a changeling who would never turn into a swan.

Last year, when I was yet twelve and the green leaves of summer were burning themselves to orange and gold, Mama burned her clothes. That was also the summer the prayer caps disappeared. Maybe they went up in the conflagration of flames also, I don't know. The relatives were treading lightly in our presence, saying little and visiting even less. I at least had my bicycle to help me flee the roller coaster of ups and downs. Last year - clothes, this year - sheets. What would be the sacrificial offering next year?

~

Miss Arlene was sole proprietor and owner of my favorite store, the fabric and dry goods shop, where the middle-aged *Mennischt* woman presided over sales and merchandise with an unusually keen sense of business. She was a Schwartz. Her family made use of their farm by launching a dairy treat drive-in in the summer and then a year-round dairy store. They were able to outfit their unwed daughter with the store of her dreams, and I must say, Miss Arlene had an amazing eye for interior design. What an acceptable married Mennonite woman could not do to her home (pride factors), Miss Arlene displayed in abandon. Her creative touch could be seen in the ruffled Cape Cod curtains, the framed "artwork" from magazine pictures, and all shades of paint and wall murals. Bolts of fabric, every color and print and texture imaginable, stood at attention in neat rows, willing soldiers ready to fall on the field of quilted dreams. Women from every denomination and walk of life flocked to Miss Arlene's, mouths agape, eyeing each and every newly displayed object, more than ready to open wide their leather Buxton wallets. Local antiques from neighborhood auctions lent a charming, cozy touch, each bearing a modest price tag. Miss Arlene spanned the bridge from Mennonite entrepreneurship to the world outside with all the passion and gusto of her calling, outfitting her world with just the right patterns, fabric, plus a complete array of notions. *And*, of course, all the local news one could wish to hear, and more.

During this short period of calm in Miss Arlene's busy day, I being her only customer, she took the opportunity to park her thin pencil-straight body on a tall stool, measuring out my mother's order of white cotton for the new sheets, while she rested her black stockinged legs. The hair around her forehead had thinned considerably from years of unrelenting domestication into the standard Mennonite bun. Now she had freed her hold on it. At first it didn't know how to respond to this kindness, but now it was curling softly and anemically around her forehead. She would have made a *goot* wife. I wondered why she never married.

I was looking everything over. A newly framed picture was centered above the thread rack. It was a curious and intriguing print.

"Miss Arlene? What's this picture about?"

She looked over, following my gaze, and laughed. I liked how easily she did that because I was not accustomed to much in the way of laughter, not at home anyway.

"Ahhh! My new Rockwell print. Do you like it?"

"I guess so," I responded hesitantly, as I did not really understand what I was seeing, but I liked the faces.

"I found that in an old October issue, 1959 Saturday Evening Post," she chuckled. "Norman Rockwell is the artist, from New England, you know," she added, waving her shears above her head as if north is always up in the air. "He's quite popular just now. He draws down-to-earth things that people can relate to."

The print showed a large leafy tree with different faces, male and female, paired up along the branches. At the very bottom was a dark and exotic pirate couple. At the very tip-top of the tree was a little red-haired boy with a cute grin. I followed the progression of faces from old world to modern.

"Does it mean something?" I walked closer, craning my neck upward while leaning carefully against the thread rack.

"Well, it shows a family line and how the family started with the two at the bottom. Look how far back the little boy got his red head of hair." I squinted and found the source of that red head about five generations before when a guy in a tricorn hat, son of a pirate, paired with a red-haired, fair-skinned Irish girl.

"It's fun to see how the family traits pop up so far along in the generations," Miss Arlene said as she carefully guided a huge pair of black handled scissors along a metal cutting edge. The crisp white cotton looked exactly like the old sheets that Mother had lopped into strips. I thought about the print and its message.

"So," I concluded, "it shows how blood lines can show up a whole lot of years after somebody fair-skinned marries, say, a dark-skinned person?"

Miss Arlene suddenly slowed her motions. I had betrayed myself. The sheers picked up their speed again after her long fingers smoothed the wrinkled cotton for easier gliding. She studied the cotton as if it were woven with Rumpelstiltskin's gold.

"Yes, I guess that is what it boils down to, Anna." She pivoted on her stool to face me, resting her hand still in the scissors. A sigh whistled through her thin lips. She removed her fingers from the metal finger holes and rubbed her thumb, a pensive mood softening her sharp-featured face. She grinned over her own private thought.

"I often wondered how I got this beak of a nose," she snorted. I looked at her quizzically. Her nose was rather...outstanding, with an amazing eagle-like quality. She gave me a profile view. Wow! I couldn't even stifle my giggle. Arlene was a good sport about it and her comical grimace added to the hilarity. "My mother and father did not pass this on to me," she said ruefully, as she crossed her eyes and tapped the side of her nose, "and no other relative has it. So I figure one of my great-great-grandfathers from the old country had once proudly announced his Roman blood that entered the line when some Germanic tribe was conquered, whereby he acquired this noble sniffer." She said it all so dramatically that my laughter bubbled over like ice cream over root beer. I heard myself belly laughing and was surprised I could still do it. Ahh, it felt good. Fortunately no other customers entered to disrupt our time. Miss Arlene, after wiping her eyes with a lace embroidered pink hanky, slid from her stool, a tentative black shoe feeling for the floor. She leaned an elbow on her cutting table. I could tell she had more to say.

"Anna Mae, I know you are a bright girl. And you are how old now?"

"Thirteen last May."

"I figure this Rockwell picture is saying something to you, and you are trying to match together some pieces in your own life." She picked up the dressmaker shears and set them in a small basket. "For whatever it is worth, I know your parents think the world of you, and we all love you." I looked away, unaccustomed to such open validation. Besides, I knew reality; we didn't completely fit in, my mother and I. Guess Miss Arlene did not know that.

"I will never know how I got this nose. You may never know about ... yourself. But, dear girl, you are one of us. And that," she vigorously shook out the cotton, quickly folding it, "is that!"

As if on cue, two blue dresses with prayer caps hustled through the door and Miss Arlene whisked herself from behind the cutting counter to attend to their needs, but not before patting me gently on my shoulder as she passed. Could she ever know how much she had just encouraged me? I picked up the folded square of white cotton and returned for one last look at the Rockwell. It intrigued me how fair skin and dark skin popped up intermittently. More than ever though, just knowing I was loved and accepted was not enough. I wished I had someone who could answer all my questions. Could this have somehow happened to me? Was I just a product, some fluke, of natural breeding along our family line? It all boiled down to this: some marriage mix along the way produced the likes of me to the likes of Elizabeth Lapp and Jacob Moyer. Maybe Miss Arlene was right. Maybe some things I would never know. But I wasn't ready to stop trying.

I waved good bye to Miss Arlene over the white meshed caps, and left the smells of fabric and old wood behind me. After placing the parcel protecting the very white yardage of cotton in my bicycle basket I kicked aside the stand and started for the outskirts of town. Home, where mama was in her cleaning frenzy. Home, where Papa was a silent visitor appearing at meals and at dark after his chores. Home, where I hid my library reading under my mattress.

As I passed Widrick's Hardware I saw what made my heart almost fail me. Adrenaline mixed with panic and dread. Who cared what home was like right now, I couldn't get there fast enough. I crossed to the far side of the street and pedaled like crazy, as far as I could get from that red and white '57 Chevy. Home, the only place I wanted to be.

FOUR

Navy blue below-the-knee culottes with matching tee shirts, the kind farm hands wear. As if seventh grade was not bad enough, the standard gym outfit was enough to undo me. I hated gym class. Oh, I was healthy enough, sturdy like a sequoia trunk, and could run and keep up with the best of them. It was the overall humiliation of the girl's locker room that tainted my existence. Turning thirteen last May of 1963 was memorable in its physical awfulness, but this…well, this plagued my life with a unique brand of embarrassment, awkward actions and responses without verbal retaliation on my own behalf. My arsenal was not equipped for this kind of warfare. Every Monday and Wednesday for fifty minutes, third period of the day was *Dread*, pure and simple.

All of seventh graders from a wide radius had been lumped together, severed from the security of our small elementary settings, bussed from various locales to be thrown into a melting pot called Creekside High School. Not very imaginative, but the name served as our label, our alma mater. It was an era of school consolidations. In my new classes I felt the painful separation from my childhood friends and cousins as we were forced to face adolescence solo. Cousin Esther and I were still able to walk the distance to our new fortress of mental expansion and conditioning, thank goodness, relieved of the trauma of riding a bus. I had heard tales likening it to a torture chamber on wheels.

At Creekside High I was thrust in with a new breed of classmates, ones who did not grow up with me, therefore looked at me strangely and whispered behind cupped hands, their eyes on me from my top to my bottom. To the male population I was invisible and that was okay with me. The female side, on the other hand, was painful in its establishment of the hierarchy. I was pegged, obviously destined to be put in my place on the manure-covered barn floor assigned to similar girls who, like me, did not conform to a certain worldly standard.

Their names were unfamiliar to my tongue: Tina DeFranco, Connie McGovern, and Maureen Flaherty, girls who enjoyed shocking the rest of us as they hung on their boyfriends, spouted foul words, and flaunted their devil-may-care attitude while smoking cigarettes and polluting the air in the girls' restrooms. As much as I was repulsed, my eyes were drawn to them, watching and analyzing their actions, their clothes, and hairstyles.

It started the first day in my ugly new culottes and tee shirt that could not hide my embarrassing pubescent growth. The barb hit hard and fast. The battle had begun.

"You look like a Sadie. Is Sadie your name?"

I looked up hoping like anything the girl was not talking to me. My shoulders slumped. Yup, she was. Black drawn-on eyes, like Egyptian art in the National Geographic, seared through me with a prim, sardonic smirk. I felt my face and ears instantly grow hot. Some snickering was going on behind me. I looked back at my white sneakers and continued putting them on as I sat on the wooden bench with the cold metal lockers on each side and a cold tile floor under foot. I had already been warned that the lockers were easily broken into and any valuables or nice clothes would disappear. No worries there. I had not been warned that any value regarding my self-worth could be stolen also. My pulse raced. The room stank and I needed fresh air.

"My name is Anna," I stated flatly, hoping my voice didn't sound scared. I almost included my middle name- good thing I had sense at the moment. "Anna Mae" would have really gotten the raw end of the deal.

"Ooooh no... No, you're not!" was the loud reply. I looked up, surprised at her terse response. What did she mean by *no*? The blond head was shaking vigorously. "No, Sadie is a better name for you. Sad Sack Sadie. Such a sad sack of...of potatoes, *brown potatoes*!" An eruption of giggles caused Tina to feel brave. One of the girls, Connie McGovern, was in my homeroom but we had not passed any words between us. She was always too fixated with her hair and Tony Martinez to notice the likes of me, and I had no reason to notice the likes of her. It was, after all, still the start of a new fall term and we were either getting used to or ignoring each other, which ever case fit. It would have been only a matter of time before those girls' homing devices would have tracked me down.

"I bet you lu-uv watermelon," Tina DeFranco continued with her small jabs at what little self-esteem I did possess. I sensed a mounting attack of words coming on and was frustratingly powerless to stop it.

"And southern fried chicken," a new voice joined in. They were coming in for the kill. *I will not cry...you can't break me.*

"Oh, and, what is that mushy stuff called? You know, like hot cereal..."

"Yeah, grits! And corn pone." My jaw was so tense my mouth hurt. I was not used to being teased or made fun of, not even in jest with my cousins, of whom not a one was here to stand up for me. I think I grimaced because my expression caused Tina DeFranco to misread my face.

"Can't even talk. Poor Sadie. Just grins like the village idiot." I shook my head in disbelief, beginning to feel fear mixed with something else. Everything felt off-kilter, like I might get hit or have something thrown at me. My laces were tied and I stood, turning my back to my tormentors as I put my things in my useless locker. Still no one spoke up for me. It was time to go out onto the gym floor. A whistle was blowing, shrill and biting. Girls began to file like cows in a slow plodding row. I was in the mix. *God help me if we have to choose teams. What will come next?* But then another feeling started to surface from deep inside of me. If this continued would I lash out with all the anger that was starting to bubble up in my innards? Would I tell them to shut up? No, I couldn't possibly. It was not a phrase that ever slipped off my tongue. My family would say to ignore and forgive them, as sickening as they were to me. Needless to say, the start of seventh grade was not going well.

I entered the locker room the next Wednesday of that week with a fuzzy head from so little sleep. I was wound up tight in anticipation of what might happen, and a certain dread that the worst was to come. Quickly I went about my business of opening my locker, which was not even latched securely, and replacing my beige corduroy skirt and cotton blouse with my inmate uniform. I heard Tina DeFranco before I saw her. Dashed were my vain hopes of avoidance. It felt like my breath caught in my throat. I feigned deafness as I continued with great earnest putting on my new white crew socks.

"Hey, Sadie! I like you so much I wrote you a poem in your honor." I did not look up. "You'll love it!" she fawned. *Left sock, left sneaker. Don't look up.* It still stank in here. Sneaker feet and sweat.

A paper rustled. "Ahem, AHEM! O-kay!" *Don't look at her.* I stood and started jamming things in my locker.

"Sadie, Sadie, Marmalady, brown as dirt and giblet gravy. Got a tan one summer day, and now she always looks that way." A few snickers, but the response was not as hoped for and it fed Tina's mean streak. My ears were poker hot and I started to sweat over my upper lip, but I'd be hanged if they'd see me wipe it off. I turned to go out into the gym, knowing I'd have to sidle past my nemesis, even though the annoying whistle had not yet summoned us into the gymnasium. Tina was not finished with me. She was approaching into my space. She smelled like an unappealing mix of fried bacon and a lousy floral perfume.

"Awww, lookie there. Poor Sadie doesn't like my poem. Such ingratitude since I spent so much time on it." My predator was so close she could have cuffed my head. Though she was much taller, I turned and looked up directly into her drawn-on eyes. They smoldered with an unwarranted hate, but then, so did mine.

A voice from one of the restroom stalls yelled, "Knock it off, Tina." To which came the reply, "Hey! You shut up, you…" and she added some pretty nasty modifiers that were new to me. That was my chance. I walked by Tina like she was not even there. I was past being hurt. That would have made me too much the victim. I was angry, and not just a little disgusted. How we would have come under church discipline for such a violation of the golden rule. I did not have any words for what I felt, but in my own small way I felt like a martyr. This is how it must feel to be a black person in Birmingham right now. Dr. Martin Luther King, Jr. was our Moses leading us to freedom. The cousins and I had heard his speech about his "dream" on Mr. Widrig's radio at the hardware store just two weeks ago. I wondered if Dr. King was afraid, if people taunted him, if he felt like he was in danger. Had he ever had the "n" word thrown at him? It all seemed a world away from Hemlock Creek, Ohio, yet it was as close as my own town and my own school. This was my world and no one else could walk this journey with me. We each have our own lonesome path to follow.

Somehow I got through the school year, those one hundred minutes every week, with reciprocated hatred passing back and forth between two sets of brown eyes. I fought to do my best outward job of not buckling under my terrible situation. Inwardly, though, I have never forgotten the sting and humiliation of those locker room encounters, and that unfamiliar emotion, hatred, that soon grew to be my constant companion.

Mulatto Marmalady. Who says names will never hurt me.

FIVE

I could sing, and I knew it. Not just the everyday belting out in the bath or along with the radio type. I felt as if there was nothing that could ever stop the song so deep inside from coming out. My mind's ear heard harmonies in every range, and out they came, surprising even myself sometimes. Like the family of robins nesting in the elm branches by my second story window, heralding the dawn in great ecstasy, I could not *NOT* sing.

One summer afternoon, in the company of several cousins, we rode our chrome-plated Huffy bikes into the town of Hemlock Creek with half dollars in our pockets, a gift from Uncle Abe. Our destination was The Valley Ice Cream Parlor. We ordered, sitting on high black-padded stools with our legs dangling. Black and white diamond tiles decorated the spotless floor. An impressive array of glasses and dishes on shelves under a panoramic horizontal mirror reflected sunlight from the large front windows. A young college guy by the name of Ned was working there. He wore a white paper hat shaped like a boat with NED in red letters on each side. The sleeves of his white shirt were rolled past his elbows and chocolate smudged his once white apron. We watched in admiration as he dramatically prepared our sundaes. With great flair he placed the decadent cherry-topped sweets before us, giving a slight bow to acknowledge our attention and applause. Without further hesitation we delved into hot fudge running over creamy hills in tall flute-edged glass dishes. Some guy in the back with an extra coin in his pocket flipped through song choices and Etta Jones scored. Soon her jazzy blues version of *At Last* began playing from the juke box. It was a doleful blend of slurs and unfamiliar progressions emanating from her mellow mezzo soprano range, singing of a love I did not know about. Could I find a dream to call my own? How was my life like a song? As my cousins slurped and scraped the fudge clean, totally unaware of the music in the background, I was totally immersed in the song, locking the style and certain words into my mind. I hadn't realized the silence around me until I felt three sets of baby blues fixed wide-eyed ... on me. Then I heard my own voice, randomly singing aloud, die down as searing heat flushed from my neck to my face. In the mirror over our heads I saw the twenty-something guy at the jukebox, a crooked grin on his stubbly face as he caught my eye in return. I quickly looked away.

"Sorry," I mumbled as I stuck my spoon in my softened mound. I stirred it around before setting the spoon on a paper napkin while briefly considering breaking all rules by slurping up the puddle, but I had lost my taste for it. Even the soda guy Ned was looking at me, his dishcloth over his hand as he stopped mid-swipe while drying a sundae bowl. Now my differences were not only visual but audible.

"Anna Mae Moyer!" a male voice boomed. Esther started giggling. *Here we go!* I really did not need Cousin Abram to start in on me now, here. Picking up my spoon, I tackled my sundae with renewed interest and feigned a surprised look as I finally lifted my head. "What?" I inquired innocently. I really think the juke box guy was laughing. Ned had sense enough to turn back to his work.

"Where did you learn to sing like *that?*"

"Nowhere. I just heard it on the ..." I jerked a pointing thumb over to the back where a country song was now twanging heartbreak and misery. Jukebox guy had moved to a seat where a bottle of cola and a mound of fries waited. I shrugged my shoulders. Why should I care what anyone thought? But I *did* care, very much. Mennonites did not sing for worldly entertainment. That was too great an emphasis on oneself. I was permitted to take piano lessons simply because Miss Lutz, my school music teacher, was offering lessons and needed to groom choral accompanists for the school choir.

"Land sake, Anna, I knew you could sing, but that, well, you are something!" Cousin Esther's eyes were wide. Her head gave little shakes side to side, and I truly did not know if she meant something good or not so good. The way they were now looking at each other led me to think not so good. Where did this come from, this ability deep in me? Once again I felt strangely out of tune with my surroundings as our arms lined the counter for all to see. I glanced up once again at the overhead mirror running the length of the countertop and, as I watched myself with my cousins, thought how I was like a crow on a wire surrounded by bluebirds.

After ingesting the last spoonful we hauled ourselves out of the ice cream parlor feeling lazy and full. We mounted our bikes and turned around on Main Street to head back home. I was eerily in tune once again, very aware of a car slowing down behind us. A fear took over instantly and I resisted the urge to race ahead of the others. Instead, I steered toward the far sidewalk to take my place away from the center double line. *Look straight ahead. Please, Jesus, please...* A black four-door Ford inched by as smiling Deacon and Betty Gehman waved and told us to ride carefully. The whole thing caused me to melt like my sundae had, turning into a puddle. The cousins had no idea what had happened last spring and I wasn't about to tell them. I let out a huge sigh and we pedaled on. That haunting song, *At Last,* became a brain worm that slithered its way deep in my recollection and I sang it to myself the rest of the day, about finding a dream and calling it all mine. It calmed me and took my mind off my foolishness.

~

"Anna, you have very pretty eyes!" Cousin Molly was staring at me. I blinked in disbelief. Molly was not one to pass along a compliment. I was at the Clemmen's house and Molly, Mariah, and I were sewing zippers in our new school skirts. The old Singer pedal machine kept Mariah's feet moving up and down and she was intent on her seams. She was paying little attention. Never in my fourteen years had I heard such a thing as that. *Pretty eyes?* As if *I* had pretty anything. I looked straight into Molly's soft sky blue ones. *Are you just saying that or do you really think so?* As if to read my thoughts she replied, "Yes, I really believe you have the prettiest shaped eyes I've ever seen. Just like the shape of butternuts and the same color as Beulah's." I scrunched my forehead. *Beulah?* "You know, our new jersey calf." Even Mariah slipped a grin and that was all that was said. It had caught me unawares to think I had even one good feature. I fought in days to come to not think overly much on Molly's kind words. Humility and all. But, oh, it was hard. *Pretty eyes, large and brown, like Beulah's.* The windows into my soul had become a little brighter.

~

School started in the usual way here in Hemlock Creek. Not so everywhere else. I reread the newspaper article three times as I sat on a comfy sofa in the library. A young black fellow, James Meredith, was the first African American admitted to the segregated Oxford University in Mississippi. He was strengthened in his cause by President

Kennedy's inaugural speech citing civil rights for all. What his admittance caused at the time was nothing short of riots and chaos. James Meredith had to be escorted to classes by federal marshals assigned under our Attorney General, the president's brother, Robert. I was oddly drawn to this kind of news since facing my own little locker room war last year. Mississippi seemed so far away, but the current events could be happening anywhere. Even with such unrest in our country, not to mention our country's involvement in Vietnam, life took on its everyday sameness in my hometown.

~

At fifteen, a girl's life often centers on clothes. That is the way of it, unless you dressed as a plain girl, which I did not. But I must add that I was conservative compared to many others who were shortening their hemlines at an alarming rate. My new skirts came to the middle of my knees and I felt I fit in, at least with my clothes. No one looked down, though, on my Mennonite classmates who dressed plainly. They were who they were. There was no exclusive Mennonite school for us to attend at the time. I suspect there were those in my fellowship who were on the receiving end of jabs and biases because of our strict adherence to pacifism, modesty in speech and dress, and our separation from ways of the world, but there was strength in our numbers and we stood up for our own.

We were all caught up in the new school year. There were new teachers to get used to and a few new pupils. Then there were the same long-standing teachers for specials like music and art, same homerooms, same alphabetical line-up. But now we were considered high schoolers. Freshmen. I was determined to keep up with the press of reading assignments and weekly quizzes. I put up with all else just to take my music classes. Miss Lutz continued to offer piano lessons on Thursdays after school. Four of us from the school choral group had back-to-back half-hour lessons; mine was scheduled for 3:30, so I had half an hour to fill. Since the library was not far, I made good use of my time.

I entered the cool, stone, Federal-style land mark with a goal in mind, and, after acknowledging Miss Ledbeder, who today was sporting a paisley silk turban over her tightly permed curls, went right over to the alphabetized biography section. In music appreciation class we learned about Grace Bumbry. I wrote her name in my black and white composition notebook, underlined it boldly, and put stars around it. This young woman had become an overnight sensation in the music world last year in 1961, singing a Wagner opera, *Tannhauser,* at the Wagner Bayreuth Festival. She was the first black woman to ever do so. Miss Lutz quoted a magazine article which chronicled Grace and her amazing success following such humble beginnings. Then we received a short introduction to Luranah Aldridge, a mulatto singer from the late 1890's.

But Grace was the one that intrigued me. What a stir she must have caused, in light of Wagner's racial stance against Negroes. Grace was major news. This year, she had made her United States debut at Carnegie Hall and sang at a state dinner at the White House. I was proud that our President Kennedy and his wife invited her. For some reason, Grace became like a hero to me and I wanted to follow her career. I did not find any biographies about her, but then, she was only twenty-five at the time. Amazing to think there were just eleven years between us. Music and singing were now secret dreams of mine, yet I kept these dreams well hidden under a bushel, wondering how my desires could ever become reality when I could not let them out. It was a very non-Mennonite dream. I would not be the girl to marry a *goot Deutsch* farm boy and have babies while canning a winter's worth of red beets and carrots.

I left Mrs. Ledbeder with a wave of my hand and no checkouts this time, saving me the embarrassment of her eyeing my choices. I was singing a Four Season's hit I had heard flowing through the radio speakers at Widrig's hardware store, *Big Girls Don't Cry*. While skipping up the steps of Miss Lutz's little brick Cape Cod home, I belted out those crazy lyrics, wondering at the same time why big girls aren't supposed to cry. I whisked open the screen door and hip-bumped the colonial paneled inner door enough to squeeze my way in, mindful to shut it quietly behind me. Then I sombered up a notch, remembering what and who I was, and that was Miss Lutz's star pupil. No amount of humility lessons could have kept that from me. I was feeling so good, ready to make that upright Steinway produce music fit for Carnegie Hall. I might be another Grace Bumbry and the world would take notice of Anna Moyer from Hemlock Creek, Ohio. I had glanced down the street as I quietly closed the front door. I did a double take. No, I could not possibly have seen a red and white vehicle two streets down. I would not let my imagination get to me this time.

At the sound of the door, Tommy Heckler sprang up and bolted as if the bench had zapped him with a mega current. Miss Lutz shook her head in resolved disappointment. Mrs. Heckler's dream of begetting another Liberace on the keyboard would never come to fruition. The door banged like an exclamation point.

Miss Lutz beamed with anticipation as she cleared the Czerny scales and Schaum intermediate books from the wooden filigree music stand. We passed some general comments about weather and school as she prepared the space for my books. Her terrier, Sparky, had escaped from the kitchen, only too eager to greet me. As Miss Lutz scolded her pride and joy with little effect and restored him to his confinement, I set out my Debussy piece, carefully adjusted the bench to the right distance, and centered myself before the keyboard. My hands began to get a little sweaty as they always did before playing in front of others, but I had practiced *Clair De Lune* on the school piano every available moment and was now eager to share my progress. Practicing fed my perfectionistic bent and I was never satisfied until I played with *no* mistakes, which was seldom the case. Miss Lutz stretched my half an hour into forty-five minutes, as the next on her schedule, Darlene Koelher, sighed in audible resignation and flipped her piano books up and down on her lap. At 4:15 I flounced down the brick sidewalk leaving Darlene to fumble through her scales. I had played to my satisfaction today and it was a terrible *goot* feeling. I faced the walk home floating on an ethereal cloud of classical and Rogers and Hammerstein melodies.

To my surprise I realized that, lately, I was not dwelling on my differences as much and was becoming less traumatized and desperate to find answers. Good thing, because Mama was in a mental shut down after her cleaning bee earlier in the summer. Afterwards, she holed herself up in her very clean house, as if ready for the winter, though the leaves were barely turning and the warmth of Indian summer still ripened the end of harvest pumpkins.

SIX

I can hardly write of my fifteenth year without dredging the bottom of the pond, so to speak. The events of that year, 1963, started a chain reaction that seemed out of control. I equate it to a time when I was just learning to ride my bike, maybe around age eight, and I did what most children do…I fell off into the gravel on the side of the road. Little stones, dirt, even a little sliver of glass embedded in my left leg and I hobbled home with the blood running in trails down my shin and calf, crying out loudly in my pain. Papa saw, or heard me coming and came to my side, grabbing the handle bars from me and telling me to go sit on a kitchen chair. He would take care of it.

"Oh, Anna, you will have some scars, I fear," Mama remarked as she scrunched her face from the sight of blood and mess. Left hand rubbed right hand repeatedly.

"Papa is coming to clean me up." I sobbed, trying hard to be stoic as Mama just stood there, hands now over her mouth while looking at my leg as if it had leprosy.

Papa had taken his clean handkerchief off the wash line and had a bottle of mercurochrome, probably from his first aid supply stored in a metal tackle box on the back porch. He went to the sink and was washing the stiff bristled hand and nail brush. I thought he was going to wash his hands, but instead he brought it over and before cleaning my wounds he said, "This will hurt like fury, but you will heal *goot* enough." He seemed to buck himself up as he said sternly, "Now, be a brave girl and brace yourself."

    I gripped the sides of the chair, my foot resting on his thigh as he knelt in prayer posture before me. I could not help crying out as tears poured down my cheeks into my open mouth. There was nothing to do but let it happen. After he washed and picked debris from my brush burns, dabbing the continual flow of blood, he gently rubbed the soapy brush into the raw flesh sending me into ragged gasps of pain. Did he have no mercy? My hands clenched the sides of the oak ladder-back chair and my teeth clamped tight at the same time. Mama, helpless, scurried from the room. All the better. Then the mercurochrome with its dripper top spread an orange stain which mingled with blood, and finally the white bandages from strips of Papa's handkerchief wrapped and tied in little knots. I limped for two days.

    The scabs that later formed were horrendous outcroppings on the bulb of my knee and downward. But within two weeks the new skin emerged, lighter and almost pinkish. Mama was right. To this day I have a small scar on the side of my knee, but for the most part, as Papa predicted, I healed nicely. The worst was the scraping of the brush against my raw wound, cleaning it out, and that was the healing factor.

That year, 1963, brought on a much more traumatic wound and once again I required a "brush treatment" that brought on such pain in my heart I thought it would kill me. When a wound seems so deep how can a person heal?

I was in my third year of piano lessons. As part of my weekly schedule I was expected to walk from school to Miss Lutz's house by 3:30, then walk home no later than 4:15. There was little variation unless the snow was too deep, or some seasonal illness interrupted the routine. Darlene Koelher had long since retired from the keyboard and the world breathed easier. Poor Tommy Heckler, on the other hand, still bolted from the door as soon as I arrived. Maybe his mother used some sort of bribery to keep him playing against his will. No bribery was necessary for me to continue. Singing and playing the piano were as natural to me as breathing, almost effortless. I no longer looked over my shoulder when walking home. Time had eased my phobias about the red and white car. But time can fade harsh realities and numb us with a sense of false security, as I discovered that Thursday in late October.

My lesson had not gone well. I was off my game and had let other things interfere with my practice time. I was considering trying out for a part in a scheduled spring musical. My school was somewhat progressive for a small town and had chosen the lofty venture of Rogers &

Hammerstein's *The King and I*. The recruiting poster caught my attention every time I entered the main lobby. What a ruckus this would cause. Nondescript me, auditioning for a singing part in a play. I thought maybe I could be chosen for the role of Tuptim, the junior wife of the king of Siam. I certainly looked more the part than a fair-skinned, blue eyed cheerleader. How silly I had been to even consider it! The character, Tuptim, was everything I was not: exotically glamorous, in love, and disobedient to name a few of her unfortunate foibles, but I wanted to give it a try. My family and church would flip, but I couldn't stop thinking about it, even if I knew I would not follow through.

Preoccupation with my lousy lesson and my quandary about the musical gripped my attention until I heard the engine slowing behind me. I turned and saw the hood of the red and white car with its now less-than-shiny chrome fender. *Don't look at them, look straight ahead and just keep walking, just like Ruby Bridges.* I did a quick mental calculation but I realized I was too far out of town to take refuge at someone's home and still too far from my own home. I wasn't even near the corner fence or the old lilac tree.

"Hey, Nigger Girl!" Another guy laughed from the backseat. "Hey, I'm talkin' to you!" The car kept my pace which had quickened considerably. I kept my head up like Ruby did, but terror took the moisture right out of my mouth and put cotton in its place. I felt like screaming but didn't seem to remember how.

"HEY, I wanna see those pretty eyes." *Don't look, Anna.* "LOOK AT ME, GIRL!" The voice that started out dripping sweet as syrup now pierced and burned like vinegar. I started to panic. There was no one to turn to anywhere. Where was everyone? The familiar world around me blurred and my eyes burned. Without wanting to I had looked. I saw the same dark hair, his head so close I saw the red around his green eyes, eyes so strangely glazed under thick dark brows. Two other boys were laughing, their heads lolling as if they were marionettes. Instinctively, I broke into a run. The railroad tracks crossed the street up ahead. *Don't trip, Anna.* I'd outrun them like I did the last time. What happened next has never come back to me clearly, thank God. I heard the brakes give a screech, a car door opened, and a rough arm pulled me backwards, causing me to spin around and trip. The voice seethed pure evil. "I SAID, LOOK AT ME!" I squinted my eyes tightly shut, turning my face away, as hands now grabbed at both my arms. I was being yanked where I did not want to go, my eyes now open and blinking rapidly as arms flailed all around my face. I screamed and was slapped so my ears rang with the impact. There was a sickening smell of strong drink and something else. The others continued laughing. The one with long brown hair felt it was all so funny he pummeled the back of the seat like a drummer. I saw him face to face, the one who grabbed my arm. The same leering smile, neck veins protruding, the gritted teeth, the dark wavy hair flung over his light greenish eyes that were narrowed in... in what? Anger to a point of fury? Hatred? Power? At me? Over me??

    I fell and was grabbed again quickly, forcefully, brutally, and shoved into the car. No! *NO!* I heard my screams, strange and from another world, but there was no one to hear me. The door slammed and another set of hands shoved a cloth in my mouth setting me to gag. I tried but couldn't work it loose with my tongue shoved back so far into my mouth. My hands were held in a strong grip that twisted my wrists behind me. A muffled cry of pain...my pain! I thought he broke my wrists. But I fought on - oh, how I kicked and mangled my body to escape the restraint of so many hands. I squirmed like an eel as I kicked. My shoes twisted off as I fought. *Papa!* **PAPA!!** But not a word other than my own guttural sounds escaped from behind that gagging, smelly cloth, its grossness threatening to make me pass out. God! Jesus!! ***JESUS!*** For a second, a vision of Christ's agony as He died with his blood flowing, covering His precious face, this vision floated in my mind's eye, then was gone. *I'm going to die.* They're going to kill me. They wanted to kill Ruby Bridges. I'm next.

    No. **No, I'm not.** Renewed determination surged through me as I resumed my fight. Then there was no more. No more memory. No more green eyes, no more laughter. No more of that leering face and the odd sickening smells. No more.

~

The face looked only vaguely familiar. I vainly tried to focus. "Anna," was all that came from the precious deep voice. *Oh, Pa-pa. I knew you'd find me.* But you should be on your tractor this time of day. "Papa, you look so worried." I was certain I said it out loud, but heard no sound come from my lips. Had I even moved them? Through a dark haze I heard a sob, like a groan, but nothing registered in my brain except that Papa was here, that's all that mattered. I closed my eyes.

The next time my eyelids struggled open I was more alert. The room was dark. Night time. Where was I? Was this my room? Yes, and this was my bed. I felt my nubby chenille spread under my fingers, my window overlooking the shorn corn fields extending over mounding hills revealing a macabre vision in the moonlight. I wriggled a bit and felt wetness in my bed sheets that I hadn't felt for years. How could I have done such a thing? I tried to get up but a searing pain shot simultaneously down my legs and up through my stomach. I heard a chair creak and a shadow passed. A kerosene lamp was lit. I heard the match strike and smelled the oil as the wick burned off its residue. The shadow kept moving very quietly towards me, hovering over me. A gentle hand patted mine.

"Anna dear," whispered a sweet, familiar voice full of care, "It's your Aunt Laura. Can you hear me?" I gave a nod as best I could. Oh, my head! So extremely heavy. What was wrong with me?

"Try to drink some of this, child." She fumbled to find my mouth with the straw. It seemed she was awfully shaky. I did my best to suck in a small amount and the broth cooled my throat, but my neck muscles gave way and my heavy head fell back. My lips felt like fever lips, dried and blistered, and my head ached like a fevered head. I must have come down with a good case of influenza. I tried to tell her about my sheets. "I…wet…"

"Don't you worry, dearie, we'll take care of it. Never you mind. Rest like a *goot* girl." She softly, very gingerly patted the blanket covering my arm and hand. Through my blurry eyes and the darkness of the room I saw her plain yet beautiful face, a crumpled mass of pain and tears. Poor Aunt Laura, so like Mama.

~

After many days when I finally felt some better, all sorts of aunties and older girl cousins came to visit. There was little conversation at first, just a patting on my hand, and a small vase of chicory or goldenrod placed in my view. Gradually, family got used to me just lying there like a lump. Mariah tried to joke that I had many people at my beck and call, but I was not up to smiling over her feeble attempt at humor. Besides, how could I be a demanding patient when I could barely speak? Even worse was I could hardly move for all the pain that seemed to come from every part of me. At some point early on, a doctor had stitched up some very delicate parts of me from my head to, well, lower parts. One wrist was badly sprained and throbbed during the long nights. It hurt so much to breathe and something caught in my chest when I'd breath out, so I took little baby breaths. I was wrapped up like a mummy across my chest, and oh, such pain in the oddest areas. My recovery was a slow, slow process, and dear Aunt Laura faced my most private physical burdens without so much as a screwed up face or a scrunched nose. I was as helpless as a babe.

As time passed I remembered a little more until I finally recalled at whose hands my pain had occurred. Upon regaining my memory, I had very terrifying dreams and tried to force myself to stay awake. My trauma was not a subject for discussion, Lord knows I tried. I was pacified with *not now, dear, maybe when you are better*. It was a road I had to travel alone. I guess my family decided to hold their tongues. The time for questions must wait.

The Clemmens sisters came often after school, but not Cousins Esther or Abram. I wondered why. We had been so close, sharing childhood. It must have been November by now. I watched the trees slowly shed their foliage until they were skeletal. I was sitting in the upholstered chair by the front window when my three carefree cousins trouped to the door and knocked gently before entering. With permission, in they entered, accompanied by a swish of cold fresh air, which felt so good to this housebound prisoner. Off came the fine wool coats and French style caps that Molly called berets, discarded on the rocker in a pile. My mama was strangely absent through much of my convalescence. She would have huffed at the sight of clothes thrown over her rocker. For me, to see their bright healthy faces was like a tonic, better than the awful medicine Aunt Laura had trickled down my throat with a dropper those first terrible weeks of recuperation.

"There you are, Anna Mae. You are looking better today," Mariah observed, patting her windblown brown hair into place. The girls now sported a trendy hair style and I was quite envious of their new, smart looks. I felt a mess, still recovering from broken ribs, and feeling generally unkempt and unclean. I think I must have smelled pretty bad, too, though Laura did her best at bed baths.

Molly was smiling with hands behind her back. "We have a gift for you."

"We had to make sure it was okay first with Uncle Jacob. It was. So, go ahead, Molly," Eva excitedly waved her sister on. Molly brought from behind her back a small transistor radio. "This is to help you pass the time. We put new batteries in it so you can listen for a good long time, I hope." Molly handed me the small black box with the dials, and the retractable antennae. I loved them so much it hurt. Music! Right there in my house. Who would have thought!

"How can I thank you for such a great gift? You cannot know how tiring it is to sit here day after day and look out the window." I found the *on* button and it clicked as I turned it, static, static, ah! An orchestra performing! My thumb and forefinger turned the tuning knob, touchy it was, to hone in on the airwaves. There! I found a station I could really enjoy. I turned the volume down and set the radio next to me. We looked at each other, beaming with smiles. "Thank you all so much. You are the best." Their faces glowed and I felt some happiness returning. They stayed for about an hour, updating me on news from school, church, and who did or said what to whom. Papa came from outside and started thrashing about in the kitchen, looking for the makings of supper. For me, it had been an untypically *goot* day, though I wished Mama could have seen me receive my precious gift of music in a little box. Would she approve like Papa did?

My days passed in a blur of similarity until I could get around with less pain, about a month later. My radio became my companion. I had seen so little of my mother. She was a subdued phantom, ghostly white. Never would I have thought I would miss her tears and her hugs, even her rocking. She saw me but didn't, and I hadn't the strength to take care of her. I just wanted her to talk to me, and I couldn't understand why she did not, not often, anyway. Now I understand so much more, but at the time her silence was just another cause for my own pain. Christmas passed with the usual family meetings and greetings, yet no fanfare of celebration in our small home. By January I would return to school. Little did I know then how much I had changed. The Anna Mae Moyer of last summer was a Spirit of Childhood Past. Now I faced the Spirit of the Present and the Future, all at once.

SEVEN

The year 1964 was ushered in on the winds of a snowstorm. The world felt hob-nobbled. Gone was our young president, murdered while I slept my time away that bleak November day. The Vice President, Lyndon B. Johnson, stepped into the nation's highest post. There was no figuring President Kennedy's assassination. It was an event that haunted everyone. The nation was still in mourning, and there was no justice served with the death of Lee Harvey Oswald. Too many questions left unanswered.

By January 2nd, just before school resumed after holiday break, I understood about as much as a fifteen-year-old could in regard to what happened to me that Thursday in late October. I never heard the whole sad drama since it was spoken of in hushed off-to-the-side whispers. Aunt Laura, after seeing signs of the handwriting on the wall, took it upon herself to clue me in. I listened as though I were hearing the story of someone else, or having a newspaper article read to me about a young girl's tragic misfortune. I could only hope and pray *I* did not make the news headlines.

I was found by a passerby who spotted my form near the rail tracks going east outside of town, not too far from the gate crossing. He thought I was dead. I must have been a sorry, embarrassing sight, but that is only what I surmise since no one spoke that graphically about it. The plea for an ambulance to come to the Boston & Ohio tracks near the east gates on town outskirts sped through the phone line. It was from Pleasant View Hospital my parents were notified, my identity tracked from my history book thrown on the bank nearby.

Papa had come alone soon after receiving the news from Deacon Gehman. He wanted no arsenal of relatives to give him support, especially not his unstable wife. He must have rushed in through the hospital doors without knowing how to find his way around, so seldom would he have needed to be in that place. He sat in the upright chair by my bed keeping a vigilant eye on me, but I did not wake up that night, not until the following day and then I was in and out of consciousness. The medical people did what was needed so Papa could bring me home on Saturday morning. While I was hospitalized, our family doctor came to the house with Aunt Laura to make sure my mother understood some of what happened before easing her trauma. She was "eased" for three months, hence the ghostly silent state I could not understand. Aunt Laura remained to care for her sister, and then for me when Papa needed to carry on farm chores. So, that was how I heard about the missing hours and days of my fifteen-year-old life as I had just started ninth grade.

Papa, outwardly always the solid though unfeeling presence in my life, became my care-giver, providing me with company those long hours, reading to me, and changing some of my bandages, along with the gross chore of replacing bed linens. The lines around his mouth looked softer, but the crevice between his eyes grew markedly deeper. Worry lines masking age wrinkles.

"There you go, Anna Mae. Mattress aired and turned, clean sheets." He always seemed a bit unsure of himself and I tried to smile but everything hurt. "All right then. Off I go to take care of the cows." He nodded at Laura, eyes downcast. Laura started smoothing the chenille spread and adjusting pillows. "Thank you, Papa," I mumbled, embarrassed about my helpless condition. He was being so gentle, so good to me.

"And thank you, Aunt Laura." I added, trying to be extra polite since she gave up so much of her time for me. She gave me a waning smile as she also turned from me to go elsewhere. *Please, don't go! I need someone to talk to.* "How's Mama today?" Laura was close enough to look like Mama's twin, and I craved her company. She reversed herself and sat lightly on the end of my bed. I think she understood my need for her company.

"Oh, your Mama is fine… jus' fine. I took her out for some fresh air. Snow has freshened things up a bit. Your mama, well, she looked up and smiled as some snow geese flew overhead. She said, 'I wish I could fly.'" Laura smiled again at me, this time with more feeling, giving me a rare glimpse of Mama, only happier, healthier, and younger. From the fine brown baby soft hair framing her oblong face to the blue eyes and the long neck, the sisters were undoubtedly *Mennischt* women, so pretty in their freshness.

How did I look right now? I had not seen my reflection for many weeks. "Auntie, I wish I could see myself. I am missing some hair still, right here," I said, gently fingered the spot above my left ear. "Could you maybe bring me the silver pitcher?" I saw a moment of hesitation followed by resignation. She nodded.

"Sure, Anna, I will go fetch it." What would I see? Did I really want to see? Yes, I realized I truly did. Laura returned with Mama's water pitcher.

"Here you go, *schveet madchen*." Auntie Laura was the only relative other than Mama who ever told me I was a sweet girl. She handed Mama's wedding present to me, handle first.

I turned the pitcher just so, as it was curved outward and really gave a distorted chipmunk look. Things didn't look much different on the outside. Sure, there was that bald spot, but other than that, I recognized my wide nose, my full lips, now healed of the weeping blisters caused, I guessed, by the awful gag cloth. I gave a ragged sigh and handed back the pitcher.

"Does the whole town know? Will everyone at school know what happened to me?"

"Oh, I don't know, *liebchen*, we tried to keep it within ourselves, but if folk like Mrs. Ledbeder found out, well," she gave me a lopsided smile, "pretty much everyone knows." *She knows everyone knows, but wants to spare me.* Her long fingers smoothed my hair, which was impossible to do, and then, with her apron she took to rubbing the finish on the pitcher. "Now, you leave this to *Gott* und before you know it, life will go on as usual." Good ol' Aunt Laura. What a gentle, innocent soul.

But life refused to resume as it had before. I came down with another flu bug before school started on January third, and spent miserable mornings with a bucket by my bed. Papa was totally dejected about my poor health. I could tell by that worry line between his brows. I hated being such a dead weight on Papa and Aunt Laura, but what could I do? My stomach couldn't stand the sight of food and I was so tired. Before long I would have to face the fact that my schooling would most likely end with the eighth grade.

~

In early February someone sent for Great Grandma Moyer. She was a spry, chip-chop kind of old country German who came right to the point and didn't bother with "beating around the bush," which is exactly the first thing she said as she sat in Mama's rocker across from me. I was properly dressed but feeling a bit fuzzy from sleepless nights, thanks to night terrors which sent me into screams. Poor Papa, in a frazzled state from being wakened so, would have to shake me out of them, losing precious sleep himself.

There sat my great grandma, Minerva Moyer, a starched female version of my father, straight backed, big bosomed in her plain garb and prayer cap over her white thinning hair. She had married into the Moyer family as a sixteen year old, and promptly took on the lead role in the partnership. Her eyes were Papa's, her mouth prim and straight across. But, for all that, she had a kind heart; that much I knew. As a child, I had never sensed a reason to fear her.

"So, Anna Mae, I see you are up and about. So I will not beat around the bush." She studied the view out the window, giving my stomach time to flutter about inside me. "I have not very *goot* news to share with you. You must be a very brave girl and take it as it is." I nodded, puzzled, expecting a very dire prognosis of my health. Nothing prepared me for what was coming.

"You are with child, Anna. This child is the result of the…the… *attack* on you." She practically spit out the word "attack". Now she paused to once again look out the window, as if to gather her wits to go on. I sat stupefied, dumbstruck. *What??* I had nothing to say, yet felt my mouth opening and closing, like a fish out of water, gasping. It took some minutes for things to make sense. I remembered thinking, in the Bible, Mary was "with child." But not me. Not Anna Mae Moyer. It's good I was seated because the room began to go around. Great-grandmother became an outline, hazy and out of focus. She stood with amazing agility for her age and brought over a tiny glass of her homemade dandelion wine. "Here, child, take a sip of this." It was bitter and unappealing, but it renewed my senses. She must have poured it in anticipation, for herself or me?

A baby! How??

Oh…of course. Now things made much more sense; the pains, the strange stitches, though I had some wonderings about it all. So, this verified it. *That* had happened to me. There again, I didn't know much, but knew enough. Yes, the delicate issues regarding my healing now made all the sense in the world. Great Grandma returned to the rocker after carefully setting her small glass on a nearby table. She sat down hard, not bothering to be delicate. It was obvious there was more on her mind. She watched me, making sure I did not black out, I guess. When satisfied with my stability, which was actually a state of deadness, she clasped her hands and prepared to go on.

"We predict you will be delivered of this…child," she cleared her throat, "come July. Until then you shall remain at home and venture out as little as possible. Do you understand, Anna?" I kept my head down, numb and dumb. "Your mother's sister, your aunt Laura, has been good enough to consent to stay on…" To my shame I felt myself completely crumbling, utterly falling apart. I could not control tears that spewed unchecked down my face while my shoulders heaved with the intensity of my sobbing. I had never known true misery until this moment. Even the attack and all its implications did not compare. *That* I could have put away in the recesses of my mind. But *this*, there was no going on, no getting over, no putting it all away. As the tears rolled, I brought my hand up to my bald spot. They had taken so much of me. Robbed me of my very life! This was too much. I should have died the minute that cursed car door closed. Through my brokenness I heard her go on in the same tone, or did I hear a slight falter, a crack in her voice?

"What you are experiencing is what many women "with child" face. You may be sick and vomiting for a while but it will ease as your time draws near." *But I'm not a woman- I'm a girl! I am fifteen years old, just starting my life! "As my time draws near" sounds like I'm dying! How can you be so calm? How can you keep talking? The sun has just stopped. Time has stopped. I can't breathe! Please - stop talking at me*! Her words trailed off and she sat, her ample arms draped on top of the arms of the rocker. She sat as I grieved. She sat through my tears of betrayal. Life had betrayed me. At least she did not rock. At one point I even screamed with my fists clenched, pummeling my lap, which caused Aunt Laura to rush to the door, always ready she was to come to my aid. Still my great grandmother sat, as if she had done this before. When I was spent, she arose and smoothed out her lap, gathering the small stemmed glass, now empty of its wine which was poured from a pint-sized Mason jar with its rubber ring and lid.

"You will get through this, Anna Mae," she remarked as she started for the door. "*Gott* will help you. You are a Moyer and we stick by our own." She turned then, and gave me a rare, almost sympathetic smile as she placed her hand over her heart, fingers fanned over her bodice. It felt as if we were connected in an unfamiliar new way, woman to woman, experiencing what only women do. With that she was gone. Hot tears came afresh but were quickly cauterized as I stilled myself. Were those my cries? What was I hearing? Holding my breath, I waited. There, coming from Mama's room, loud sobs and wails of agony. Behind her closed bedroom door came sounds so deeply felt I could only guess she had overheard the outcome of my life. Then the soft murmurings of her sister as Laura set about calming the unstoppable tide of misery.

~

Winter days passed as I simply survived, allowing life itself to take over. I had no fight. No drive, no anger, no nothing. Mama would open her door and peek to see if I was downstairs. If I was awake she'd come out to sit in her rocker. Back and forth, back and forth. It became a rhythm of our life, as it was when I was a child being rocked in her thin white arms. Words started coming, then tidbits of conversation.

"My dear Anna, are you well?"

"Yes, Mama," I lied. "I am feeling fine."

"What can I get you?"

"Nothing, thank you. Is there anything I can get you?" *Is this what we are reduced to, this chit-chat?*

"I am tired. I think I will lie down now." *Alright Mama, but I wish you'd stay. I am so all alone.*

~

Spring inevitably came, then May, my favorite month, my birth month, though I was giving it little thought. I was feeling better and very eager to get outside. The Clemmens sisters told me yesterday, after wishing me Sweet Sixteen greetings, that the high school musical production, "The King and I", was scheduled for this Friday and Saturday evening. I asked them about who was chosen for what roles and if they thought the singers were strong enough to project through the entire auditorium. Only time would tell, Molly had answered. Oh, by the way, had she shared with me that Tina DeFranco landed the part of Tuptim, the exotic junior wife of the king? Dear Molly had no idea she was salting open wounds by discussing my locker room enemy and the part I had coveted when I was a different person, a young innocent girl.

A pang of envy speared my heart. Oh well, why not and more power to Tina DeFranco. Life has a way of turning and biting us. Later, after my cousins left, I thought of seven short months ago when I was conflicted about try-outs and my desire to star in the role of Tuptim, which I never revealed to a soul. Who was that young girl with the silly hopes? What had I been thinking? May as well have been a lifetime ago. Any song that was there inside me had been doused like an oven fire. I feared there was no ember remaining.

Yet, this day as I slowly walked the periphery of the house, the beautiful warm sun on my face, the clean, clear air issuing its promise of better days to come, the lilac scent heavy on the breeze, I felt something rise up in me. A hope, almost akin to a faint glimmer of joy, had germinated with the warmth of the sun. With careful steps I walked toward the meadow, awash with fuzzy headed grasses, and I put my arms up to the sky.

"*Mein Gott*, do you still have a plan for me?" I spoke out loud to the burgeoning white clouds." Did you cry with me? Were you there? You saved my life, but for what reason? I want to go on. I want to be healthy and young again." Throwing caution to the wind, I spun around and around, my stomach with its bulging weight felt like a balloon filled with water. I became so dizzy I needed to plop down onto a bed of grass. There I remained, hugging my stomach and thinking of the verse in the Old Testament book of Jeremiah - about God's promise of His plans for our good, not for evil.

"Does that apply to me, God? I will have a baby this summer and I will give it up to a good home. Then will you show me your good plans?" Sadly I heard no reply, yet even as I listened I felt God reassuring me in my spirit.

The bees were busy in the grass heads, barn swallows swooped down to keep me company, sunlight shone into my dark corners. I arose and walked the lane down to the road, not yet ready to face walls and Mama's sadness. I was young, and there was so much I wanted to do. I wanted to sing! I would have the baby, it would be placed in a good home with a husband and wife, and then I'd find my life's direction. An old hymn came into my mind and I tried the words aloud.

Whiter than snow, yes, whiter than snow. Lord, wash me and I shall be whiter than snow. Oh, Lord, how I long to be perfectly whole...cast out every heartache, cast out every foe, now wash me and I shall be whiter than snow.

I did not remember the words perfectly but the melody rose up in me without bidding, and I found myself singing out loud, head back, serenading the clouds as the barn swallows swooped around me. The life inside me fluttered.

EIGHT

The summer of '64 came on with a hot, dry vengeance. Papa's corn grew inches during the warm nights, and the laundry on the line was folded within several hours. Parched yellowed stems of daffodils and tulips bowed underneath the majesty of daisies and peach hued lilies. Woodlands were surrounded by tall phlox the color of fuchsia, startling our eyes with such flagrant color. I grew with the season of growing things. Though I was not big like some of the young wives with their first endowments, I was decidedly ... "with child." The morning sickness passed with the lilacs. I was healing inside. That had to do with Mama.

~

I kept my distance emotionally from the tiny being inside of me. In the spring it had flitted like a butterfly, tickling my ribs and stomach. Now it stretched and punched. *Let me out*, it seemed to yell. I inwardly yelled the same plea. Night was once again a restless monotonous time. While all living things rested, I kept vigil with the crickets and the night insects, pacing, reading, sewing, walking... no, more like plodding around the perimeter of the house. Now and then a vision of whiteness kept company by my side and Mama and I walked in silence, or she quietly talked of the time I fought inside her to be free. She was preparing me for the day, *my* day of delivery. *Deliverance.* Time weighed heavily on me, as did this growing protrusion. Protrusion - intrusion, both apt nouns describing my condition, the "in" and "out" of it.

The red and white '57 Chevy had become the enemy of the town. The Clemmens sisters told me that daily the neighbors and town folk searched for that symbol of evil that had shattered our peaceful existence. They could not get over the shock of some drugged hippie, so termed by the town folk, having done that to Jacob Moyer's precious Anna-girl. The car became like a face on a wanted poster offering a substantial reward of justice served. Miss Arlene had become a sentinel on the porch of her fabric store. She placed a wicker chair by the door so she could keep watch during customer down times. Mr. Widrig kept a hand gun, very hush-hush, within reach in a cabinet at the hardware store. He was a Lutheran and they had no issues with forceful resolutions. On the other hand, every *goot* Mennonite was raised in a life style of pacifism, and I was not sure *what* would occur if that Chevy showed its colors in town. Molly seemed to think the driver would be arrested on the spot, no time for rights, no nothing. Off to the maximum security prison in Dexter City without bail. She was most dramatic about it and I wondered how she could know of such things. She made a veiled allusion to keeping my father under control as he would likely "go off the deep end." That made sense, though my father was a peaceable man. What father would not want vengeance for such a violation of his daughter's entire being, Mennonite or not.

Almost every day, one, two or all three of the sisters came by to lighten my spirits and bring some diversion to my dull, hum-drum days of confinement, as the elder women called it. How I missed riding my bike into town and visiting Miss Lutz, and Miss Arlene, even Mrs. Ledbeder, who was always kind and talkative with me. I ran out of choice reading weeks ago, and though I received new books from the sisters, their selections were not mine. And my advocate, Miss Arlene, the validator of my being...oh, how I would have loved to run my hands over the fabrics and smell the dyes once more, and to look at that family tree print, then glance back and study her beak of a nose. I smiled to myself, but it quickly wiped itself away as I realized how soon the top of our generational tree would have a nameless face growing over top of my face. A single limb bearing an offshoot, an uncertain hybrid. Or would the little face be excluded completely, a memory to erase from the records? Not a Moyer, not loved enough to even inherit a name. I placed my hands over my stomach. Could this baby really be a part of me? Which part? Would it have dark hair, light skin, brown or green eyes? A deep sadness filled me as I thought of this innocent victim of horrendous out-of-control violence. Sometimes I wanted to hate it—but found I could not. Both of us were victims of the sinful nature of another human being. I rubbed up and down on my tight itchy protrusion, and the baby shot a hand or maybe an elbow as if responding to my touch. I stopped. The less thought of this little one, the better.

The calendar days progressed in relentless but merciful fashion, and I welcomed the passing days as I readied myself to be freed so I could go on with my life. Since schooling was probably not an option here in my town, I saw good sense in relying on family support. Maybe there would be opportunity to move in with Mama's older sister in Pennsylvania and finish school there. Or maybe take on an apprenticeship under Papa's cousin, Marian, who ran a successful bakery business that catered to family restaurants in Lancaster. I was considering my clean slate carefully, truly wanting to follow God's good plan for my new and different life to come. *Deliverance.*

~

Eva rode a bike over, not uncommon except it was mid-afternoon, and a warm one at that. She was noticeably agitated and the ride had mussed her up considerably. I waddled out to meet her. "Oh, Anna. Something has happened!" She was so winded I felt a dread enter my soul. "Miss Arlene saw the car and was on the phone line quick as a blink. The sheriff has him at the town hall. Oh Anna, what's to come next?" I instinctively put my arms over my belly. "You must be ready…" She panted and sat right down on the ground, her skirt billowing as she let the bike fall to the other side. I wanted to run into the safety of my house and bolt the doors. Mama, how could she face this? What of Papa? How could *I* face it? In my case justice demanded a stern price in the reliving of such an agonizing experience.

The door unlatched and Mama rushed out, wide-eyed but calm, calmer than usual. She was over her spring cleaning frenzy, but this year's took on a different aspect. She removed every object in the side pantry, cleaning and scrubbing with a vengeance. Not one iota of dust survived. A braided rug from scraps was fashioned as her fingers worked tirelessly while the sun's rays evolved like a watercolor wash, from light egg yolk yellow to reddish-orange, nature's proclamation to the watch hours of the day. Yellow gingham curtains tied back at the small windows greeted us with an unfamiliar cheer. Such a fuss for a lowly pantry. Poor Mama. Reality completely eluded her.

"What is it, Eva. You must tell me, too." Eva, still winded, held up a hand. "Just a moment, Aunt Elizabeth," she gasped. So I proceeded to tell Mama, wondering if she would catch the significance of any of it. Would she remember what the red and white Chevy meant?

That woman was starting to surprise me. She looked at me directly. In a decisive manner so unlike her she said,

"Anna Mae, you must clean up. Fix your hair, put on your blue wrap-around skirt and the white short-sleeved blouse. If it needs ironing I'll do it." Ironing? Who cared about that at a time like this? "Come in, Eva. You need a drink." With that she turned and bustled into the house. I helped Eva get the bike propped up against the porch and we went inside to do as Mama had said. For the third time in my sixteen years I felt as if I was blanched white, and it was not a natural feeling.

We waited for the summons. Papa was home now and we were readying ourselves to receive a telephone call. At 2 o'clock, the shrill ring made me jump. We were unaccustomed to this loud intrusion into our lifestyle, but Papa felt it was a necessary encroachment. He moved uncommonly fast to pick up the receiver. Any more than two rings was two too many for him.

"Yes? Yes. All right. Give us about fifteen minutes. Yes. Thank you." Papa hung up and looked at me.

"It is time to go, Anna."

"I will come, too. Anna needs her mother right now." Did Mama just say that or had someone entered, masquerading as Elizabeth Moyer? Papa seemed confused at first before nodding in agreement. Last month I had looked out the window and wondered who parked their shiny black automobile in our drive. I should not have been surprised when I discovered it was Papa's purchase, that solid looking Oldsmobile made in the early '60s. We silently harbored our own fears of what was coming as we took our places, me and Mama in the backseat. Papa started the engine, moving us onward toward an uncertain ending. But, we were together, the three of us - the Jacob Moyer family against the world.

~

The courthouse had the smell of old cigarettes and body odors. Queasiness brought a vile burning up into my throat and I felt Mama's solicitous eyes on me as I coughed it back. We sidled past protruding knees before slinking down into three straight-backed solid chairs. Mama placed her hand over mine on my thigh. I was so hot I felt dizzy. A man in a black suit leaned over to say something and Papa nodded in return. The man went up to the elevated chair where another man sat in a Lutheran choir robe, so it looked to me.

I heard words bantered around me but was more aware of the little one protesting my stress on its life. Mama's hand kept up its continual pat, reassuring me of her support. Papa leaned over, "Anna, the judge is talking to you." I was asked to stand which I did clumsily. I answered questions with my head down and my voice wavering on the verge of tears. My tongue seemed thick and oh so dry. I don't know what I said in reply to the questions, nor do I remember what was asked. I felt separated from my body and my brain felt disengaged. Then I obediently sat in shaken relief when told to. A young man was ushered before the judge while the sheriff held him by the arm. From the back I saw nothing that triggered a memory. His answers were not cocky or angry. He was scared, very scared. Was he a witness? Or one of the friends who wrenched my wrists back and shoved the vile cloth in my mouth? That must have been his parents over on the other side. The woman was crying. As well she should be if her boy had been any part of my attack. I heard my name again and was told to stand. My parents stood with me and held me on either side. Good thing. Fear made me too weak for much good.

"Anna Mae Moyer, have you ever seen this young man before?" My breaths came in gasps as I reluctantly raised my eyes. My parents' hands in unison tightened encircling my elbows. The sheriff forced the boy to turn. I looked into scared blue eyes, taking in the clean-cut dark blond hair, the lean tall body of a teenaged boy wearing a striped polo shirt and blue jeans held up with a leather belt with US on the buckle. He was gulping and his pronounced Adam's apple bobbed up and down. I shook my head and, still looking at him replied, "No, Sir. I've never seen him before." I heard murmurs, Mama swayed slightly. The two suited men leaned close to whisper. The boy's mother released the hold on her shoulders and they drooped as she closed her eyes and continued to dab each one with a floral handkerchief. The sheriff kept his restraint on the thin arm and said something to the judge who then told the boy to talk, to "say something."

"I don't know anything. I already told the sheriff I would never attack anyone, let alone a girl. I just bought that car from a guy in New Berlin for $50. My summer job paid for it." He was babbling quickly, the words falling over each other. His parents nodded emphatically. I knew he was not one of them.

"Anna," the judge said in his serious tone, "Have you ever heard this voice before?"

"No, sir. It wasn't him. He was not one of them."

"Look again, Anna, and think hard. Then give us a final answer for the books." I looked at that poor young man and just knew.

"He was not the one. He was not there." There was a corporate release of tension, audible in the atmosphere of the room. The judge sat back in his throne-like chair.

"All rightie then. That settles that!" He placed both hands splayed open on top of the file folder. "Sheriff, hand that boy over to his parents." I heard someone behind me say, "They should sell that car. It's marked." The boy and his family left quickly, but not before the mother clung sobbing to her boy's neck as the father wiped his face with a handkerchief he whisked from his pants pocket. My parents and I sat back down, drained from the encounter.

"Are you feeling okay, Anna Mae?" Papa sat with his large hands clasped before him.

"Yes, Papa." He nodded and stood. Mama placed her arm around my shoulder protectively.

"Maybe Anna needs more time to gather her strength, Papa," she said to him while watching me.

"No, I want to go home," I said decisively, and we stood. The man in the black suit came over and beckoned my father out of our hearing. After some words between them, Papa nodded and returned. The sheriff came, looking important in a uniform that fit tightly around muscular arms and chest. "Well, folks," he addressed us, holding his hat, "Jacob, Elizabeth, we will not stop the search for that boy, I want you to know that." Then to me he said almost tenderly, "Anna, you may be called upon to do this again. And hopefully, one day you will say, 'Yes, that's the one.' Then we will put the scum behind bars for a good long time so he can't do that to any other girl." Something the sheriff just said had mightily agitated Mama. She began shaking her head furiously, making little sounds.

"No. No, Michael." I did not know Mama even knew that man, let alone his name. He gave his full attention to her. "Anna will not go through this ever again. Do not look for him, do you hear, Michael?" She challenged him with the authority of a school teacher. Sheriff Michael turned to my father. "Jacob?" Papa studied his hat, the brim going 'round and 'round in his hands.

"I guess Elizabeth is right, Mike. This is too much for Anna. She is weak. Let's end it now and call it all off."

Sheriff Mike asked them both, "What about Anna?" as if I was not there. The hat stopped its orbit. I watched my father, wondering if I had the gumption to be disobedient if asked. Papa sighed. "She's old enough. Ask her yourself then."

"Anna?" Sheriff Michael studied my eyes. "Do you want us to call off the man hunt? Or shall we go on 'til we find him?" My mind raced through the options before I answered. It was eight long months ago. The boy had supposedly just disappeared leaving his car behind. But if this had happened to me right here in our little town... well, I started shaking. I couldn't stop. Mama's clasp grew stronger under my forearm. She must have felt me sweating profusely. I could feel her slight tug on my arm and, once again, I could tell she wanted to close the door and leave the pain behind. I knew what I had to say.

"I just don't want any other girl to go through... th-this-ever." My whole body shook out the judgment. I felt like I just released a guillotine blade. Mama let out a defeated groan, then checked herself. *Land sake, would these tears never stop gushing from me?* I embarrassed myself.

"One last question, then, and I'll leave you be. Anna, if you saw him, would you recognize him *for sure* after all this time?" the sheriff asked as gently as before.

My head moved up and down. Very certain I was, of that answer.

"That settles it. Okay. Go on home now and just get on with life as best you can. I will not rest until my job is done." *Get on with life. Gladly!* He put his navy blue officer hat on and worked it into its proper place. "Jacob...Lizzy...Anna..." and with those words of closure he was gone. *Lizzy?* Never had I heard anyone call Mama "Lizzy". There was a side of my mother that was unknown to me. I guess no child is completely familiar with a parent's life outside of their own. Mama was stoically swabbing my face with her cotton handkerchief. My, how this woman could turn around. "There now, Anna." She shoved the wet cotton back in her black handbag which hung from her elbow. With untypical leadership, she steered me out the door. "Jacob, let's get her to the ladies room."

The black Oldsmobile sat like a solitary domino in the row that had only one vacancy when we arrived. It looked as alone as we were. But as great grandmother Moyer said, "We are Moyers and we stick together." There was strength in that.

Little One shot out a foot, testing the boundaries of its cocoon. *Alive, active, with a heart that was beating.* Isn't this baby a Moyer, just like I was born a Moyer, even though I was obviously someone else's too? I had some thinking to do on the ride home from the courthouse.

NINE

"Mama, did you have any idea before I was born that I would have dark skin?"

"No, Anna, I never gave it a thought. Your papa and I were so glad to be having our baby."

"Does anyone on Papa's side have my features?"

"Grandmother Lapp was rather short and stocky…"

"I mean my skin, my hair," I reached up and felt the tightness of my curls, then brought my fingers to my face, "my nose, my lips. Even my musical ability is a feature that no other Moyer seems to have."

"Oh, I don't know about that. Aunt Catherine is very musical."

"Yes, she plays the organ but I mean, really musical, like a performer."

"Oh."

"Mama, please answer my first question, about my features."

"Anna," she said with a huff. "You've been to the family reunions as well as I have. You are... You! God made you very unique." Such a motherly answer. This was getting me nowhere.

I settled on the bed, Little One heavy in me and due any day. "I really need to know these things because, well, this baby can go either way. Maybe fair, light brown, green eyes, brown eyes, a straight nose or one like mine." I folded a tiny snap-down undershirt and placed it on the small pile with two others. I planned to have two of every needed layette item to take to the hospital.

"What does it matter if you are not going to keep it." Mama shook out a washcloth with more energy than necessary. She was upset and her reply was testily spoken.

"Mama!" What was going on here? I just assumed I had no choice. Why *would* I keep this baby?

"Are... are you telling me I have a choice?" This had not even been mentioned before. Mama hugged a towel against her chest and turned full face at me.

"We always have a choice, daughter. If I were you...well, I'm not. So you are free to make up your own mind." The towel was being folded vigorously, and she in a huff with me. I was left on a cliff hanger, confused and anxious.

"If you *were* me, what would *you* do?" Feeling exasperated, I threw down a tiny yellow washcloth. This was like treading water in a vast ocean, just keeping my head above. She pursed her lips in a line and sighed through her nose.

"I already did what I would do if I were you." She whisked her armful of clean clothes off my bed where she had been folding, and quickly turned to leave the room. Had she just insinuated that she chose to keep me? But why wouldn't she? How many times had she told me she had never been with any man other than Papa. Now it sounded like I could have been given up for adoption. My mother had clamped her lips shut and was already down the hall to place the linens in the hall closet. This new revelation had given me great cause for thought. Maybe I was barking up the wrong tree all this time. Maybe Papa was the one to talk with.

Was there ever a good time to broach such a subject? I quaked inside as I did when Papa told me to never bring up the subject of my origins. But, this was a different Papa, one who had become my protector and caregiver. Mama was still tending to her laundry while Papa was taking a break downstairs, a glass of iced tea in his large hand. I descended the stairs slowly with the railing for my balance. After some small talk, two-way communication finally kicked in. He was filling his pipe, tamping down the tobacco, and seemed receptive. I shared what passed between Mama and me. He said little as he drew in, the pipe stem clamped between his strong even teeth.

"But Papa, how could I even dare to ask you and Mama to take on a baby? And what about the church fellowship? This child would not be accepted." The bowl of the pipe in Papa's large hand was emitting a smoky scent of cherry.

"Anna, when it all boils down, *you* have the choice to give away part of yourself. You, Anna. It can only be your decision."

"But…does it still count as part of me," I waved both hands in the direction of my huge stomach, "if I was forced? Or, might that cancel me out, since it was an unwilling taking from me." This was not easy to articulate. I guess I did not think any child conceived outside of marriage was considered a viable family member. Talk about speaking in riddles. I was glad Papa was following and I did not have to attempt an alternate explanation.

"Anna Mae, did you have any conscious part in the conception of this baby?"

"No, Papa, you know that."

"Yet could this Little One, as you call it, have happened without you?"

"No, but it would probably have happened to another…"

"I'm not talking about the act of...of... conceiving," his dear face was growing flushed. "I am talking about this," and he pointed adamantly to my middle, "this *particular* living being growing inside of *you,* Anna Mae. Whether it was chosen or forced, it is growing within *you.* Now you decide whether it is worth keeping or not."

"Papa, this is so cold of you. As if we are talking about a, a...puppy!"

"Exactly."

"Do you and Mama *want* me to keep this baby?" I felt like I yelled at him. Is this what they *wanted*? My loudness served to quiet him down. He was not one for tense verbal confrontations and when he finally got to his reply, it was calm and direct.

"Anna, look at what your mother did to our pantry room. Now ask me again how we feel."

I hadn't realized why Mama had done that. To me it had been just another obsessively compulsive cleaning spree. Now I felt *I* was the one not living in reality!

"But - who is the father?? We are Mennonites! Blood line is very important..." I cut myself off before I blundered any farther. *Schtupid of me!* How could I say such a thing to this man when I am mulatto yet Elizabeth and Jacob Moyer kept me.

"Yes, we are from a long line of God-fearing Mennonites and we have had our share of persecution in the past, but we came through because we had each other and we had our faith. We place our families just under God and we care for and protect one another. You are your mother's child and, therefore, you are ours because we are one in the sight of God. You do not see the whole picture yet, Anna, but maybe someday you will. Until then, think long and hard before you release a part of your Mama and a part of yourself to a world of strangers."

My father had never spoken so many words to me before in my life and may *never* have except that this awful circumstance forced his hand. I understood for the first time that this gruff yet gentle man whom I called Papa was definitely not my biological father. *Dear Gott, what are all the ramifications of this new discovery?* All the questions yet unanswered, all the humiliation of my past, whatever it was… with all that still mystified me about my birth, one thing had become clear as summer rain because of this conversation with my father ... I was not unloved, or tossed aside. I was my mother's baby.

TEN

"Robert Lee Moyer, I dedicate you in the name of the Father, the Son, and the Holy Spirit, Amen." Bishop Lapp returned my son into the arms of his grandmother Moyer. The look of love on my mother's face was a thing to behold. With my parents, Cousin Molly, and Aunt Laura surrounding him, my son made his Christian debut, while all the other Mennonites of good name looked on. Then the congregation of Hemlock Creek had a picnic in the grove of maple trees near the cemetery. I was overwhelmed by the approval of my decision to keep Robert. I chose to never wonder about his father, not who he was, where he was, or what awful things he was doing. Robert was a part of me and Mama. Period. His little arms were fair and soft, and he was perfect in every way from the dark head of hair to the rosebud lips, as Laura called them, right down to his teeny toes in a straight row. Papa placed my small infant bed with rounded spindles in the old pantry room, and Mama set her rocker by the window. One night as I nursed my baby, rocking in the darkness in Mama's chair, I thanked the good Lord I had no recollection of the moment he was conceived. Mama took to Robert from the start, while Papa took more time to warm up, being a mite clumsy with such a fragile being. The hospital staff must have known of my situation. All were kind and patient as I faced head-on the unrealized pain of contractions and delivery. I no longer waited for God's good plans to reveal themselves to me. I knew Robert was part of it all. *Deliverance.*

At night I sang my bundle to sleep. I sang songs I learned on my radio all those long lonely days. During the sunny days while Robert slept, I washed his tiny clothes in soft herb soap and hung them to dry, his diapers in a neat row on the clothesline. I'd stand back and soak up the contented satisfaction of seeing them arranged so.

A month after Robert was born, in the warm dog days of August, I was asked to sing during a Sunday evening contemporary service geared toward young people. The church was changing with the times ever so slightly. We now had a piano up front on the platform with the communion table and the pulpit. Two of us could actually play the thing to accompany hymn singing. Tommy Heckler, who had dropped the boyish Tommy for Tom, made good on his mother's bribery and now played quite decently. Still amusing to me was how quickly he'd close the lid with a thud and flee to his seat when the singing ended. That never ceased to bring a smile, but now I knew him to be a naturally reticent young man, to the dismay of many of the young girls. One could never tell if he actually enjoyed playing the piano or simply suffered through it as his allotted fate. I, on the other hand, lived for the day I was asked to play or sing.

~

At eight months, Robert could crawl almost as fast as I could walk. I had to watch his every move, or something would end up in his mouth, like a match stick or a peach pit. And the stairs were a constant dread. He'd be up them in a flash, and down them even quicker. Oh, the screams that followed, but he was a tumble bumble little guy who quickly forgot pain. He was the joy of my life.

I hadn't given any more thought to the manhunt on my behalf, until a cold March day when the howling wind delivered Sheriff Mike to our door. He knocked and I opened to see him there gripping his hat,+ his navy blue tie blown over his shoulder, hair askew, and a nose wind-whipped to a crimson red.

"Anna, we may have found the fellow in the Chevy that did you so much harm."

"Oh!" It was so unexpected and I had gone on with my life. "Come on in, Sheriff." He took over our small living room with his bigger than life presence. Mama came in from the kitchen, drying her hands and removing her apron. I was surprised to see that Sheriff Mike looked at her with such softness. He actually became shy in her presence. How interesting.

"Lizzy."

"Michael." They nodded at each other in greeting. "What brings you here today?"

His professionalism took over. "We think we found the fellow that...uh... hurt, well, attacked Anna. He's been shacked up over New Berlin way. It took a bit of detective work on my off-hours, but I think I found him." Mama motioned him to sit on the sofa and I took the matching upholstered chair. Then *Lizzy* perched on the opposite end of the sofa, half turned toward Mike. We sat waiting for him to continue.

"I brought him in today. We got him on embezzlement charges. I followed up on the Chevy title, but he had changed his name. Took on his mother's maiden name." Robert was asleep and I hoped he wouldn't waken yet. I had to concentrate on what Mike had to say.

"If you can, Anna," he pointed his hat toward me, "would you come to the station tomorrow and tell me if you recognize him? I want this guy behind bars for a good long time, so we want to nail him on several serious charges, along with endangering a minor and leaving the scene of a crime." He said it with malice. The man took his job very seriously, and well he should. I would have added *destroying* the life of a minor, but that would have sounded vulgar. As if I was ungrateful for my baby. I kept my conflicted thoughts to myself.

"I think I can get there. The station in Hemlock Creek?" He nodded.

"Best if you can bring your folks for moral support, but don't bring your baby." I gave him a look. Like I would do such a thing. What was he thinking?

There was an uncomfortable pause. "Well." Sheriff Mike slapped his hands on his knees and stood. "Must get back to work. See you tomorrow, Lizzy, Anna." He left us to ourselves with a lingering gust of cold air to counteract the heat from the kitchen stove.

"So," said Mama, "Michael really took this to heart. I honestly hadn't thought this day would come. Actually, I hoped it wouldn't, for your sake," she added.

I didn't know what I felt other than a strange sense of loss which leeched its way through my body. I hoped I would recognize the face and get it all behind me. Robert need never know what his Mama went through. No more wondering, no more nightmares.

~

Once again the three Moyers sat in the small local courthouse room with the judge presiding from his elevated position. And once more Sheriff Mike escorted in a young man of average height, dark hair falling over eyes filled with anger and an apathetic world-be-hanged attitude. I knew instantly. Anger bubbled up in me like a boiling tea pot as I stared at his back, almost willing him to turn and see the "Nigger Girl" whose life he had violently stolen. *You sorry excuse for a human being, see ME, Anna Mae Moyer. I am standing, my family around me. I was not ruined. You, on the other hand, will be. Thank God!* Anger and vengeance were morphing into sheer hatred, a feeling that seemed right and deserved.

The legal words droned on. No family here for this young man, no legal representation. The court would have to assign one. I was not shaking this time, nor was I in a sweat. I felt an unearthly calm. This was good for me, to face this person and see him for what he was, and to know I was stronger than he because I had the Lord for my strength, and I had my family. The baby boy that resulted from this animal attack on a young innocent girl will not grow up like this angry, violent, unloved young man. The chain of his life's events which made him like he was stopped right here in this courtroom. My little Robert would have no part.

My name was called. I stood without help this time, stood straight up with my chin firmly set, mouth closed tightly, in the face of the perpetrator. He turned, saw me standing, and there was no sign of recollection, no remorse on that unshaven face. No emotion. He was an empty shell. His presence prompted unhidden memories: the smell of strong drink that I sometimes noticed exuding from Mr. Widrig, the other smell - a loathsome burnt mixture of something acidic, like leaves, the dirty cloth smelling like gasoline that was shoved in my mouth, the pain of the fight, the intense fear.

Narrow green eyes showed a soul full of perverseness and emptiness as he squinted in the sunlight streaming through the long window with its bars of protection. He did not seem to care that he was in a very bad way.

"Anna Moyer, have you seen this young man before?"

"Yes, Sir, I have. He is the one who attacked me October of 1963." There was power in the pronouncement. A moment's silence followed during which some woman, off to the side, typed like fury. Papa leaned forward, his hands in tightly closed fists. Mama was as still as Lot's wife.

"Young man, do you have something to say on your behalf?"

"Got nothin' to say, never seen her before," he spat out. "She's a liar! Look at her! *Course* she's a liar!" He stopped himself short of spouting any more incriminating insults. The muscle in Sheriff Mike's jaw protruded. In the silence brought on by that shocking statement, my mother made a strange sound as if stifling a scream and my father shifted his position. I stood with my head up in defiance of the statement, looking directly at the judge, who in turn, was watching me.

"Miss Moyer, do you recognize that voice?"

"Yessir." I spoke firmly with assurance. "He is the one who attacked me and left me for dead." I probably shouldn't have added that last part, but I was coming in for the kill. Sheriff Mike nodded and whipped out his handcuffs, then joined the wrists behind the wrinkled denim shirt that was hanging over black jeans. Rights were read.

More legal words, more charges, a jury of peers will be assigned, bail set at... It was over, but not before I heard the judge say, "Robert Maurice Malone, you are a menace to civilized society..."

Oh no! Please tell me I did not hear that name... *Robert!* My shoulders slumped. The irony cut through me like someone had opened a cauterized wound. All the starch was wiped out of me. Mama grabbed my hand and said repeatedly, "You did not know - you had no idea." She addressed Papa in a hissing whisper, "Why hadn't we thought about that?"

Don't bring your baby. Don't bring little Robert. The words resurfaced, a mocking echo. Of all the names in the world. Never would I call him Robert again...only Bobby.

~

Life is always future bound whether we are ready to move forward or not. I knew it was time to go on as that fateful March ushered in a gentle spring. I fought to get past the courtroom scene which played over in my mind, past the uncertainties of who I was, past my mother's issues. How I desired to leave all that behind and move forward into my life with Bobby.

My life found its center in my religious heritage. Being Mennonite was a lifestyle as well as a religious belief. Community formed our strong foundation and we faced our world not as individuals but as a group. Often the fellowship pooled monetary resources to help any that needed medical care since we did not carry any insurance such as our worldly neighbors purchased. When large jobs needed completed in short order we, like our *Amisch* brethren, banded together and worked until the job was completed, no matter the size. I had seen barns go up in a day and acres of orchards plucked clean of their harvest in an afternoon. My Fellowship, the folks who worshiped with my family on the Sabbath, seemed to swarm around me, protecting and supporting like a suit of armor during my difficult time. There were no judgmental remarks about my attack or my ensuing plight. Bobby was accepted from the start and I was reinstated into my church life as soon as my confinement ended. I loved that church building as much as I loved the people. It was my refuge.

Such a beautifully plain building, my church, made of solid red brick. Unlike the library, no shutters adorned the long, wide windows of clear glass. The interior was also a simple affair containing three sections; the middle of long bench pews, the side sections with wooden folding chairs. Overhead, lights hung from chains, the light diffused by milky glass globes. New to the scene was a small spinet piano off to the side in front, a simple table front and center, and a wooden pulpit opposite the piano, all this on a slightly risen platform.

"Church members must maintain close unity with one another, remembering separation from the world, nonresistance to evil, mutual burden-bearing...then we shall be able to retain proper relationship with our Lord, our church, and our society about us," to quote Bishop Lapp in 1947. There had been great emphasis on the "no resistance to evil" part. According to Papa, these beliefs came into play regarding my personal attack and its outcome. He also made a veiled allusion to another close relative's life, which left me with even more questions.

I had been faulty to think the church would have tossed Mama out on her ear for any deviation from "proper conduct." On my part, I had been a victim of a great evil and it was imperative for me to just go on in the face of it, as Great Grandma Moyer reminded me. The church did indeed bear my burden in a mutual way, though some of my acquaintances were ill-at-ease in my presence and it showed up in their stilted conversations. It must have been tricky to know what to say or what not to say since I had experienced traumas they could not even begin to understand.

On a Sabbath morning, unmarried young people sixteen and older sat separated on each far side of the church, their families filling the middle. I posed a gray area in the seating arrangement since I was still an unwed young person but also a mother. Where should I sit? My dilemma resulted in a decision made by our bishop: I was to sit with my parents, my son by my side. I missed my position that identified me with my cousins and friends. Even this had been stripped from me. I was no longer a part of my peer group. Cousin Esther and I locked eyes as she filed into a row of folding chairs with others my age, while Cousin Abram, now courting Ruth Good, took his place opposite them. Cousin Eva was soon to be married to a young man of good German heritage who was sadly not from our denomination, but our family held out hope that we could shift his Lutheran alliances. The Jacob Moyer family, my family, filled a miniscule place on a bench pew surrounded by large families with stair-step children, all so familiar and dear to me. Bobby would grow up as I did, knowing his place in the Fellowship.

A large white banner hung over the communion table. "Ye must be born again," it read in blaring uppercase letters. My eyes always gravitated there and I thought about those words of Jesus. I wanted to be born again, believe me, if only to come out with lighter hair and skin! I knew this is not what the Lord meant, but as a young person it was hard to concentrate on the inward when the outward needed so much attention. It was a maturing process, as most things are. I prayed for heart cleansing and the renewing of my mind to face this earthly walk, though not certain what it all meant. But it was expected of me to be of this mind, and there was great security growing up within the confines of our church fellowship with its lofty beliefs.

On the other side, I was ill prepared and uncomfortable facing the outside world. This, too, was a maturing process that had to come about in order for me to pursue my music, my dream of singing, mostly. Where was I to go with this passion of mine? Where would it lead? And now with the care of Bobby as he toddled into trouble, well, he consumed my time, energies and fears. I hoped he would survive all the falls, scrapes, and choking hazards. Would God ever see fit to bring my desire to sing into actuality? I had my doubts.

This mindset of "nonresistance to evil" influenced our decision to drop charges against Robert Maurice Malone. He was facing other ones that would incarcerate him for a good many years. I was not up to a grilling on the witness stand during a court proceeding, reliving the pain, seeing that dark empty face. It was enough that he was the one, he was apprehended and could no longer haunt me, terrorize my nights, or hurt another as he did me. Sheriff Michael was not happy about our decision, but not surprised either. Though not a part of our fellowship, the sheriff seemed very familiar with our beliefs. It was not the first time there was an attack against peace loving people. Sister communities like Lancaster, Pennsylvania, had recorded attacks as did Lowville, New York. But here in Hemlock Creek? Mine was a first in two ways: an attack on an under-age female and the color of my skin that may have labeled this a racial attack.

~

"Mama, you seem familiar with the court proceedings. Did you ever sit in on a court case?"

"Of course not," came the acid-laced response. The silver clattered onto the drying towel. I grabbed them and wiped them dry with little thought or thoroughness. A far smarter girl would have stopped right there, but not me. I was ready to tread where angels fear.

"I feel that you know something about my birth that you are not telling me, Mama."

She put down the dish she was washing with a deliberate heavy clunk against the counter. I was not in the habit of seeing my mother with anger on her soft face with its lines forming around the blue eyes. Now her brow was drawn in sharply between those eyes, her mouth a prim line snapped shut from tight jaws. Oh boy. What had I done now? Her blue apron was taut under the strain as she repeatedly rubbed her hands over it. I reached for a plate and dried with great focus.

"Anna Mae Moyer," she ejected, hands defensively placed on her thin hips. "You are sixteen now, and have experienced an awful thing that I couldn't protect you from." I knew what was coming next, the wagging finger.

Sure enough. Her pointed index finger started waving at me. "You have strength of character and a stubborn streak that would cause pride in your pilgrim ancestors, but I have little time for it! I will not, I repeat, *will not* let you badger and harass me with your accusations. It is enough to let *Gott* be the One who knows such things. You best not bring this up again, you hear me, Anna?"

This passionate rush of words assaulted my ears and squelched my willful pestering for answers. I did not know my mother had a sharp side. Could this be the same woman who cried and cried, rocked and rocked all through my growing up years? She had fire inside that frail, pale little body. And it was beginning to flame up. In my younger years, what had smothered the flame? What was rekindling it? My mother was an enigma to me. Yet, this was progress in a hard, challenging way. The impenetrable shell around my mother was cracking.

ELEVEN

"Would you consider working for me part-time, Anna?" Miss Arlene asked me after Thanksgiving. "I am finding it a bit hard to keep up the hours here all by myself. And now that quilting and cross stitching are so popular I could use the extra help." She rubbed her lower back, which I knew was causing her pain. "I wanted to ask you first before considering anyone else." I smiled. That was a flattering consideration. I told her I would let her know by the week's end.

Would Mama be able to keep up with my high maintenance son? He was trying to walk by hanging on to things, but in moments of sheer determination would plop back down on his diapered bottom and crawl like crazy, little knees and feet all red from friction against the hardwood floors. Would it be right of me to even ask if my mother could handle such a responsibility? Wouldn't know 'til I tried.

"Mama, I was at Miss Arlene's this afternoon. She is having so much business that she needs an extra hand. She asked me if I was available." No answer. Time to introduce plan B.

"Maybe I could ask Molly if she is up to a little extra money babysitting." After a moment Mama's head bobbed.

"I think Molly would be a good caretaker for Bobby." I smiled to myself over her terminology. I was used to words getting jumbled up. Well, *goot*, that settled that.

"Shall I take him to her place or can she come here? Which would work best for you, Mama?"

"Oh, she can come here. That would be easier for Bobby now that it is getting cold out."

Molly was happy to earn a little extra which I gladly parted with from my meager pay. I was excited to get out of the house for a couple hours every day. I trusted Molly with my son and also with my mother. She knew Mama's history and would not be unprepared for mood changes. But I was unprepared for my reception by Miss Arlene's regular non-Mennonite customers.

I forced myself to be outgoing and extra courteous. "Good Morning! May I be of assistance?" The eyes under the winter fur hat checked me over suspiciously. "I'd like to consult with Miss Arlene about what she thinks is the best fabric combination." Snubbed, I was. Often. Was it my skin color? My wide nose? My dark tightly curled hair? Poor Miss Arlene had more attention than ever. I was sometimes invisible, sometimes ignored, sometimes just smiled at and then overlooked.

Thankfully, not all customers were rude. Familiar faces greeted me just as warmly as I did them. I found I had an eye for matching fabrics for quilt patterns, both for beds and for wall hangings, and before long my advice was sought as frequently as Miss Arlene's. I tried my hand at a couple of crib-sized quilts since time played on my hands when customers were lacking. I made a wonderful coverlet for Bobby's bed appliqueing a Noah's Ark theme with the animals by twos. Up at the top I placed a white dove with a twig in its mouth as the rainbow faded off to the other side. It received good reviews from others who seemed to eye it with admiration as it hung on a dowel gracing open wall space. I was flattered at the response but was eager to take it home for its intended use. All in all, the job with Miss Arlene was good for me, and helped me learn social astuteness as I dealt with all sorts of women. I was not even seventeen years old yet, but I felt much older and wiser than the giggling gaggle of girls from town.

Always a song in my head. Always. I would sing as I rode to Miss Arlene's on my new bike. Papa had found a *goot* deal on a taller Schwinn with gears, to replace my old one. I often polished the bright glistening chrome over the tires with the blue kerchief I wore over my hair and tied under my chin. I felt quite grand on that new bike, let me say. Singing and riding became my two favorite things to do. What could anyone do to me now? No fears of a red and white Chevy haunted me as I rode into town. Though I missed going to school, I had my little job and my child to keep me busy, along with church functions. But with so much of life looming ahead of me I was restless and impatient. What would come of me? My dream of being a famous singer began to seem like a girlish fancy. How would God work things out for me? My dream couldn't happen here at this store, or anywhere here in little Hemlock Creek, Ohio. At times I still felt keenly like Mulatto Marmalady whose tan would not wash away.

~

That Christmas I accompanied much of the congregational music and also sang a John Peterson song written seven years back called "No Room." Everyone's attention was on our children as they acted out the Christmas message. I was well off to the side, mostly unseen, and it was fun to hear visitors asking who sang that song. Life was returning to the norm. Bobby grew as quickly as everyone said he would, judging by his big puppy paw feet. Mama's moods no longer swung to the helpless, despairing side. I was growing too. I was now as tall as Mama, which wasn't saying much, but my feet and hands were cumbersome compared to her dainty build. I kept my hair trimmed to my neck and maintained a daily fight to smooth it. When I smiled at customers they saw a nice white row of teeth past my full lips. Full was a word that seemed to apply to an awful lot of me. God didn't make much on me or in me that was scant. Mama said even my dreams were 'way too big and I'd better 'trim them back to size.' But I did not know how I could ever do that. I wanted so much more than singing in church now and then.

Hope surged inside of me when Miss Arlene shared about Mrs. Ledbeder's grown daughter who was a private music instructor some fifteen miles away. She had attended Brown University to major in voice. Here seemed part of a good plan for a new direction falling into my lap. I felt hope that hadn't shown its face in a while. I stopped at the library one cold January day after New Year 1965 rolled in with all its bleakness and chill.

"Hello, Anna, how are you?" Mrs. Ledbeder was wearing a screaming loud paisley tunic over her version of bell-bottom pants. "How's little Bobby?" Her hair was a new tint, more reddish than usual. She smelled of Shower to Shower body powder and Cashmere soap. She always spoke in a whisper even if there were no patrons sitting around. I figured she was not able to talk loudly so she made up for it in her apparel.

"We are just fine, Mrs. Ledbeder. Bobby is walking now. Yes, he is a handful." We chit-chatted about baby milestones and such. "I came with a question for you, but it's not about books."

"Alright, dear." She settled back in her swivel chair on wheels. I planted both arms on the tall wooden counter and smiled. "Miss Arlene told me about your daughter, the one who teaches voice over in Alba."

"Yes. Amanda has a lovely soprano voice. I think she has a full schedule of students now." My shoulders slumped. "And you interested in my daughter?" she went on.

"Oh, well, I was hoping to get in touch with her to see about voice lessons."

"Ah! And do you still take piano from Miss Lutz?"

"No, that ended before Bobby was born. But I play at my church now, me and Tommy Heckler."

"Ahh, Tommy. I used to feel sorry for that boy. His mother even checked out his library books for him." We chuckled, quietly of course.

"Well, I would love to take voice lessons. Do you think there's a chance with your daughter?"

"I can't say, but why don't I write down her telephone number. Would you be able to give her a ring?"

"Yes, I can. We have a telephone in our house now."

"Good. Very handy, isn't it? Do you have a party line?"

I nodded. "With the Alderfers, but they are so seldom on the line. We are not Chatty Cathies, either of us." Mrs. Ledbeder nodded, smiling as she handed me a piece of memo paper with "From Your Librarian" at the top and the phone number in precise print. I rode home quickly to make my call.

~

"Miss Ledbeder's School of Voice." In the background a female was singing a choral scale, faintly off-key.

"Hello, is this Miss Amanda Ledbeder? Hello, my name is Anna Moyer and I received this number from your mother, our librarian. Do you have an opening for another voice student?"

"Well, let me see, I am pretty well booked up, but do happen to have an opening now on Saturdays. Anna, did you say? Alright, Anna, I could place you on Saturday mornings at 11:30, if you can make it at that time."

"Yes, I'll take it. Write me on your schedule. I love to sing, Miss Ledbeder, and this is part of my dream."

"Yes, well," she replied hesitantly as if she heard that all too often, "we will see how your first lesson goes, Anna. You must work hard and practice your scales every day. Do not expect too much too soon. The voice box is a muscle that takes time to develop." The poor girl in the background wasn't yet developed as was proven by her final high note and Miss Ledbeder gave a little sound that made me think she just groaned and rolled her eyes.

"I will work hard, I promise, Miss Ledbeder. May I start this Saturday?"

"Sure, and call me Miss Amanda. Goodbye, Anna. Let's hope we do not have snow to hinder your travels here."

That's how it all started with Miss Amanda. I became bold and asked my father to teach me how to drive the Oldsmobile so I could get a license. Mama was stunned. After the initial shock, Papa said, "Well, why not!" and on clear evenings he'd sit on the passenger side, his big old knuckles white from clutching the dash board as I practiced turning corners on our deserted back roads. It was with a feeling of triumph that I faced another milestone toward self-independence.

~

What a strange year in our nation, this year of turmoil, 1965. The war in Vietnam escalated with more ground troops sent overseas at the decision of President Lyndon Johnson. On our nightly national news, Alabama was the scene of gruesome interest. Voting rights were on the line for African Americans, resulting in protest marches, some footage so bloody I was glad we had no television. Martin Luther King, Jr. was headline news with amazing speeches on behalf of equality. Recently I had heard his latest, "How Long, Not Long" and was touched to my core. News traveled to Miss Arlene's, and she, being of open mind, shared many topics for intense discussion.

On a more local scene, we were once again sucked into the outside world as the trial of Robert Maurice Malone was scheduled. Though we pressed no charges on my behalf, that young man had enough others to keep him in the state penitentiary for a long time. The jury convicted him on three major accounts and the judge "threw the book at him," so said Sheriff Mike. There was a write-up in the daily newspaper, but fortunately there was no mention about Bobby or me. It was as done as Christmas in June. There was one little visible thing that remained of the whole terrifying ordeal: for some reason, that patch of hair never grew back over my left ear. I had to work my hair to cover it. Other tell-tail signs were not so visible.

~

We had a snowstorm in March. It was a doozy with huge drifts and power outages. Bobby, almost walking now, was feeling as housebound as I was. The trains on the Baltimore and Ohio lines even had trouble pushing some of the drifts from their tracks. Nightfall arrived around 6:00, dinner time, and Mama and I were setting the serving bowls on the table. There was a triple knock on the porch door off the kitchen. Often we do not hear when a visitor knocks out there, since it is a room away. Bobby was in his high chair ready for mashed potatoes, peas, and squash. It seemed a rudely inopportune time for someone to come calling.

"I'll see who it is," I said to my parents as they were ready to be seated. I went through the inner door to the outer one, but stopped before opening it. It was not a person I knew or had seen before. He was middle aged or elderly, scantily dressed, scraggly, without a hat, and he had his arms wrapped for warmth around his skinny body. I yelled through the storm, "Can I help you?"

"Can I spend the night in your barn?" a raspy voice forced to be heard. I did not know how to respond. Should I ask him to come in and wait on the porch? Or leave him there while I asked Mama and Papa. He looked totally miserable. I remembered Cousin Abram saying about the Christian thing to do for hobos.

"Come into the porch." I unlatched the door and the wind threatened to blow it off its hinges. One whiff told me this man had not been in a civilized state for a long time. "Wait here while I get my father." He only shivered in spasms and looked at me with hollow eyes, scant gray hair all askew. A weak purple hand tried to comb it back.

I rushed back into the warm kitchen bathed in its amber lamp light. "There's a hobo out there…" I never finished my sentence. Papa sprang from the table and almost pushed past me. Mama said, "What does he look like?" Of all the strange questions! I started to ignore her since it didn't matter what he looked like, but, to appease her I said, "He looked absolutely frozen."

I scampered after Papa, thinking about what plate to use if I were to get him some food, and should I dig out a picnic fork so he wasn't tempted to steal our silverware. Papa confronted the poor man who was still shaking from the cold.

"Go on with you. Get away from here. We have no food or shelter for you. There's a house down the road to the left that will give you something." The man said nothing and turned quickly as if escaping the barrage of denials. Papa yelled against the wind, waving his arm as if shooing away some stray dog. The wind and snow howled around the back stoop.

The skinny slumped body seemed hunched over as he faced the cold once again. He had not tried to catch the door as the wind whipped it back. Papa kicked snow away and brought the door back into place while the shadowy figure plodded through a large drift covering our walkway. The whiteness of the swirling snow brought the only light to the scene and the form soon disappeared.

How could this be my peaceable Christian Papa? He just refused this poor man a place in our barn while the snow gobbled him up. I followed Papa into the house mutely. A strange anger started simmering in me, one that I was not accustomed to, particularly regarding human injustices. These were becoming very visible and very rampant in my young mind. The more I lived, the more I saw. The more I saw, the angrier I got.

Before reentering the kitchen, Papa dragged an old table in front of the porch door, as if the frozen man would somehow gather the strength to return and break in. " Anna, you are too trusting. There are many things you do not know about." *I know more than you think.* Returning to the table he sat heavily in his chair, leaned forward on his elbows and brought both hands over his face. It was a minute before he seemed composed enough to give a perfunctory grace and begin his meal. By then I had lost my desire for food. How could he dare to thank God after what he had done? I know I was sulking. Mama pecked at her food with her fork, then gave up completely.

"What did he look like?" she whispered again, with that look like she often had when I was younger. It was a crazy person look, a furtive look. I hated to admit that, but that is what it was. Papa ignored her or did not hear her, maybe both. I was irked.

"What does it matter? Mama, does it really matter?" I countered her question crossly, so saddened I was by the whole scene. Bobby had his spoon in hand and winged some mashed peas across the table. I reprimanded him too harshly which brought tears. Mama's eyes went from face to face around the table. Then she sat in silent resignation, her question unanswered, watching Bobby as I fed him. Papa ate quickly without the normal second helping before retiring to his chair in the living room. The only sounds came from Bobby, and we were all used to that.

The entire occurrence happened in only five minutes but it colored the entire week and lodged in my memory for all my days.

TWELVE

Miss Amanda Ledbeder did not know what to do with me. I could see it in her face. I fear she had not much hope when I first approached her door and entered her small music studio that doubled as her living room. Me, just an inconspicuous all-too-hopeful excited little wannabe. If my skin color surprised her, she did not let on. After introductions, she had me stand by her studio upright with properly folded hands, elbows slightly extended from my body at mid-torso. In this posture, she asked me to sing in echo what I heard her play. She played a scale in thirds. I sang. She upped by a whole note and played the next triad. I sang. Higher and higher, then lower and lower, in attempts to find my perfect range, which I could have told her had she asked. Finally, her hands rested on the keyboard as she looked up at me. I was having a wonderful time and wanted more of those challenging echo scales. Her look was inscrutable and left me feeling a bit uncomfortable. With sudden defeating discouragement, I thought... *she is disappointed.* I was not good enough after all. I should have known.

With as much courage as I could muster, my lower lip starting to tremble, I said, "I am sorry Miss Amanda. I really thought I might be good enough to pursue my dream of singing as a career. I..." I did not finish my sentence for fear I might embarrass myself by crying, so I turned quickly saying over my shoulder, "You have been very kind to hear me." I walked the several steps to the coat tree, reached up to the hook where my coat hung in a forlorn fashion by the neck. After feeling in the pocket I set the $4.00 fee on a little entry table before grabbing my woolen beret with the ridiculous pom-pom protruding from its gathered center. I heard rustling behind me.

"Anna, wait! Where are you going?" Miss Ledbeder rose from the piano bench. She seemed truly puzzled, her small heart-shaped face pinched in confusion. Had my own insecurities caused me to misread her? "I am sorry you have misunderstood my silence or my expression." She came to me, replaced my coat on its hook, and gently guided me back to my place by the piano. "Please, Anna, you must sing some more for me." She opened her piano bench and removed some sheet music and books. "Tell me, what kind of music do you enjoy singing the most?" She fanned her selections on top of the unadorned piano lid. Show tunes, operatic scores, religious, even some Negro spirituals, but no jazz or blues. So I had misunderstood. I quickly recovered my composure.

"I like all kinds of music but I especially enjoy singing Nat King Cole songs like *Chances Are*, and Henry Mancini's *Moon River*."

Ah! I had struck a common chord and watched as Miss Amanda leafed through her sheet music. Right now she resembled her mother as she searched her papers, but only in organization skills, definitely not in looks or dress. With a flourish she flung the sought after piece in the air in front of me.

"*Moon River!*" she said with triumphant enthusiasm. "I love playing this piece. It's easy but so beautiful. Almost haunting, the way Audrey Hepburn sang it in *Breakfast at Tiffany's*, though not a movie of good moral repute," she added shyly. A smile broke out on her soft face with its laugh lines and her deep-set brown eyes laughed also. She excitedly lined up the pages, checking the order. "This may or may not be your best key, but let's give it a try."

I did not even need to look at the words. When I heard the piano decrescendo, I did the same. As Miss Amanda increased her volume, I followed. When she slowed I stuck with her like a bur. As I finished singing the last line, the piano ended softly and we were silent as the chords faded on their own accord. I watched my teacher's face.

"Oh, Anna, that was… Oh, I have no words…and you are so young! You have not had voice lessons?" I shook my head, smiling and flushing with embarrassment by her praise. "Ever?" No, my head again responded. Then I laughed from deep inside myself. Miss Amanda placed song after song before me and I sang, encouraged and strengthened by her enthusiasm over me. She taught me how to hold my chin down to keep from straining my voice, and to feel the sound coming from deep within, to protect my throat. When my first lesson was over she thanked me for calling her. I had not felt so light-hearted in a long time. I left with an assignment booklet, some scales handwritten on score paper, and a song, *The Lord's Prayer*, to learn for the following Saturday.

God was showing me His plans for my life, me, ruined and left for dead, little mixed-up Anna Mae Moyer. Maybe this was an example of how the Lord works all things for good for those who are called according to His purpose. Papa was waiting for me in the Oldsmobile, a patient man who set aside Saturday morning chores to wait for his daughter to emerge from a little Cape Cod in the small town of Alba.

"I heard you, Anna Mae. I could hear you right through the closed windows," he chuckled. Was that a good thing? I checked his face. Yes, it was a very good thing. Papa's smile and nod showed his approval. It was enough. Good thing, or else I would have never known. He was a man of few words and even fewer compliments.

On my third lesson, I had perfected *The Lord's Prayer* to memory and was willing to perform at the recital in the spring. Normally a new student was asked to wait a year before a solo performance. "This is not a time for prima donnas," Miss Ledbeder warned. "Each must earn the honor of performing." It was the end of March and my life was full. I was almost ready to try my hand at the driver's test. For now Papa worked his schedule around my Saturday lesson, shifting his chores aside to devote an hour to my singing.

~

Black ice, they called it. Black because it was undetected. Black like sin and evil. The big old Oldsmobile hit that patch and we careened off the road. We had been traveling about fifty miles an hour when we hit that patch. Over and over I screamed, Papa frantically fighting the wheel for control. Then, a huge old tree sprang up ahead, wide from years of growth. The final impact, metal against wood, right against the front driver's side, and that big old tree didn't give. I was slammed against my father's arm and hip. That solid old car was built before seat belts. My father's head seared through the windshield. When the emergency workers arrived we were both covered in blood. I was chattering uncontrollably, my whole body vibrating with the shock. Poor Papa's head wound sent blood all over the car, it seemed. I must have screamed until my God gift was silenced, and nothing but a raspy hoarse voice issued from my injured throat. I lost my song for many months after I lost my Papa.

THIRTEEN

For some time, it was as if I had lost both parents. Over and over like a trapped droning bee, her blue eyes swollen with the skin underneath patchy and red, my mother muttered to herself, "*Ich sterbe, Ich sterbe.*"

No, Mama, you are not dying, not without me you aren't. And I think we will have to live on without precious Papa, your precious Jacob. We have little Bobby to care for. Was it only in the last two years that Papa and I had become so close? How did that happen and what prompted the change in him from an absent to a present father figure? From the time Robert Malone attacked me, he had been like a different person toward me. I had the father I always wanted for such a short time.

Our Hemlock Creek Mennonite fellowship did not allow caskets inside the sanctuary, but instead assented to the use of a smaller chapel area recently built in the huge wing off the original building. The reason for this was that many outsiders would probably attend the service and bring with them their worldly ways, and everyone knew how Deacon Gehman hated cigarette butts on church property. Papa was known and respected in town, even though we led a rather solitary life together. After the service, a great retinue of both family members and friends walked out to the cemetery. We held each other up, my cousins and I. Molly held my Bobby, dressed in a miniature suit under his winter coat, with small black shoes. Seeing the dirt flung over the box almost did me in, as I couldn't bear to see my Papa forever removed from my sight in that cold dark hole. My aunts cloistered around Mama, who by this time was totally spent of tears. Her eyes were closed and the frosted air from her breath joined with those around her. Then we dwindled away in plain shiny black vehicles, to meet once again for moral support at our home.

Back home, on the front porch, were steaming pots filled with coffee alongside huge platters of freshly fried donuts and an assortment of sandwiches arrayed on trays held up by a makeshift table. The crowd converged onto our land, up on our porch and into our home. Relatives and outsiders alike. I felt nothing, saw little, ate less. Once again the sun needed to stop its winter journey, the shadows should have been frozen in time. *How could those men be laughing over there? Tell them to leave. Tell the children to stop running. Why is there food here like we are celebrating a birthday? Go away, all you people!*

"Anna." I felt a hand on my arm and looked into the dear plain face of Miss Lutz, with her familiar, kind voice. "Anna, I am so sorry."

Oh please don't give me sympathy – I'll start crying all over again. But cry I did. She held me, offering a tissue dug from the depths of her massive black handbag. "I lost my father when I was twenty-four. I thought I'd never live again. It took me over a year to get past my grief." Tears afresh. There was no end. The scene of the accident so vivid, so awful, kept replaying in my tortured mind.

"He'd be alive if I hadn't had that crazy notion to be a singer. He was bringing me home from voice lessons," I sobbed into her shoulder. "I don't think I will ever want to sing again." There is no such thing as dignity in true grief. I was undone. Another arm came around my shoulder but I did not look to see. "I am so selfish, Miss Lutz. I can never forgive myself," I said through ragged breaths.

"This is probably not the right thing to say," my old piano teacher replied, "but in time you will feel like yourself again and you will sing. It is who you are, Anna. And you will realize there is nothing to forgive."

"That is right, Anna Mae, your father would want you to sing again when you are feeling better," came the musical voice of Miss Amanda Ledbeder, whose lips were near my ear. "The good Lord will allow him to hear you and he will be so pleased." For some odd reason this last statement gave me some iota of comfort and I sniffled and patted away the remaining tears. Tissues were pathetic replacements for cloth.

"And your mother," Miss Lutz continued, " well, she will need you to go on eventually. Bobby, too." Miss Ledbeder nodded in agreement as I wiped my nose and searched the crowd at the mention of my little boy's name. I needed to hold him. "Where is he?" I asked. Miss Lutz pointed, "Over there, with your cousin Eva and her husband."

I stumbled over, tripping on the end of the rocker foot, but at least I stayed upright. "Eva, here, let me take him." Bobby reached sleepily for me and nestled against my shoulder. *My little man, my dearest baby.* Somehow the day ended, all the people went their ways, aunties cleaned up our home, the men finished up chores in the barn, and only Aunt Laura stayed to care for us. Mama was given a pill, I'm sure, for she slept hard all through the night. In the morning my cousin Abram would be moving in with us to keep up chores until the time we decided what to do with this farm that Mother and I could not handle on our own. He and Ruth Good agreed to postpone their wedding for a short time, giving us a chance to think things through.

~

Sheriff Mike stood once again on our porch with his hat in his hand. His police car parked at the end of our walkway looked like an alien, so out of place and unwanted in front of our home. I watched and listened as Aunt Laura invited him in and asked him to have a seat in the living room. Bobby was playing on the floor on our green and tan braided rug, his wooden farm set all around him. I had parked my tired body on the sofa, watching him or looking out the window as each day brought a flurry of new growth to the budding trees. Mother, as usual, was in her room. We had buried Father only two months ago but time tricked my mind. Sometimes it seemed so long ago that he sat at the table or read his papers in his comfy chair. Other times, I couldn't imagine where sixty days had gone. My son was growing, running, talking, and feeding himself. Sheriff Mike patted Bobby's dark brown hair that stuck up in soft cowlicks on top. Mike asked him which farm animal was his favorite, to which my son replied "the cows, same as Grandpa." *Oh God, will this loss and pain ever go away?* Sheriff Mike stood up after making Bobby laugh about something to do with cows, and rejoined Laura in the entryway. I only caught bits and pieces, but tried not to care.

He had asked to see Lizzy, to offer his condolences. I'd never grow accustomed to my mother being called Lizzy. He was on duty the day of the funeral and then thought it best to wait a while before showing up. I realized I had tensed, expecting some report about Robert Malone. I breathed deeply and relaxed into the sofa cushions. In the distance with the midafternoon sun on his back, I watched lazily as Cousin Abram scurried from the granary to the milk house.

Aunt Laura's voice was quiet. "She has not seen visitors often…had to start giving her….. was this a personal visit or business?" To which came the reply, "Nothing urgent ...just a friendly visit....sorry to hear ....relapse." I felt like I was dozing off. Nothing was clear anymore and I was, oh, so tired all the time. When Bobby napped, I did too. From my fog I heard my name. That figures, they were talking about me. I did not really care. I wasn't in the mood for visiting. I had not been in the mood for much of anything since Papa died.

"....news....Robert....sent to.... never worry again...always wondered.....Jacob would attack again..." I roused from my reverie as curiosity took ahold.

"You can stop whispering, Sheriff Mike," I said aloud, causing them to turn their heads in my direction. Something about hearing first Robert's then my father's name and 'attacking again' forced me wide awake.

"Tell me, please, I want to know what you are saying to Aunt Laura." He hesitated, looked at Laura, and returned to the living room. Laura scooted Bobby into the kitchen for a little snack before nap time, and Mike once more seated his muscular bulk of a body in our chair that matched the sofa. I shook my head to get rid of the cobwebs and smoothed my crazy hair with my hands. Hopeless. I hadn't taken any time to do it right.

"So, is there some news I should know about? This isn't just to wish us condolences, is it?"

"Well, Anna, I wanted to wish you and your mother my sympathy." Shaking his head, he seemed at a loss for words. "Terrible," he said sadly under his breath. He bolstered himself up. "Your dad and I were good friends in school, in fact, all our growing up years. I thought the world of your father, and your mother too." Once again, he fidgeted. Every time he faced my mother or even mentioned her name, he fidgeted. *What was behind that?* "Your dad and I used to play ball together, and swim at Bergey's Pond all summer, jumping off the wooden pier and doing cannonballs. He was a crazy fun guy." His face lit, lost in memories that I would never share and could not even imagine. My father a fun guy?? Are we talking about the same Jacob Moyer? "We also skated a lot in the winter at Bergey's, and when we were fourteen or fifteen your mom and her sisters and your aunt Laura, joined us sometimes." He smiled, his brown eyes lost somewhere out our window, enjoying fond recollections of a carefree time for all of them. I did not know this fun-loving, playful side of my parents. It intrigued me. I forgot all about news of Robert Malone.

"Sheriff Mike?" I shifted my position for a better look at this man. "Were you sweet on my mother?" I watched the smile disappear. There was no denying Mike was a handsome man in a rugged kind of way, even now in his forties, I guessed, going by what he said about school days with Papa. He frowned ever so slightly as if thinking. Or debating whether to say. He tossed his hands helplessly in his lap, jingling his massive set of keys hanging from a belt loop.

"Anna Mae, I was crazy about your mom. I wished like anything she had liked me, but I was not of the Fellowship. I am not even Lutheran." His lips set in resignation, and he finally returned my stare. "It was always Jacob, Anna. It was always and only your dad."

"Always *only* my father?" I dared to question. I could not let it go. "Sheriff, there had to be more to my story. Do you know why I am not full German Mennonite?"

Again I lost his eyes. He kept closing the windows. For being a law man he sure was timid. "I know I am a mulatto," I rambled on. "I even heard my aunt Jeanette use that word. She was trying to explain me to a newly married relative at the Moyer reunion one summer. I was only fourteen. But I knew anyway. I read about it the summer I turned twelve. Aunt Jeanette would have been mortified if she knew I overheard, but I did and I need to know about myself." I could not stop. Maybe he had some answers for me.

"Mama and Papa would not talk about it, so I always waited for the right time to ask my father again…after we became closer," I broke down. "That opportunity was gone forever. The wound, still so fresh with grief of loss, opened wide and I gushed. Mike waited, probably relieved for some extra time to formulate his answer. After I controlled myself, I pushed him again.

"Do you know anything about me?" I pleaded. I must have looked pitiful.

The crew-cut head nodded slowly before opening the windows again. "I do Anna, but," here he leaned toward me, arms on his legs, his hands open as if sacrificing something, " I feel it is something that should not come from me. I am not family." He stood very quickly, ready to bolt. "I am sorry, Anna, I'm just not the one to tell you." He skirted the toy farm set still scattered by his huge feet. "I hope and pray someday your mom will recover and…maybe she'll be able to…" His hands turned in and out in an apologetic gesture, as he left his sentence dangling. He turned from me and headed for the front door when I heard the words, "she only loved Jacob," said to the empty air around him. He was out the door. I watched him head down our walkway, putting on his hat as he returned to the alien craft parked in front of our house. The engine started on the second try and he backed with confidence out of our yard, back to Hemlock Creek and out of my life again. I was tired of my life, so tired. I had finally found a person with some answers and he refused to reveal what I needed to know.

Aunt Laura rushed into the room, holding Bobby. "Oh," she said dejectedly. "He's gone." She peered out the window. "I really wanted a chance to thank him and say goodbye." There was a strange yearning in her voice.

FOURTEEN

I saw the longing in my aunt's eyes. She had never married, neither had he. Sheriff Michael Weber. Laura Lapp. Elizabeth Lapp. Jacob Moyer. Great Day! What a tangled up mess. Life now reduced the equation by one, and still the math was not working out right. Couldn't Sheriff Mike see that Laura was available and so similar to Mother in looks and in many facets of their personalities? And more to her credit, Laura was the steadfast and stable one, a real plus in my opinion. What kept those two apart? Was the family so against marrying out of the Fellowship? If I knew how to play matchmaker I'd give it a try. These things were on my mind as I walked into Hemlock Creek this June day. I was newly turned eighteen, older and wiser and more in tune to the things of the heart, so I thought.

The flowers were a riot of color erupting in every garden, bees everywhere with incessant buzzing to keep us away from their turf. I walked into town on these fine days just to smell the scents and keep my mind clear, as I readied myself to face the customers who were all abuzz about the world. For so long our sleepy town was not very conscious about the rest of the universe. Now we were assaulted rudely out of our stupor.

It was June of 1966. There were fewer young men in Hemlock Creek these days. They were taken from us and sent to a far off unfamiliar mountain country full of brutal guerrilla soldiers called Viet Cong. Vietnam was the talk of the daily news; young men were being killed in droves. Killing and war - concepts that were not even in Mennonite thinking. We were taught that "nobody could be a good Christian by Force," to quote a founding bishop. "Turn the other cheek" was an oft quoted verse from the Holy Bible. Our young men were conflicted but standing firm in the strength of the fellowship of Mennonites, Amish, and Quakers, all of us pacifists to the core of our being.

Ruth Keyser and Jennie Lukens were the first through Miss Arlene's door that day. Their names were always said in couplet since they were children, so seldom was one seen without the other. Ruth and Jennie, in that order. In agitation they started right in on the news.

"Oh, Arlene, did you hear the awful news? Hemlock Creek has its first war casualty." Jennie, in her frenzied mental state, kept dropping things, first her handbag, then her pattern, and her fabric samples she brought to match scattered like a mosaic on the linoleum floor. In age she was about five years older than me, and had married a local boy who became the father of her two blond-haired girls. The slender willow twig she used to be had matured into a strong hefty branch. She and Ruth were respectable community matrons now.

"*Ach nein!*" *Oh no!* Miss Arlene set her small box of spools on the counter to give her full attention. "Tell me."

"Harry Widrig's middle son, Carl. The hardware store will be closed for the remainder of the week, I am sure," added Ruth as Jennie dropped her handkerchief. They grazed heads as they both bent to retrieve it.

"Poor Harry and Mabel. I cannot imagine losing a child to a needless thing such as a war. We in the States are in no danger from that country. Why are we allowing our boys to be sacrificed?" Miss Arlene was very politically minded compared to many of her peers. But foremost she was a Mennonite and the tenants of our doctrine were firmly entrenched. I had to agree. I abhorred violence of any kind, even to animals. When my father had turned the hobo away in the snow storm, I was appalled. It seemed an act of violence and was unconscionable. It did not fit with the man I had known my father to be.

"Here," said Jennie as she handed Arlene the newspaper but dropped it instead. "Oh, I am sorry. I am all thumbs today." Ruth bent over and handed it to Arlene, then noticed me.

"Oh, Anna, *goot* morning. We have brought such sad news that it has taken all else out of our minds." Ruth and Jennie always talked in plural. Such a funny pair. I gave my perfunctory greetings of the day, acknowledging them both individually before returning to my first daily responsibility of straightening the shelves. Having lost our first local soldier, a boy I knew from school days, I felt bereft from this news.

Carl. Twenty-one. Just three years older than me, a junior when I finished eighth grade. Quiet, athletic, a good boy who enjoyed playing his trumpet in the band, his shock of reddish hair always the friendly joke of fellow classmates. Gone. Like Papa. Where were they? Where was heaven? If part of living is dying, why bother? But life is not an option. We are born. That is all. Like Bobby. Yet, where would my heart be without my boy? It would be empty and lonely. Then we are all destined to die causing loved ones left behind to wonder where we went. I know there is a heaven, but I wondered *exactly where* it was located. Someday I would know. But for now, I was here. The here and now. God gives us gifts in the between time that He expects us to use... Papa had a gift of caring hidden deep inside. He took care of Mama, then me. He gave glory to God caring for us. I guess now he was being glorified *by* God for his earthly troubles. Carl had a gift of loyalty and light-heartedness. Now, gone. It was all too deep and I wanted to stop thinking about it.

The bell jangled over the door as another woman, obviously not in our Fellowship, entered hesitantly. She smiled at all of us as her eyes scanned the group and the store. A new face, very pretty, clean of any make-up with a healthy glow to her cheeks and a tan on her arms and legs. Long straight brown hair parted down the middle was held back from her face by a pair of large white-framed sunglasses. Her brown eyes, rimmed with dark lashes, smiled in unison with her lips and seemed to take in all her surroundings at once. "Oh, good, wasn't sure you were open." A yellow tee shirt was tucked into jeans shorts with flower appliques. Her sandal clad feet were tan and rather exposed. I found my eyes drawn to very pink painted nails between the sandal straps.

"Oh my yes, promptly at 9 a.m. every week day and Saturday," Miss Arlene assured her, proudly.

"I'm here visiting family and just thought I'd stop in," the young woman said.

"Anything you need help with, just ask," I offered from behind the rack of upholstery fabric. She looked at me, then *really* looked at me. I suddenly felt very conspicuous, a feeling that did not happen too often lately. *My features are that obvious,* I thought as I buried my head in the bolts. Ruth and Jennie kept some running account of town life with Miss Arlene and I did my job, happy to be able to blend into the background. Over my head was the Rockwell print of the family tree, taunting me as the ill-fated results of happenstance. Where else could I go to get away from myself? I could not move away from Hemlock Creek, Ohio, not with Mama in her state of mind, and with my little boy just a toddler.

"Excuse me, I could use some help now, if you are free," the young woman asked over my shoulder. She smelled like something floral, very soft and pretty.

"Certainly," I smiled, pleased that she had asked for my help. "What do you need?"

"I am not really sure," she laughed, "I don't do much sewing, but I do like to do macramé. Do you have any of those supplies?" I felt her eyes on me again, but I averted mine. Did she realize she was staring which is both rude and very uncomfortable?

"Right over here," I led the way, hoping to make a fast escape. "Miss Arlene tries to keep up with the latest craft projects. Here we are." I held out my arm toward a section of colored rope yarns, ceramic baubles, and project books.

"Thank you," preceded that award winning smile. "Please, excuse me, I am sorry to stare." *Here it comes.* "But you have the prettiest eyes!" Sheesh! I did not expect that. Flustered, I said, "Thank you," and made my escape. Not since Molly had told me the same thing years ago had I heard that remark repeated. As I returned to my work, I looked up at the family tree in its wooden frame. Where did these eyes come from?

~

Many attended the service for Carl Widrig a month after the newspaper featured his death in its headlines. His battered body was shipped home and the casket was draped with our flag which was later carefully folded with much pomp and handed to his crushed and weeping mother. World War II and Korean Conflict veterans honored their fallen comrade with a gun salute, their uniformed presence a somber reminder of the realities of war. Mr. Widrig, himself in sad shape, was hardly able to keep his wife on her feet. Over in the Widrig family circle, standing in a tight group after the interment service, was the young woman from the fabric shop, her long brown hair braided and wound at the back of her neck. She wore a dark mini skirt and a gray blouse. She stood out in a crowd. Obviously so did I, an oddity in a group of blond heads with prayer caps. She saw me, and gave a small wave, smiling and replacing her sunglasses. As we walked back to the Presbyterian Church for a post funeral gathering, I wondered which young man would be next and how long this war would plague us with death.

"Remember me? The macramé queen?"

"I do! You are a member of Carl's family?" The brown eyes softened. "Yes, I am his cousin." She put out her hand. "Nancy Widrig."

"Anna Moyer."

"It is nice to meet you, Anna Moyer. Were you one of Carl's friends?"

"I knew him from school but he was older. He was a very nice guy," I said, "and everyone liked him. He was often teased, in a good way, about his red hair." We smiled and studied our punch cups. "Nancy, do you live far away?"

"Actually not too far. I live in Sugar Creek. I assume you live here in town?"

"Sort of, outside of town, on our family farm."

"Ah, it must be very nice living in a peaceful country setting." I had a flashback. Minding my own business before being beaten and hauled inside a car.

"Yes," I said behind hooded eyes, "peaceful. Well, it was nice to meet you, Nancy. I am so sorry about your cousin. Let's just hope the war ends soon."

"Yeah, that is my prayer." She was not ready to end our conversation. "I have a boyfriend over there now. Jerry. I almost can't concentrate on my job because he is always on my mind." A hand with pink nails whisked away a stray strand of brown from her tan cheek. She actually looked very nice with tanned skin. How I wanted to put my arm next to hers.

"What do you do? Your job, I mean." I was ready to hear dress store clerk or waitress. "I am a clinical psychologist."

That's not a job, that's a *calling*.

"I work at the hospital in downtown Bluffton. Ever been there? Pleasant View Hospital." Sirens went off in my head. I was there two times, nine months apart.

"I am familiar with it. A good hospital," a lame response on my part. "Do you enjoy your work?"

"I really do. It is fulfilling to help people who are trapped in their own minds and unable to reconcile past events." She popped a stick of gum into her mouth after rolling it up. "Want a piece?" I shook my head no thanks. "Sometimes I feel like I do absolutely no good, but then there are times a patient is able to get past their mental issues and live a good fulfilling life. That's rewarding." She shrugged. "I pray a lot," she whispered. Instantly, I liked her even more.

"Sounds like you are a very caring person."

"I try to be. I want every single person to feel they are valuable."

Now this is a fascinating person!

I heard my son even before Molly brought him over to where we were standing. He was fussy and I had the feeling Molly was done with him for the day. She thrust him into my arms.

"Here, Anna, he is too overwound. I think you'd best take him home and get him down for a nap."

Molly had watched Bobby so I could attend the service. She had not known Carl and was not one for funerals anyway. My boy twisted and wrestled in my arms, wanting to get down and run. Nancy watched as a smile played on her lips. "What's his name?" I told her.

"Hey there, Bobby," she said, vying for his attention, "aren't you quite a handsome little guy." My son stopped and looked at her before offering a huge smile. "Is he your little brother, Anna?"

"No, he is my son." Nancy looked blank as a silent moment passed. She reclaimed the moment quickly, to her credit. "Well, Anna, what a wonderful boy God has blessed you with. Is your husband with you?" She started surveying the crowd. Oh, this was so hard to explain to visitors.

"He has no father." I might as well just say it simply and let the chips fall as they may. This time Nancy was quicker on the rebound. "Well, I hope you have some family members to help you out," she ventured. "He's quite a handful, in a good way," she laughed.

"Yes, I have lots of aunts and cousins. We are not alone." Funny, I hadn't thought to include my mother.

Thankfully, Nancy knew when to leave things as they were and after many attempts to get Bobby to wave goodbye we took our leave, my son fighting me as we left. He was becoming stubbornly independent as he faced his twos. No wonder God planned for a mother *and* a father. Both energies were needed just to get through this age. I placed him in his stroller which Molly had left waiting by the rear exit from the fellowship room. He was asleep by the time we passed two blocks. I thought of Nancy and her boyfriend in Vietnam. How she must worry. Did they plan to marry and have kids someday, I wondered? Had she been at the hospital the first time I was there, a beaten and broken little girl? Did she hear of my case? There were probably many sad cases she had to face. I was not the only girl who was attacked and left for dead, though I pray there are not too many others. I had gone on with the help of my family and my own stubborn will.

Bobby looked almost angelic with his dark lashes against his pudgy cheeks, sleeping deeply as the stroller rhythmically jostled over seams in the sidewalk. *Make this war end, Lord, and please keep our country war-free when Bobby is of age. I couldn't bear to give up my boy, especially to a war. Oh Gott, have mercy on this country, for we seem to have lost our way.*

FIFTEEN

Mariah was getting married. Not an unusual event for a twenty-one year old Mennonite girl, but always a cause for great celebration. Eva and her husband were to be in the wedding party, and, of course, Molly. Now for the unusual part: Mariah asked me to sing. *O Perfect Love*, no less. Her family had a piano in the guest living room, which was where she and John Longenecker would be married by our own Bishop Lapp. John was an interesting young man, kind of wild, maybe a bit irresponsible, but so good-natured and a friend to many. Mariah had been swept away by his good looks and charm and he was indeed so blessed to have a lovely, kind-hearted Clemmens sister for his very own. Of the three sisters, only Molly would still be living at home with David, now an incredibly handsome seven year old. Their father, my uncle Henry, was a carefree Mennonite, not given to over-work or great ambitions. Somehow they always had lots of money and could dress the girls and David in the height of fashion. At one point they had two homes, which they called their town home and their country home. In the end, the old farmhouse lost out to the town home and was sold, all umpteen acres plus the family woods, to a developer.

"Oh, Anna, you must! You cannot say no." Mariah used all her powers of persuasion before I finally gave my consent to sing. I was insecure, afraid of doing a poor job of it.

"But… you know, I do not have the proper clothes for a wedding."

"Oh, nonsense! Most will be in their Sunday dresses and will all look alike. Just wear your Sunday dress, the floral shirt-waist with the navy belt."

My reluctance was not so much my dress, but my singing. Since Father's death, I had lost my self-assurance. My nerves caused me to blunder and sound weak. I heard nothing pleasant come from my mouth anymore.

That week I paid a visit to Miss Amanda Ledbeder's home. She greeted me warmly and asked about Bobby and my mother. When I told her about Mariah's wedding and the song chosen, she clapped, saying that was the best thing for me, to ease me back into public singing. She had a copy to lend to me which she pulled from a file drawer labeled "Weddings." After playing it through for me, she urged me to return for weekly lessons. I had a driver's license, thanks to Eva who picked up where my dear papa left off, but I'd have to see about borrowing a car and finding a sitter for Bobby.

My next hurdle was a proper dress. I was never vain about my clothes, but I needed all the support I could get, and a new dress would bolster my self-confidence.

"Miss Arlene, I am going to make myself a dress for Mariah's wedding."

"Good girl! I know just the pattern for you," and she propelled me to the pattern books to show me a McCalls semi-formal with very pretty lines, simple but somewhat elegant.

"You are right, Miss Arlene, this is the one."

I found the pattern envelope number in the large file drawer and took an hour choosing the right fabrics and notions. Thankfully, Miss Arlene told me to take a little out of each paycheck to cover the cost.

~

Mariah was simply beautiful, as beautiful as the warm summer day. Her brown curls hung on her shoulders and her white lacy dress came to her calf, showing white stockings and small white leather pumps. The effect was nothing short of angelic. She carried her small confirmation Bible and a single rose with a ribbon wrapped around the stem, the remainder in two streamers down her front. Her head was covered with a lacey veil that outlined her oval face like a halo. It was not the normal Mennonite wedding. John wore his Sunday suit and cleaned up his dress shoes.

He had tamed his hair with some kind of hair dressing gel, giving a slick, shiny look. Eva and Molly wore matching sister dresses the same length and style in a rose color, which suited Molly's olive complexion very well. Neither wore a head covering over their dark shoulder-length waves. Eva's husband, Sam, standing at John's side, towered over all the others, a good four inches over the groom. Bishop Lapp was a short, squat, elderly man. He seemed to get lost in the wedding party. But what he lacked in stature, his voice made up in volume.

I was to sing after the vows were exchanged. I felt my nerves taking over, causing my knees to shake and my hands to become clammy with a cold sweat. Why did I let myself be talked into this? *Next time just say NO.* It was my cue. I had to start. I numbly propelled myself to the piano and arranged the music sheets. How could I ever play or sing when I was rattling so. My knees literally knocked together. *Oh boy, Anna, you're in for it.*

After a rather choppy introduction, it was time to open my mouth and sing. My mother was there, one of her first social excursions since Papa passed. *Sing to Mama.*

"Oh perfect love, all human thought transcending...." I was so conscious of my faltering voice at first, but singing did something to me. I forgot how much I loved to sing! I forgot everything but singing. The three verses passed without incident, thank God, and the piano died down. I gathered the sheet music and returned to my seat near the piano. My knees did not know it was all over and continued to shake under my new light blue tea-length dress with its matching lace bodice and capped sleeves. I was thankful its length covered my traitorous limbs.

Afterwards, I wished people would stop praising me. Kind, yes, but too many compliments, too much attention, many I doubted were sincere, just words. I did not need all that. I may have been surprised I could still do it and that my voice did not fade away, did *not* leave me when Father died. I guess what is in my heart comes out of my mouth, for good or bad. I had grumbled about singing, brought on by the weight of my lagging self-esteem. Today I had conquered my fears. I felt a hope for my future.

John's friends were whooping it up on Uncle Henry's sprawling front porch. I smelled a slightly familiar smell that triggered…what…I couldn't place it. Molly and I had gone out to "join the fun," as she called it. I felt a strangeness come over me. What was wrong with me? I could not join in with this jostling and joking atmosphere. A young man, one of John's many buddies, kept staring at me. I was not a flirting type, and his look unnerved me. I tried to keep my attention on Molly, but she was enjoying another boy's attention a little too much. I sneaked another quick glance. Those eyes were still studying me. He looked somewhat familiar, maybe from school? That seemed so long ago. I had lived through a lot and matured much more than these carefree young people could imagine. Then, it struck me. A glimpse through a mirror dimly, as the Bible said. *I knew his eyes.* I had seen his eyes before. I backed into a folding table and some drinks spilled. *Sorry. Please...let me by...* I mumbled apologies and attempted to skirt my way back inside, into the living room.

"Anna, is something wrong?" I heard Molly ask.

"I just need to go back inside. Stay on the porch and enjoy yourself," I replied. *I must get away from here.* My heart felt like a hundred pounds as it strained to keep the rhythm of my surging blood. I knew those eyes. And he knew mine.

SIXTEEN

My mother was coming around. The summer with its warmth and newness seemed to bring her back to herself. No frenzies of cleaning, no burning of clothes or household items. Just a day-by-day return to the world around her. I knew she was on the mend when we received our yearly post card reminding us of the Lapp family reunion scheduled for a Saturday afternoon at the end of August.

"I think I would like to go, Anna. But only if you and Bobby come too." She looked at her sister. "And you, Laura, you love the reunions, don't you?" The very thought brought animation to my aunt's expression.

Aunt Laura, the steadfast one, the sister who seemed to spend most of her adult life caring for other people. For her, little things like a day away brought much excitement into her otherwise monotonous little day-in, day-out world. She immediately began planning for the dish to pass, and the two sisters shared choices back and forth until two recipes were settled upon as if the reunion were a week away instead of an entire month. I would ask Miss Arlene for the day off and see if Molly, though not from the Lapp side, wanted to come also. She had grown quite attached to Bobby, and would be a help keeping track of my speed demon, not to mention she was my closest friend.

This was a daring invitation on my mother's part, including me and Bobby. It would mean introducing her grandson who had no father, and it was one of her first public ventures as a widow. This branch of the family was more stringent about adhering to pure principles, but in my case, if judgments could be delayed until after an explanation, it would prove them a fair and compassionate people. My son was his own person even at his young age. Like most toddlers, there seemed to be a devil-may-care attitude in him. "No" meant "yes" to him. "Don't do that" meant "go ahead." His sturdy strong little body was in continuous motion, here and there, up and down, in and out. Even in his sleep he often twitched and jerked. Genetically speaking, he acquired neither the shape of my eyes nor my cautious disposition. In fact, I did not see much of me in him at all, except maybe, my nose. Time would tell.

Bobby was a climber. Stairs were a favorite of which he never tired. I taught him to come down on his bottom, figuring it was better to teach him safety rather than fight to keep him away from the inevitable. I had just barricaded the stairway with chairs which forced him to play with his toys in the living room. He was screaming in dismay, which he did more and more. Mother and Laura often shook their heads over his tantrums and left him to scream it out. He did not have much contact with other children except on Sundays when we gathered for worship with our increasingly large fellowship. I made a sudden decision. "It will do Bobby good to meet his cousins. He needs diversion, too. Sure, we will come." And it was settled.

~

One August afternoon when the lowering sun cast amber shadows, Sheriff Mike came back. This time Mama was out in her garden tending her lavender which had, in June, given her a huge bundle of purple stems for drying. I had Bobby out for a ride in his wagon. Aunt Laura was taking down the dried laundry, snapping the towels to rid them of bugs and wasps. Mike walked slowly to the garden, took off his hat, and squatted by Mother. I glanced at Laura and saw her eyes glued on the two. No smile crept on her face. She was the ignored sister. Piece by piece she kept taking down laundry and looking over her shoulder at them. Bobby, of course, had to climb out of the wagon and run over to the "pleace man." What my son lacked in verbal skills he made up for in the physical. Mama and Mike both stood, and Mike followed her to the lawn chairs set around a metal table, as Bobby clamored about the blue uniformed legs.

Something in me rose like the fur on a dog's back. This wouldn't do. Mama, now a widow, well, she had had her life's love. Papa should never be replaced in her heart. But Laura, at thirty-eight, never had a chance at marriage. What was on Sheriff Mike's mind? He already confided to me his feelings for "Lizzy," even if that was years ago, and I sensed those feelings had not died much over time. I ran after Bobby and called Laura to free her hands and join us. She shook her head and doggedly pulled the last sheet off the line, throwing it into her basket and heading for the back door, her eyes set in a resolved intensity.

"Hey there, Bobby!" Mike made a grab for the squirming mass of energy. He set his hat on the little dark head and was rewarded with a jubilant laugh before Bobby snatched it off and tried putting it back on its owner. I did not think to see my mother laughing again only six months after Papa's death, but there she was, thoroughly enjoying herself in the company of old friend, Mike. *Hmmm.* I sat with them to make sure they did not have too good a time. After all, Mama was still likely to have unstable moments when she would either go like a house afire, or shut herself away. She needed care, but not from Sheriff Mike.

"So, Sheriff, any news to share?" I asked. I meant nothing in particular, only making conversation. He answered while rough-housing with Mr. Squirmy Pants. I couldn't stop my smile.

"Got the looter who broke into Widrig's store while everyone was at Carl's funeral. The punk stole Harry's hand gun and some money. Then the jerk broke into the gum machine." He laughed. "Stupidity. Guess he thought he'd strike it rich in dimes, or else he was into jaw breakers." Mama giggled. Yes, giggled. I wanted to give her one of my "knock it off" looks, but refrained. She was acting like a high school girl with a crush.

"I hope it wasn't someone we know," I said.

"Not unless you know another punk from New Berlin." He instantly regretted his choice of words. It showed on his face. Bobby thwacked him with his officer hat. *Good boy!* How dare he insinuate I knew my attacker! As if I ever had a civil word with the likes of Robert Malone. I was only raising his son…

"Another war casualty from Tremaine area. Not sure what good ol' Dick Nixon is trying to accomplish, now that LBJ has stepped down." He shifted his focus back to my mother and his face became gentle. "How are you doin', Lizzy?" His voice became softer, quieter. Bobby was getting more pronounced in his attempts for male attention. I pulled him back, and he fought my grasp, feigning a cry before escaping and running as fast as his pudgy rolled legs could take him. I rose to the chase, having no choice but to leave my helpless mother with this old "friend."

I had toyed with the idea of calling Pleasant View Hospital in Bluffton. "Miss Widrig? You may not remember me…." I practiced my dialogue, "but we met at your cousin's funeral. Would you be willing to see my mother?" No, that sounded strange. "Would you be willing to counsel my mother?" Better. "You see, she had some kind of a traumatic experience that she does not remember." No, how do I know she had a traumatic experience? "She suffers from sudden and long-lasting mood swings." There, that was really all I was sure of, but as I held the receiver, I hesitated, lowering it back into its cradle. How would I get Mother to agree to such a thing? "Almighty *Gott* must deal with it," she would say. There had to be a different approach.

~

I chose the moment carefully. Bobby was napping in his bed, the door almost closed, Laura had walked to town for needed items and Mama was in a lazy mood, staring out the window.

I parked myself near her after handing her a cup of her favorite orange tea, with two small cookies on the saucer. "Oh, thank you Anna." As I sipped at my mint tea, I studied this woman the world knew as Elizabeth Moyer, her soft profile half darkened into a silhouette against the daylight coming through the window. Mama was still a pretty woman. There was a fragile transparency in her fairness that revealed a faint purple network of veins at her temples where the light brown hair was now slightly silver. I wondered how long her hair was by now. She would not have considered cutting it while Papa was alive. Lately she seemed to be warming up to the idea of a shorter style. Enough time had passed making it easier to bring up Papa's name, and go on with life.

"Mama?" She turned back to me and took a sip of tea, watching me over the rim. "How long were you married before I was born?" She set her cup back on its saucer.

"Oh... a little over three years. Why?"

"Just wondering. So you were my age when you and Papa started dating each other?"

She smiled, warming to the topic. "I was eighteen when your father asked to come calling. We never used the word *dating* - that was a word for the worldly couples. When a boy came calling he was serious about that particular girl."

"Did you go places together?"

"We usually went to young people's events at the church. Sometimes we went with a group of friends to each other's home, or the county fair in summer, or on a hayride in the fall. Come winter we would go sledding or skating, always in a group. We had wonderful times." Her eyes again focused on the view out the window, a cookie poised in her hand.

"Were you disappointed about not having a baby right after you got married?" I spoke softly, not wanting to spook her out of the moment.

"Well, not really. Not for the first year. It was fun just being the two of us. Your father worked hard, but we took an hour together for lunch, and then ate dinner around 7 o'clock, so he could spend the evenings with me." She nibbled at a cookie. "Did you make these or did Laura? Not you? So that's why these are so good - Laura always uses lots of butter." I gently brought her back to topic.

"So, after a year or so, did you wonder if you could have a baby?" This took some thought on her part and I gave her time.

"About, say, after our second wedding anniversary, I began to have a nagging thought. Every month came and went and no sign to give me hope." She shook away the thought and smiled at me. "But, here you are! I needn't have spent any time thinking on it." I did not want her back in the present just yet.

"When did you find out you were going to have me?"

This caused a change on her placid face. Her head cocked slightly to the side, and her brow drew together in a confused expression. Her hands were motionless as they embraced her warm cup which rested on her lap, except for one pointer finger which kept a rhythmic tap on the cup rim.

"Um, I guess…umm…it must have been, let's see, you were born in May, so it must have been in early fall, maybe …September? October?" She clearly could not recall, but felt she should be able. I pressed on.

"You and Papa must have been so excited! Did you have a celebration and tell everyone?"

Suddenly she was getting clearly agitated. Her lips set in a line and her features formed into a scowl. "We don't do that kind of thing. Only worldly couples do such things."

Not true. The Mennonite couples I knew always shared the joy of a first pregnancy. Oh, not in the worldly way of elaborate baby showers and monthly doctor visits, but a sharing of the excitement nonetheless. The cup and saucer clanked on the window sill. With quick flutters Mama brushed imaginary crumbs from her lap, stood, and said, "I have sat around long enough. It's time I picked some squash for dinner." She turned with a swish of her skirt, her white tennis shoes making a small squeak against the wood flooring. With a muted shutting of the screen door behind her, she was gone.

I slowly finished my tea. Bobby hadn't made a peep. I was going to bask in my quiet time and think on these new thoughts. My different angle of questioning led to what appeared to be a traumatic time after all. I might just phone that hospital in Bluffton and renew an acquaintance.

~

Mariah and John, newlyweds, were hosting a housewarming party in their four-room apartment above the village ice cream parlor. Just a small group of friends, Mariah said. Eva and Sam, Cousin Abram and his wife, Cousin Esther and her husband, then the singles: Molly and me, and two of John's friends. Twelve did not sound like a small number to me, considering the size of their rooms.

But, being my cousin Mariah, in all her happiness, I could not say no.

I arrived with my cousins, each female holding a platter or bowl of something to share. Mariah had a talent for making things comfortable. Her blue eyes gleamed as she showed us some of her wedding presents displayed here and there. John stayed seated in his favorite chair, his legs sprawled out. Poor Eva's husband, Sam, was hard pressed to keep from hitting his head on overhanging lights. He, too, found a sturdy dining room chair and settled himself, sharing work experiences with John and Abram.

Molly was not against being matched up with one of John's single friends. I could not have cared less, and was already feeling like the odd one out. She prattled on about a good looking *Englisher* she'd met at the wedding. I remembered the one who stared so blatantly, the one whose eyes I had seen before, and prayed it was not him. Her description did not match so I breathed easier.

I should have known better. When did I ever have good luck, as the world calls it?

John's two single friends arrived. Molly was preening. I wanted to hide. I know Mariah had no matchmaking schemes up her sleeve. Just another of life's crazy coincidences, believe in such a thing or not. In an attempt to be civil, I allowed myself to be properly introduced to the young man whose eyes I knew from somewhere, and John's other friend, but all contact ended there, I hoped. I averted eye contact with the young man whose eyes I recognized, wanting to appear icily disinterested. His name was Bill Meyers, the boy with the bad staring habit. The name was new to me and did not trigger any recollection. A card game called Blitz started up and six gathered at the dining room table. I set out the food on the kitchen counter and as I searched for plates, I knew he was behind me. I turned and handed him a stack saying, "Could you please set these next to the pies?" He gave a curt reply and did as I asked, but I knew he'd be back. The rooms were small. No place to hide.

"So, Anna Moyer, you are from Hemlock Creek?" Bill asked as he returned empty handed.

"Yes," I replied, finding busy work wrapping the forks in paper napkins.

"And you sing at weddings?"

"Well, for my relatives," I replied. "That's the only one I've ever sung at."

"And how do you know John and Mariah?" It was not stated like a question but with emphasis on the "how."

"I don't know John very well. Mariah is my first cousin." I handed him twelve rolls of covered forks. He took them but did not move. "So, you are Molly's cousin, too." I nodded.

"I would not have guessed you were cousins... no offense," he added. *Too late.*

"Do I *know* you?" he asked, his eyes squinting slightly with the question. His light brown hair was straight and combed over his ears, like the Beatles' style. His lips were wide as he smiled at me, his teeth straight and white, though the front two were large. His greenish-brown eyes were a bit small and his face had some blemishes along with a spray of freckles. He wasn't bad looking, if you didn't mind the arrogant sort.

"Well, *I* don't know you." I shot back, but then could not resist following up with, "Where did you go to school?" It had been a while and faces change.

"New Berlin." Man, *that* place again. It must be cursed, like Sodom.

I was finished in the kitchen and finished talking with Bill. "Nope, we never met," I edged my way past him and joined the others. Why does that town keep popping up? New Berlin was a good hour's travel time to the north of us. I only ever heard it associated with Robert Malone and the dumb thug arrested for robbing Widrig's hardware during a funeral. Some places just seemed to harbor the saddest members of society. Maybe the city needed some good churches.

I was ready to leave long before the others, but was not afforded that opportunity. My cousins asked me to sing. From the bedroom, John retrieved a guitar on which he could strum some major chords. He knew *Scarborough Fair* by Simon & Garfunkel. I only knew it because I heard it often on my transistor radio and liked the minor bluesy folk sound. So John strummed and I sang, glad to do something I was decent at. Then I asked if anyone heard Andre Crouch's *Through It All*. No one had, but Mariah asked me to sing it anyway without the guitar. The song fit my life to a tee, with all the sorrows that Jesus helping me through it all. I simply... sang. When the last words left my mouth, I became aware of my surroundings and realized all eyes were on me. It was very quiet. I couldn't wait to sit down and be inconspicuous again. I gave the hangnail on my thumb all my attention, though I couldn't stop the upward turn of my mouth as the group applauded my efforts. I felt as shy as a little girl.

"No one, but *no one*, sings like our Anna," said Abram, who himself had natural musical talent. "Wow, can that girl sing."

Murmurs of agreement floated around the room. Compliments were as hard for me to take as Philips Milk of Magnesia. Thankfully John, who loved being the center of things, started with a jazzy rendition of *Sittin' on the Dock of the Bay*, and I got up to refill my cup.

"Hey, *girl*, you sing like you have it in your blood," Bill said, sending my blood curdling. I had heard that phrase once before and I hated it. It set me to boiling. No one called me *girl*.

SEVENTEEN

A car load of us traveled across the state line to the 125th Lapp reunion, Cousin Abram at the wheel. This side of my family was even more strict than the Moyer side about dress propriety. Molly and I looked like sunflowers in a bed of forget-me-nots. Mother had dug out one of her plain Sunday dresses and, though she did not go so far as to resurrect her white mesh prayer cap, she had pulled her soft brown hair into a severe knot. My little boy was in his glory, his round-cheeked face a picture of health, running with the other children, fitting in from the start. I felt some stares, some behind-the-hand whispers, some side glances. Though I had tried my best to straighten my hair into submission, it was useless with the car windows open the entire long drive. It would not have mattered anyway. Other features were conspicuously apparent.

Aunt Laura and Mother proudly set their casserole dishes among the long line-up on end-to-end picnic tables, and began renewing old acquaintances in earnest. Molly and I kept up with the children, not feeling free to allow Bobby complete independence in his play.

"This is a very large family, larger than our Clemmens side," Molly remarked, surveying the various family groups among the elm covered picnic grove.

"The Lapps did very well for themselves in many ways, but…" I faltered, "I am not really a big part of this family, maybe about one-eighth." She nodded absentmindedly, her focus on the laughter from the playground.

"There are some Asian children," Molly remarked with a jut of her chin in their direction.

"Adopted." So obvious I hadn't needed to say a thing.

She nodded. The Mennonites were broad minded when it came to the Great Commission of Jesus - to go to the entire world and tell the good news of salvation. They were also eager to do their social part in the Kingdom of God by caring for the widows and orphans.

"Pretty children, aren't they?" Molly said. "And the women seem a hardy lot," she added. We laughed at the old fashioned term.

It was true many of our Lapp female relatives were of a short stocky build, broad across the shoulders with smaller hips, the classic inverted pear shape, unlike Mother and Laura.

"Look at that," Molly pointed to the group of children on the grove playground, "about three sets of twins."

"More, when you count the adult sets," I took note of at least two female pairs of look-alikes. "At least I was not a twin," I responded in as carefree a tone as I could muster. "Two of us would have really sent my mother off the deep end." I grimaced as I sent a knowing look to my cousin.

"Do you know any more about what happened to her before you were born?" Molly asked. I had finally told my cousins about my quest to discover my background.

"Just a little." A light breeze picked up and toyed with our skirts. Molly's silky, fine, brown hair seemed to float around her oval face. "I believe something traumatic did happen and she has shut it out of her memory," I replied, still spellbound by such soft hair that lifted with the gentlest of wind. Mine only budged when we had hurricane force gales.

"I heard something interesting from Mother, about the time you were three months pregnant. Maybe it had to do with your mother's condition, maybe not," Molly said, watching some children swing high on a huge swing set, their bare feet sending up wisps of dust. Bobby was climbing a metal turtle shell contraption. His little brown tie-up shoes gave him a climbing advantage over his cousins.

Did I want to find out more, right now? I waited as we strolled around the perimeter of the play area. Dandelion seeds disengaged from their stems and drifted toward us as two little barefoot blondies, both in purple dresses, blew the heads clean.

"Some time before you were born," Molly said as she dissected a daisy while we sauntered, "your papa attacked a man in your barn, a trespasser."

I stopped dead. "What?" It was almost laughable.

"Maybe I should not have told you," Molly said, scrunching her face in regret. We had stopped walking.

I had never heard of such a thing. *Papa - using force?* "Are you sure you have the story right?"

She nodded. "His hands were covered in blood, according to my mother."

I shivered. His blood or someone else's? Even while I shook my head, unwilling to even consider such a ludicrous thing, I had a nagging wonder about it all.

"Oh, Molly! Maybe it was just an awful rumor!"

But I remembered when I was younger and faced a silent ominous Papa who almost scared me. Could it be? She shook her head sagely.

"He went before the elders and the bishops." A small airplane hummed overhead. She watched its flight. I watched her. Papa before the elders, like going before a judge.

"You heard this right from your mother's mouth?" Yes. "Was the man a Mennonite?" She shrugged. "How was Father disciplined?" Questions came on each other's heels. But Molly knew no more. I asked her to question her mother further, but she didn't guarantee more information.

"Mother was pretty tight-lipped after saying as much as she did," she said.

We were a silent couple as we returned to the picnic. Papa! Why?? That was my biggest question.

~

The meal was, of course, wonderful, even with all its noise and commotion. Food was followed by a prayer time and a short family business meeting. The roster of this year's attendees was completed, as a clip board went around requiring the head of each family to write every name in legible script. On to old business, then new: deaths, marriages and births. All was said so somberly, Molly and I had to chuckle.

"What do these people do for fun?" she whispered in my ear.

"Go to family reunions," I replied. Prim faces showed annoyance at our disrespectful giggling, and tried to stare us into contrition. It worked.

Of more interest was the rousing discussion on adherence to proper dress and disciplinary action required upon deviation. The fur flew, the feathers ruffled; even God had a say through the voice of Deacon Fretz. Young Preacher Souder earned my respect by his simple statement, "When discipline is strict, undue attention is given to externals, and young people are driven from the church..." I wanted to applaud. This flowed into great emphasis on the *Gemeinde* or Fellowship of our denomination and maintaining our individuality in the face of the Great Commission to "go into the world." Some voiced an approval of turning to the Amish ways of isolation, in the face of the '60s youth revolution. A few Mennonite boys, not of the Lapp family line, were said to have enlisted in the armed services, disregarding our strong pacifistic stance. "Treasonous," I whispered to Molly. The older family members in our Fellowship were unbending in their religious heritage regarding the externals, such as men's simple collarless shirts and coats, and prayer caps for women and girls. Never was a female to wear male clothes such as pants or a man's shirt. "Sounds rather comfortable to me," Molly whispered in my ear. Her breath tickled and I giggled into my hand. I tried to picture Molly in trousers with suspenders and concluded she could make it work for her. With her hair in braids she'd look like Rebecca of Sunnybrook Farm. The talking droned on and on and my attention was lost.

I was hearing between the lines and what I heard was fear in the older voices. These current issues were indeed a dangerous tight-rope walk. To be or not to be. To wear or not to wear. To fight or not to fight… until finally all were talked out and there was the shift into the next part – the singing. Bobby, sleeping in my arms, woke into a crying jag as two enthusiastic accordion players transitioned us into the family hymn sing, my favorite part of any get-together.

    What kind of a world would my son face? Would he remain part of our religious heritage, or be driven out by strict codes of action and conduct. He was already a little firebrand, stubborn as the day is long and lording over children twice his age. I, myself, felt a chasm ever widening between the generations, yet it would be difficult for me to leave the *Gemeinde*, as long as I could worship, pray, and belong without conflict over these external matters. As I held him and sang, Bobby quieted and rested in my arms. Oh, that I could have such peace.

EIGHTEEN

The sign, Bluffton Correctional Facility, its very name announcing in large letters its mission statement, hung over a young man's head with his straight brown hair cut in Beatles style. His greenish brown eyes took in the ragged, dark, leering face of this person seated across from him. With a start he realized he did not know that angry face anymore. The sullen eyes were bloodshot and stared at him suspiciously, adding to his discomfort. Though never a big guy, the form in front of him looked skeletal now, clad in a worn orange jumpsuit. He had to ask something from this angry young man who was once a big part of his teen years. He hoped it would set his mind at ease. It was eating at him from the inside out.

"I've seen her before, Rob. You should see her now. Real pretty - considering. She's got a kid. Two years old. Ring any bells? Dark hair…dark…"

"If you remember, Billy bud, you were the one who had a grand old time. Me and Ed got nothing to do with it. And who's in jail? Was it the guy havin' a party? Nope. Just the sucker, me, the guy with the record and the mug shot. You,

BUD, should be right in here with me." He ran fingers through his dark bangs, back over a greasy head of shoulder length hair. "Get outta here, you gutless moron," he hissed through gritted teeth. "Get outta my sight! Unless you got something stashed in that jacket don't never come back."

"Now wait a minute, Rob, are you sayin', about that girl..."

"I'm in here cuz of you, you loser. Now get outta here before I call the terminator over here. You make me sick."

"I'm goin', I'm goin'. But...the kid kinda looks like you... Are you *sure*?"

"I'm gonna kill you one of these days. Wait 'til I bust outta here, Loser... I'll make sure you don't see the light of day!"

"You're crazy, Rob, you turned into a real nut case, man. You'll never see me again!" The greenish brown eyes sought the exit door while pushing away from the reinforced Plexiglas-divided table.

An armed warden stood in the doorway. At the sound of a buzzer he barked, "Time's up! Visitation's over." There were immediate sounds of chairs scraping back and heels clicking toward the exit sign while listless, noiseless feet shuffled to the opposite barred door and formed a jagged row. None looked back – it was useless to prolong the ache of separation.

"Time for you mynahs to fly back to your cages." A sardonic edge in the guard's voice was unmistakable. The thick metal door was bolted behind them as he proceeded to prod the inmates back to their cells.

~

"Miss Nancy Widrig's office, please... Oh, yes, Dr. Widrig, please. Thank you. Yes, I'll hold." I had reached the hospital switchboard. My heart was pounding. What had I planned on saying? Would she even remember me? What if we needed a referral? I must remember her proper title since she was a medical doctor. She had looked so young. An older woman's calm voice picked up on the line.

"Yes, hello, my name is Anna Moyer and I am calling concerning my mother."

"Are you a patient?"

"No, but I am a friend of Dr. Widrig's," I sort of lied. *Lord, forgive me.* "No, no appointment, but I'd like to make one - for my mother." More questions. "No referral either and no, no insurance. I'll pay cash."

I listened to the nurse or receptionist, whoever she was, run through the cost for different time increments. I cringed inside. I'd have to get a full-time job just to pay for this. "Is there any chance of speaking to Miss, uh, Doctor Widrig person to person?"

"I will write her a note. Phone number...Name again... and what sort of challenges are you facing?"

"My mother has drastic mood swings."

"Has she tried to hurt herself or others?" *Had she? When she had her "traumatic experience" was she hurting herself?* What a sad question, one to which I could only reply, "I don't see how she could, so... no, I don't think so, and certainly not at present."

I could only wait now, wait for a return call. In the meantime I would go on with my life. I seemed to wait a lot: waited to recover, waited to have a baby. I continued to wait on God to guide me into my future, waited to get over grief, to get answers about my birth and about my mother. Even my singing was on hold. Now I waited for a phone call that might help open what seemed like a tightly closed door behind which all my mother's secrets were tightly guarded.

NINETEEN

My son did not do things halfheartedly, not my Bobby. When he fell down the stairs that awful day, he spiraled, propelling full speed ahead from top to bottom, his head hitting every one of those thirteen uncarpeted steps. Laura telephoned Miss Arlene's to let me know. For my aunt to use the phone was nothing short of a miracle, so I knew she had concerns. Arlene told me to go on home which I did in record time, thanks to my bike. Laura was right to call. He was a lethargic little soul who just wanted to fall asleep on my lap. The Benner's had lost a child years back to a fall down their stairs. No way would I just sit by to see if all turned out okay. Eva and Sam had a car. Though I knew Eva would be behind her desk working on the ledger books at the lingerie factory, I asked the operator to connect me to the factory office number and, after several switches to numerous phones, I heard my cousin's voice.

"Valley Lingerie Manufacturing, this is Mrs. Schaffer. How may I help you?"

"Eva! Bobby took a hard fall down the stairs and isn't acting right. I think I should take him to Doctor Miller's."

"Did you call the doctor to be sure he can't come to you?"

We were at the tail end of physicians' home visits. I phoned, but the doctor, since he was at another house call across town, felt it would take less time for me to bring Bobby to his office. I called Eva back.

"Can I borrow your car? I can ride my bike into town, come to your office to get your keys, drive it home to load up Bobby and take him to Doc Miller's." I spoke quickly because Bobby had fallen asleep despite poking and prodding from my frantic aunt. It was around 2 pm. I was sounding a bit frantic myself.

"Anna, just stay put. Someone will be over real soon to take you and Bobby over to the office. Just stay put and don't panic." *Don't panic* said by one who was not yet a mother.

True to her word, she had telephoned her sister, Mariah, who, with her husband John, arrived in short order. We wrapped my unresponsive boy in his Noah's Ark crib quilt and headed over to Doc Miller's. After an examination, he suggested we better head for Pleasant View Hospital in Bluffton. He would call ahead so they would be ready for us. I became so anxious I was near tears. My healthy active little boy was so uncharacteristically still. A nasty purple bruise was radiating from a large goose egg on the side of his forehead, just above his temple.

Mariah and John whisked us back into the car and John drove like a madman all the way to Bluffton, defying traffic and taking our breath away. Doc Miller's call enabled staff to be waiting with an emergency room ready. Another man and two nurses were in and out, checking vitals, and examining Bobby. Mother came with us. Since the court appearances, crises seemed to snap her out of her own world, and she responded with surprising clarity and level-headedness. Now I was the numb, unfocused one and Mother was talking with doctors and nurses, asking a string of questions.

"An x-ray? Are you sure he needs that?" I hated the thought, but I could not delay because of my medical ignorance. Again, Bobby was wheeled away from me, bed and all, into a room where I could not follow. I leaned against the wall, waiting. He was returned to the emergency room and we waited once again. I could hear a huge clock ticking on the opposite wall. A metal-framed picture of a spring garden, sun faded and discolored, did little to create a peaceful atmosphere.

The doctor returned with results. There was blood trapped inside Bobby's cranium. Should they release the pressure or see if it passed on its own? This was the dilemma we faced. What do you mean by "release the pressure," I asked. "How is that done?"

The explanation made me feel like I might pass out. Mama asked for the surgeon's advice. I sat woodenly on an odd orange hospital chair which made hissing noises as I compressed the cushion. I leaned as near as I could to my small white-sheeted Bobby in the metal pediatric bed, a bit like a cage. *My baby.* The dark hair curling all over his head, the knot even bigger and darker than it was earlier. *I left you in another person's care. I would have stopped you. I would have barricaded the stairs, I would have...* Over and over I beat myself up in my mind. I was not paying any attention to the fancy medical words and Mama's questions. *Please, Gott, don't let my Bobby die like the Benner baby. Please, Gott.* The decision was made to follow the doctor's advice. Release the pressure.

I spent the evening in that hissing chair or pacing the hall. For several hours Bobby was in another area, his little bed on wheels pushed by an orderly who did not talk much but briskly and methodically did his job. I followed as far as allowed, walking the corridors outside the room. Mama and I waited. John and Mariah stayed for several hours but left for the night after I promised I'd call with any news. Aunt Laura was breaking a record by using the telephone twice in one day. She called and asked the switch board to connect her to our waiting area telephone. Mama gave her the updates while I rocked back and forth in the chair that made sounds.

My heart was being torn apart. I heard praying going on around me, and I tried, I really did, but prayer was not in me. So Molly and Cousin Abram, who arrived as soon as they could get there, kept vigil with Mother.

Was this some kind of judgment? Anxiety turned my faith to mush. I already knew the answer to that, in my head. God did not work that way. Still I could not fight off worrisome thoughts in my heart. At eight o'clock the sight of the attending surgeon coming toward us as he unmasked his face made it impossible for me to stand. He rubbed his face and his eyes as he searched me out. Mother was up out of her seat and walking toward him. He was going to tell me first, that was evident, and Mother scuttled back to reclaim the seat next to me, grabbing my hand closest to her that had lain unmoving on my lap for ever so long.

"All has gone very well with the procedure," were the first words from his mouth. He gave us a very doctorly smile using few facial muscles.

I closed my eyes in relief. Mother squeezed my hand. "Your little boy is sleeping, still under the anesthesia. He's in recovery and as soon as he comes around, we will let you know. Then you can see him, Mrs. Moyer." He lightheartedly addressed my high strung mother saying, "You too, Grandma." She made sure to tell him earlier of her relationship to Bobby.

I was glad no one corrected his misuse of my title. He turned and added, "He's one healthy little boy. I think he will pull through just fine. We'll keep close watch on him." I gave a smile to at least acknowledge the doctor's encouraging words, but I was weak from the emotional ordeal. The atmosphere now changed from tension to profound relief. Mother left with Molly and Cousin Abram whose farm chores were still waiting. I refused to go anywhere. Within an hour Bobby was wheeled from a recovery room to another room where he would spend a couple of days, his mama right by his side.

When things quieted down around me, I tried to mold myself into another reclining hospital chair at great cost to my back. I was given a pillow and white blanket. Lights were turned down and I finally slept fitfully in between nightly checks on Bobby's vitals and his partially shaven head with its square of white gauze. In the morning, my little one was looking at me when I opened my eyes. My smile echoed on his dear face and I knew God had answered my prayers. As I bent to kiss his cool cheek a woman's voice addressed me.

"Anna?" I looked toward the door and saw a face I recognized with dark hair pulled back from its center part. "Do you remember me?" Cotton candy pink lips opened in a warm smile.

"Miss…oh, sorry, Doctor Widrig," I stammered. "Yes, of course I remember you…" I scrambled to right myself, but my back and my hair had paid a hefty price for the honor of a restless night in that chair.

Bobby then realized there were tubes attached to his arm so my attention was divided as he started to whimper. I rang for the nurse. The staff was kid-proficient, taking care of his immediate needs while engaging him in fun chit-chat, thanks to a Mr. Monkey hand puppet. I was soon able to greet Dr. Widrig properly. I rubbed the small of my back, smoothed my curls and apologized for my appearance. The doctor dismissed my words with a wave of her hand.

"Oh, you look great for what you've been through. And, please, call me Nancy," she said, pulling a chair close to mine and settling in.

She wore a white jacket over a blouse and skirt, and her practical penny loafers sported eye-catching copper pennies in the flaps. "I saw the name Bobby Moyer on the new patient roster and wondered if he was your little guy, so I thought I'd take a peek."

Little surprise she was so successful, being the warm and caring individual she obviously was and I found myself wanting to share my ordeal. With some residual tears welling up, I spilled out my turmoil over the whole head trauma incident and how relieved I was this morning to awaken to a pair of questioning eyes studying me. She rose to scan Bobby's chart, looking pleased with what she saw, then she resumed her seat and spoke softly.

"God has certainly heard and answered your prayers for your son. And I know you have prayers for your mother, too, Anna. I got your message about her mood swings, and how serious they have been. I am here to help, but I have a proposition that may work out better for all of us. I imagine you are clueless as to how to get her here."

I nodded and admitted sheepishly, "You are right about that." My family would not consider such a thing as attending a doctor for mental health.

She went on, "I wondered if it may not be better for me to pay a call to your home. I'd love to start a friendship with the two of you. That way your mother can open up on her own terms in the security of your home. Of course I want her to eventually know I am a psychologist and that you arranged for me to come by, all very casually, if you know what I mean." She studied my face. "What do you think?"

"I think that is a great idea. But of course I will pay you. You will require more for having to make house calls?"

"Not on my own time. And let's not think about cost right now. Your mother may not cooperate and in that case you and I will simply have a nice friendly visit."

I recalled her saying she lived in Sugar Creek. "You don't mind the distance?" A mental calculation put her drive at about thirty minutes both ways.

"Not if you will let me share some dinner when I get there." Dimples cut into her lower cheeks. I could not deny that smile.

"I do not often have a good home-cooked meal and that would mean a lot to me," she confided. "Besides, I could drop in on family, my aunt and uncle, on those days we have dinner." How could I say no?

Nancy took notes in a small spiral notebook as I replied to her questions about Mother. Before leaving she asked if I had any questions for her, but I was flustered over Bobby's flaring agitation once more over his attached tubes and I came up blank. She left me to my son with a promise to be at our home the following Wednesday at suppertime, after a quick visit with her aunt and uncle Widrig.

"Bobby will be released in a couple of days, don't you worry," she reassured me, adding, "Your little boy is strong and he came through the trauma nicely. Look how he is vying for your attention!"

It was good to hear his jabbering, with *Mama* emphatically coming out loud and clear. I could only hope my mama would cooperate with Doctor Widrig's kind endeavors.

TWENTY

A man came to our church one beautiful Sunday in late summer and preached out in the open. Benches and fold-up chairs seemed so uncomfortable at first, but most of us soon forgot all about our creature comforts. The beauty of the day even paled in the face of God's words presented to us. What happened this day did nothing short of turn my life around. Bishop James Clark and his pretty wife, Rowena, had me spellbound. James was ordained ten years ago in Chicago - the first black Mennonite minister in the history of our denomination. Could I have even considered taking my faith to racially mixed areas of large cities? Starting Bible schools? I doubted it. Bishop Clark was very intelligent and spoke like a highly educated man. That was evident to all the moment he opened his mouth to speak. But what was more evident was the power in his preaching. His style was unlike any our church had ever heard. It came as little surprise to find he now stood before us as a newly elected Bishop in the Mennonite Conference, one of the highest positions attainable.

Racial issues in the church were, as of 1968, foreign to us. We had not yet faced the question of inducting black members into our tight ranks. Yet we knew of many Mennonite groups, in Pennsylvania especially, where blacks accepted the plain coat and cape covering which were still the standard ministerial garb of our conference.

Now Bishop Clark stood before us, a straight tall man with tight graying hair, dark, clear, smiling eyes behind wire glasses and a matching gentle smile from which emanated a powerful voice. Bethel Mennonite Community Church in Chicago was his home church, but due to a fire four years ago, the inner-city congregation was without a building. The membership, about sixty strong, was ready to rebuild, requesting help from denominational brothers and sisters, like us here at Hemlock Creek Mennonite.

The preacher in Bishop Clark was a persuasive voice for the Lord. The banner we faced every Sunday, *Ye Must Be Born Again*, became a living thing, a desired happening. Little had we heard the word "revival" in our meetings. Every now and then we sang the word in a hymn, but there it ended. Until today.

I was eager, my soul so thirsty I thought I could not drink in the bishop's words fast enough. "Do any of you have a hidden room in your heart that you will not allow God to enter? Is sin abiding there, nurtured, unattended, making you hypocritical before an Almighty and pure God?" Sins? Yes, I had many keeping God from my life. I hated, yes, **hated** Robert Malone. I hated his friends that were a part of it all. I hated the girls who taunted me at school. It was a little cancer that had grown inside me, unseen, unchecked, unguarded. And like any cancer it overpowered the good in me. My sin of hatred, no matter how justified, was more injurious to me than anyone else.

I listened raptly, unwilling any of the good bishop's words to elude me. I started to feel shaky, my heart pounded, and I licked my lips continually. I needed to right myself, *now*. I needed a new birth inside myself, and I desired that more than anything that morning. The sun started to beat down, and as it rose above us the great elms' shadows leaned away from our gathering of seventy-five or so. But it was not only the sun's heat but the heat of God's Word, and all evidence of God's mightiness compared to my all-too-human nature, that singed my heart. I wanted a renewed and transformed mind. I wanted a heart white as snow. I wanted with everything in me to believe God loved me with an everlasting love and that He knew all about me. The circumstances of my birth and my son's conception were not news to the Almighty. He had taken pains to make me special, unique, like a snowflake.

How would I go about this? Did I simply ask God to change me? To give me a new birth inside my soul? I hung on Bishop Clark's words, waiting for the way to go about talking to God, little realizing I was the object of another's scrutiny.

Since our chairs were in a semi-circle arrangement, Rowena Clark, the bishop's gentle wife, was seated off to my right toward the handmade wooden podium. Every now and then I would glance her way, and we would share a smile as our brown eyes connected, but I was quite engrossed in other matters. I was ready to do business with the Lord of heaven and earth! The minute I heard the words, "If you are ready to ask God to forgive you, if you are ready to ask Him to truly become your Lord and Savior, this is the moment. Arise from your seats, O People of God. Arise!" I stood instantly, my hands clasped desperately in front of my chest, caring not a mite what was going on around me. "Come, let us pray over you ... Come!"

I was stumbling over big black-booted feet, over black handbags, over someone's cane, for heaven's sake. I quickly approached the podium for prayer. I saw with surprise I was not alone, but all that mattered at that moment was me and God. A gentle hand was placed on my arm, and Mrs. Clark began earnestly praying over me. She told me I needed to talk with God myself, which I did with such angst and agony of soul. "Lord, please rid me of this terrible hatred I feel. Please wash me clean of all my wrongs against you," I cried. How gross that I wiped my nose on the back of my hand over and over. I did not stop pleading with God until I was limp and washed out through and through. My tears completed their cleansing purpose. I finally looked up, reluctantly once again a part of the world, part of the reality around me. The elm trees no longer offered even a smidgeon of shade. Mrs. Clark told me to stay in my place until I was sure my business with God was completed, and after another gentle pat on my arm, she walked on to another poor soul in need of a Savior.

I was emotionally fatigued. I turned to go back to my place next to Mother, but found myself aware of a young man, now familiar, to my left, up front, praying with Bishop Clark. I saw the thin shoulders, the shock of brownish blond hair, his profile outlined against the dark green trees. What was *he* doing here? I turned away and with my head down, returned to my seat as the beating sun chased many of the brethren from our outdoor meeting, the soft grass silencing their exit. Mother and Aunt Laura sat patiently, heads bowed as if in prayer, but their eyes were open. Somberly, we sat for another five minutes. I was trying to make sense of seeing John's friend here. Bill…Bill Meyers, yes - that was the name. Before long, we took our leave to join the others in the church fellowship area for a light luncheon. I was unable to rejoin the world just yet. My experience set me on a higher plain, and I did not want to leave.

~

A brown hand reached out to hold mine within her two. Rowena Clark's beautiful warm brown eyes were like mirrored pools reflecting mine. Her grasp felt like an acknowledgment. There was no generational gap, no stranger hesitancy. Instead we were spiritual sisters, fellow believers who had experienced a similar life change. She could have been my mother, so close were the shape of our eyes and the tone of our skin color.

"Thank you for praying with me," I responded to her warmth shyly. I felt my mother press close to me, taking my other arm. "Oh," I looked from Mother to Mrs. Clark, "This is my mother, Mrs. Jacob Moyer," I beamed. With dismay and embarrassment, I watched as my mother, with averted eyes, ignored the extended brown hand, replying to the introduction in a chilly, civil way only as manners required. Rowena Clark, if surprised at the icy response, did not let on, but looked calmly into our faces while I shifted uncomfortably, still reeling from the unwarranted snub. I heard Mother express her thanks for being our guests today, and for their ministry in the city church. She added something about giving money toward such an excellent inner-city mission field.

My parents' actions baffled me: Papa toward the homeless man, Mama toward this Christian sister with skin the color of mine. Even before the last word left Mother's mouth she was steering me in the opposite direction toward our family group. Cousin Abram and his little wife, now in early stages of pregnancy, had been keeping an eye on Bobby as he escaped with the other children an hour after the outdoor service started. The children's saving grace was the playground newly built on church property, eight tall swings and a sand box, all shaded in a grove of oaks. I had been oblivious to my son until now and thanked my cousins for their vigilance. We all looked out for one another. It was our way.

I went to retrieve my son. I had no thought but to see him having fun among the group of children, enjoying their playtime. As I exited the side door of the church, with the playground in sight, I was shocked to see the young man, Bill Meyers, squatting near my boy as he played in the sandbox. Alarm made me hasten my steps, until I was running to Bobby's side. Bill stood as I neared, and he bent to wipe sand from his knees. He had the audacity to say hello. At least he was not leering at me like it seemed he did at John and Mariah's party.

"Come, little man," I said jokingly, but the sharp edges to my words were biting with severity. "Now!" My son recoiled at the demand and, of course, chose to ignore it. "Now, Robert!" I instantly wished I could have eaten the name. I had vowed to myself to *never* use that name. Glancing at Bill I wondered why he wore a strange confused expression on his face. What was he thinking? He looked down at Bobby with a sad but sardonic smile.

"His name is Robert? Oh yeah, I guess it would be. He told me his name is Bobby." The strange quizzical look remained on the young face with a splotching of unshaven whiskers on his chin.

"We do not call him Robert. He only goes by Bobby." Why was I telling him anything? I owed him no explanation, but my open nature often betrayed better judgment. Bill looked at me with those eyes that I knew from years ago. I decided that this day I was a new person, so I'd act like one and put my timid nature behind me. If there was the tiniest root of hatred still remaining in me, I wanted it gone. I needed to face it down, so I took the initiative and thinking to catch him off-guard, threw out the question we both harbored. Bobby was engrossed in burying his Tonka truck in the dirt.

"When we were at John and Mariah's, I thought I had never met you before, or seen you, but I think we did meet, so to speak, about four or five years ago. And I have a feeling it was under terrible circumstances." I stood with my feet firmly planted, my mouth stern. I spoke matter-of-factly. If he took the bait, maybe he could solve some of the mystery of our acquaintance. I believed he had been in that red and white Chevy. I braced myself for the cocky, arrogant look. I never expected to see him drop his head while his thin shoulders started to shake. There he was, hands at his sides, sobbing. I just stood there, unsure of what was happening.

Bobby looked up, and studied the face before him, scrunched in grief. "Mommy, he's sad." A low animal kind of cry came from Bill. He was trying to say something, but his wrenching sobs interfered. It would not do to have Bobby subjected to this, hearing whatever it was that might pertain to his circumstances. "Stay here and play, Bobby." This time he did as asked.

"Bill, let's step over here, by this picnic table." But he couldn't move. His chest heaved in gulps of air while trying to say, "I...I..." he shoved his hands deep in his pockets after swiping at his eyes, But he could not contain himself. He just stood, shoulders slumped, weeping. I had never seen a man cry. I had seen tears form in my Papa's eyes which were annihilated on the spot, but nothing like this. Finally Bill followed me to the table and sat opposite me, five planks and a whole world separating us. Gone was the arrogant disturbing young man from Mariah and John's party. Gone was the young man who called me "Girl." Here sat a broken soul, wiping his eyes with the ball of his hands like a little boy, now and then looking to the sky to regain composure. At least he had shirt sleeves at his disposal. I curled my lip in disgust at the thought of my hands. More gulping sobs. What was going on here?

"I am so sorry, so sorry..." he said jerkily, in a hiccupping way. *Oh, here it comes, true confessions!* He *was* there, maybe the one who shoved the smelly cloth in my mouth, or the one who almost broke my wrists ...he was remembering October of 1963. *Dear God help me!* I tried to collect myself and speak calmly.

"Sorry for what?" My words had a sting to them.

He met me gaze for gaze, and I will never forget what I felt next. It was as if a film had been removed from my sight and I saw it all too clearly. Those eyes! I gasped. "Oh no," I said out loud. "No." Now I sounded like the wounded animal.

I knew his eyes. *I knew*. The revelation made me feel sick. "*No*," I said for the third time, feeling as broken as he was. I brought my hands over my mouth. While looking into Bill's eyes I was looking into Bobby's eyes.

~

All I have written so far, and there is more before I have laid it completely before you, has not come easily. In fact, I have cried over my journals, as I am now. Though decades have passed, following my memories has brought me right back in time. I relive my heartbreak as if it were in the present. Yet, I continue to re-write these entries and share my experiences on a very unfamiliar computer keyboard. My fingers many times refuse to respond, but I press on. From all this sorrow came my revelation of God's goodness in the face of terrible tragedy. More than anything, I wish to show God's presence in the life of a common ordinary person, which is just what I have always been. God does have good plans for us whether we are aware of it or not, but at times He uses the brush to clean out the debris. He wants us to heal properly.

TWENTY-ONE

My spiritual experience that summer Sunday was not a once and done deal. I fought against my tendency toward hatred, but as time passed it felt like a watering down of the original deep-seated, dark tendency. My hatred was turning into a milky vague emotion, and I knew that was because of God's hand in my life. Bill had a true heart change. I was skeptical at first, but as time passed, it was evident to all who knew him that he was not the same guy. I will never forget that fateful Sunday when truth came into the light, the truth about my son's biological father. It felt as if my soul's enemy had brought a counter attack to minimalize my God-experience that morning. I told no one about Bill Meyer's confession and felt the overpowering weight of carrying that knowledge alone.

Bill kept crying for my forgiveness that day as we sat at the picnic table, our son, oblivious to all the goings-on, playing dump truck in the sand box. Children's laughter filtered by us as we sat, two broken human beings, attempting to sort out our shattered lives. Me, feeling angrily gypped out of my youth because of this young man's sorrowful, sinful life. Him, trying to clean up his life while drowning in so much rotten baggage. It took everything in me to say the words he needed to hear. Rather, I wanted to scream at him, to shout in his face. Why? Why me? Did he know I was fifteen?? What kind of pervert would do such a thing? But my heart instead began to feel at first a sick pity, then a compassionate pity, until I finally croaked out a weak, "I forgive you." I may have felt sincere at the time, but I really hadn't meant it just yet, because hatred can be a very insidious thing.

"It was not you," Bill had said. "It was not…personal." I just stared at him, fighting anger. How could he say that? It *was* me and it *was* personal, very personal.

"Well, that's pretty hard to believe." I had replied sarcastically, my self-control stretched to its limit. I really wanted to scream something awful at him and walk away. I wanted to take *my* son and go home, inside the safety of our walls. This must be how my mother felt when she hid in her room for days on end.

"It was not because you were…are…a black girl. We were stoned." I stared at him, not comprehending. *Stoned?* What was he talking about? Stephen in the Bible was stoned!

Seeing as I was in the dark about that, I asked, but not before saying, "By the way, just so you know, I am mulatto, my mother is white." He looked at me as if I had just grown another head. I guess to him a person was either black or white, or he just didn't care what term I applied to myself. He studied his knuckles. I was sorry he felt the need to purge his conscience by going on and on because I really just wanted to turn my back on him and leave him there in his misery.

"We were stone drunk and high," he answered. Again I had no idea. I opened my hands and shook my head to show my incomprehension. "High - on drugs. How stupid can ya get!" he rushed on. "I didn't know what I was doing. Man, so easy for Rob to get anything from the dealers in New Berlin." He ran his hands through his hair and rubbed his eyes. "Rob was the one who kept us goin', high, I mean. That's how he made his money, from us, me and Ed, and lots of others." I had not heard the name, Ed, but remembered the very first time I ever saw the red and white Chevy. There were three inside. "I asked God to take away any desire for the stuff. I gotta get myself straightened out, or I'll be joining Rob one of these days…in prison." He looked miserable. *Good.* I straightened my back, feeling strengthened by my self-righteousness. What a mess he was. But, for me, there was still an unanswered question that needed clarification. Otherwise, the unchecked wondering would foment and haunt me all my days. It was a dreadful thought I harbored, and one I hated asking for fear of the answer. How do I ask such a thing? I folded my hands, the knuckles tight,

"Was it *just* you? Or could Bobby's father be one…. of the others?" Angry tears fell on the heels of this humiliating question. To think that I could have been so molested! The question hung out there, and now I didn't want to know for fear of the truth. How could I live with that truth if the answer was the most dreaded? "Never mind," I back-pedaled. " DON'T tell me," I lashed out at him. "You ruined my life! I can't take any more pain!" I felt a mixture of anger and wanting to hurt him to the core, adding more injury to a wounded man. Strike him while he's down, *just like he did to me.* The Bible version of stoning was starting to sound pretty good.

"Wait," his red-rimmed, greenish-brown eyes looked directly at mine. "I can tell you that part, now that I know for sure. It was me...just me," he choked and broke down once again. I rubbed my forehead. I wanted to hate him even as he brought some closure with his assurances. "God, how sorry I am," he cried loudly to the oak trees. Everything pathetic thing about him seemed to mean that. But my old companion, hate, once again tried slithering its way back into my psyche. "I will never be able to forgive myself..." he whimpered. *Your problem. I said the words you wanted to hear.*

A single shred of dignity had been left in me. Now to end this horrendous experience, really truly end it. One more thing needed to be settled before I ran from this place. The meeting grounds had always been my refuge, my place of acceptance and security. Now, on this August afternoon, I wanted to flee from there, take my son and hide him away. After experiencing such a good morning, the place now felt tainted. From holy ground to heinous ground in one hour. Thank you, God, I did not name my son Robert William, like I considered. I would have had to legally change it to annihilate any ties with my attackers.

"Okay, at least you could clue me in on that much." I spewed with as much venom as I could muster. "But now hear this! I NEVER," my voice cracked with emotion and anger, "want you to talk to others about that day. Not your friends, not Elder Clark, or our *dienaren*," at his puzzled look I clarified, "our minister, and not any counselor you might need. AND…you are NEVER to come see Bobby or talk to him again. If you do I will tell the police and they will arrest you," whether they would or not I didn't care, I was babbling. Sheriff Mike probably would have in his ongoing attempts to bring justice into my life. I turned my head from him and I think I held out my arm, hand poised to push his very being away. *Get out of my life, forever!* "Do you PROMISE me that? Because I NEVER want Bobby to know this, or to know **you**. Understand? I swear I will have you arrested." I stopped instantly, my hand flew to my mouth. Never was a *goot Mennischt* to swear an oath, *Gott, forgive me!* There was no stopping me now and I felt power and vengeance in my cruelty. "You ruined my life, my mother and father's lives, and Bobby will have a hard go of life." I stood, agitated and shaken, "but NEVER speak to him again." I jabbed my pointer finger at him emphasizing every word like the thrust of a knife. If his head hung any lower it would have been on the table. A twinge of conscience reminded me of why I went up for prayer just an hour ago. My hatred, deep inside, was baring its fangs and roaring like a lion. But I had every right to tell off this poor excuse of a human - he deserved no mercy. *Right, Lord?*

I felt something tug at my dress. There he was with that precious little face and those brown eyes with green flecks that showed up in the sunlight. Double sets stared up at me, man and son. I reached down and scooped up my baby, shovel, bucket and all. I jogged back to the fellowship room, causing Bobby to laugh as he dropped his shovel, then the bucket onto the brick walk way. Upon seeing us, Mother, with her instinctual insight, left her one-sided conversation with Mrs. Gehman, touched Laura on her back saying a short word, and soon we were both in Cousin Abram's car heading back home. I was rattled and out-of-sorts, quite unusual for me, but obviously apparent to all. It was a quiet ride home. No one questioned me, either about going up for prayer, or about whatever had triggered my anxiety. Maybe I needed to talk with Doctor Nancy Widrig as much as Mother did. Wednesday could not come soon enough.

By the way, the old adage holds true. Never say never.

TWENTY-TWO

Nancy was as much at home in our kitchen as she was at Miss Arlene's store that first day I met her. At Pleasant View Hospital, she was a professional, here she was a friend. And I prayed she could wear both hats to help Mother and me through our issues. She charmed the socks off Mother and Laura, being introduced as one of Harry Widrig's nieces, Carl's cousin, and a friend of mine. Out came a plate of cookies and the good tea cups as we visited, aware of the comfortable smells of apple pie and chicken baking in the oven.

September bid a cursory back-handed wave to the lush green of August. It now stole the show with spectacular sunsets, flaunting a large ball of red fire sinking rapidly behind the hill. Eerie were the nights when the moon, equally as large, created lapis shadows across our yard. Autumn never ceased to bring a melancholy that seeped unheeded into my being, no matter the beauty of the leaves or the color of the blazing setting sun. They were dying, those beautiful leaves. At times I felt the same. Certain things had not healed so well as a result of that October in 1963. Was it really that many years ago? Often I had to remind myself how God could and did turn things around in a person's life, but sometimes I had to will myself to believe it. Yet watching my son leafing through picture books or pumping his short legs like crazy on his swing, singing to the clouds and the sunbeams, all this was proof enough of God's goodness in our lives, though how easily I forgot to see the good in things.

Nancy and I took our tea out onto the porch where the wooden slatted hanging swing beckoned us. Soon, its rusty chain creaked rhythmically. I missed my father terribly sometimes, like right now, which added to my autumn melancholy. Nancy missed her father also, a victim, two years ago, of a massive heart attack at age sixty-two. We shared some good times and fond memories. She asked how close I was to my father.

"I was not all that close to him before I was fifteen. It was mostly Mama and I living out life together."

"What do you think caused a change in your relationship at that time, Anna?" She was running her finger around the rim of her cup. The sheen in her brown hair reflected some of the pinkish-orange from the sunset. I wondered if my hair could ever shine like that.

"I was attacked when I was fifteen." I said. She drew in her breath, so unexpected was my answer. It took a moment before she could go on. I could see her shake her head as she watched the sky dim. Her voice returned, soft and compassionate.

"Oh, Anna, I am sorry to hear such a thing. Do you know who attacked you … if I might ask?"

"Some older boys from another town had been harassing me, starting when I was about twelve. They would yell terrible names at me as they drove by. One day in October of 1963, I was walking home alone from school and I was forced into their car. They laughed as they hurt me and I was scared witless. Then I blacked out and do not remember much, just how they gagged me and I tried to fight. But I was no match for their strength. They beat me up and…hurt me…" A bat came out and swooped around the tree tops, or maybe it was a barn swallow rejoicing in the cool of evening. I was only half aware of my surroundings. "I met Bobby's father just last month." There. I had said it. I glanced over at her. She slowly repeated my last sentence to make sure she had heard it correctly. Sorry to say she had.

I know I had spoken matter-of-factly, but the pain on her face pierced me like a knife through a chink in my armor. I did not want to yield to useless tears any more. It was all behind me, history, dry and brittle, but still with the potential to ignite.

"Do you think this happened to you because you are a black girl?" I had wondered myself if that was so, being the only black girl in a town of white people, until Bill Meyers set me straight on the facts.

"The guys were high, "stoned" was the word Bobby's father used." Nancy slowly nodded, studying her glass and understanding all too well, it seemed. "The verbal attack when I was twelve just got worse over the years, I guess, but I don't think the physical attack was motivated by anything other than guys drugged senseless. If Robert Malone had been...the one...well, that would have been different. He called me terrible names. He *exuded* hate toward me. But I found out that the guy arrested and in prison, which is Robert Malone, was not my Bobby's father like I thought he was. Robert's was the face that gave me nightmares afterwards." *Dear God*, I heard Nancy whisper. *You are the girl.*

"What did you say? I am the girl?" I asked, not sure I heard her whispered words correctly. She had spoken to the air. Nancy closed her eyes for a couple seconds, then slowly set her cup on the small white wicker table, and turned on the swing so she was facing me. I did the same. "What girl?" I pressed, feeling something big was about to come up, causing me to feel kind of jittery inside. Nancy rubbed her lips together like *Englishers* do when they put on lipstick. I think she was deciding how to begin.

"I was an intern four years ago at Pleasant View Hospital, while working toward my doctorate. The nurses were so concerned about a very young girl who had been attacked. She was very badly injured. It was touch and go for an evening, but the next day the doctors were certain she'd recover in time, which obviously happened as predicted." She patted my arm. "My medical instructor had told me that it would take extensive counseling for this young girl to recover emotionally. The only person who sat with her was her father, a white man. So, you were that girl, Anna." Tears threatened my eyes, the picture so poignant. "How God has worked this out is just amazing to me!" she added, though far from an exuberant praise.

We let the pieces of the puzzle work their way into place, swinging slowly as we heard dishes clanking and the oven door opening and banging shut. Our feet pushed off in tempo. "I am at a loss for words, Anna. Here I came to help your mother, and well, frankly, you could *both* do with a good listening ear." I agreed. We were a mess, each in our own way. A low rumbling mooing was heard off in a distance and soon a chorus of others echoed. It was a secure, familiar sound. "But," I continued, "Mother's problems don't stem from mine, Nancy. She has a set all her own." *At least I think her problems started way before I came along.*

"Right, I do see that." We continued swinging in silent companionship.

"Anna, you said this was when you and your father grew closer. That is …rather unusual, given the circumstances. How did that happen?"

"Mother was unable to help me in any way. She was sedated for three months, actually. Papa and Aunt Laura were the ones to care for me. I had to drop out of school after finishing just two months of ninth grade." I felt a surge of self-pity, which I had every right to feel. Nancy studied me.

"Did you understand the nature of your attack, seeing you were only fifteen?"

"Not really. My great grandmother and Aunt Laura had to be rather straightforward with me. Things had to be explained, but only to a point. By February I knew I was having a baby, no getting around that fact."

Our conversation ended abruptly as Aunt Laura called us to supper, but we remained seated for several moments after. I had shared some unnerving events and we both had a hard time leaving them hanging mid-air, so to speak. Mother was fussing over the table, concerned the potatoes were cooling down. Nancy gave me a quick sideways hug and we reluctantly left our swing.

The table looked nice with a vase of newly picked miniature sunflowers bending their heads over the rim. We long ago stopped using table cloths since the time Bobby pulled it and we lost our glasses and dishes that evening. Bobby was already in his wooden booster seat, banging his child spoon on his melamine plate. We took our seats, said grace, and started passing the serving dishes. I watched Nancy enjoying her meal with gusto. For such a petite thing she could pack in the mashed potatoes and chicken with gravy, and still have room for pie. She had stuffed her long hair down the back of her blouse so it wouldn't get into her food. Mama and Laura were enthralled with her, and asked about her family life, her boyfriend in Vietnam, even her job. If either was surprised that she was a doctor, there was no sign. Mama asked if we should call her Doctor Widrig. She laughed her endearing laugh and chided us for such formality, saying we better not, or she wouldn't answer!

Mother invited her to come the following Wednesday, which caused Laura to glance at her sister with raised brows. Mother seldom if ever invited anyone for a visit, much less a meal. Things were kind of tight at the farm. We had had to lease out much of the land to Abner Derstine. The herd of dairy cows we sold to Cousin Abram who now managed his own family farm. There was equipment to auction off, and if all went according to plan, we would be able to stay in our house with a little over two acres for gardening and yard. But there was little money to spare. I now worked full-time at Miss Arlene's putting my dream of a singing career out of my mind. Nancy said she'd love to come again next week and wouldn't miss one of mother's good meals for anything. How good to see Mother taking an interest in the kitchen, or in anything, for that matter!

We reluctantly said our good-byes all too soon. We had enjoyed each other's company, and the stress of her job had been wiped from our guest's face. Nancy, when stepping off the porch stairs, turned and winked at me, and I knew she held hope for helping both Mother and me. Even Bobby, who, at our prompting, called her Miss Nancy, started whimpering at her departure, calling out for her to stay. He wanted to show her his pajamas. He wanted her to read his bedtime story. He wanted Miss Nancy to bring him a glass of juice. My little conniver. Always the gazillion excuses for not going to bed. She kissed his dark head and promised to be back soon.

We waved as the little blue Volkswagon threw up dust and faded from sight. As I helped Bobby get ready for bed, I reviewed the evening in my mind and felt an expectation of hope. It had been good to share my life with someone. How much better Mother would feel if she could do the same.

TWENTY-THREE

Bobby was my daring, pumped up four-year-old and there seemed no place on our couple of acres that was not his territory to explore. Oh, I had the energy to keep up. After all I was only twenty. His favorite haunt was the barn. I had not spent much of my childhood exploring its nooks and crannies; it seemed a dismal building that smelled of hay and manure. The sunbeams, relentless tentacles forcing their way through the many seams, lent little light to the area. Dust motes became visible as they floated through these shafts of light. Bobby loved it in there, yet at his tender age I was not going to just leave him on his own. So we both explored. Mama never entered this building, and I remembered Molly's hushed revelation about my father's attack of some unknown man. Molly could get no more out of her mother; it was mysteriously guarded information, if even true.

"Mommy, look!" My pint-sized Amerigo called me over to examine some treasure. Papa had long ago started clearing out the area, but his work had been sadly interrupted, and I saw only wide boards before me with tufts of hay here and there. I had pushed back the massive sliding door, not an easy task with its rusty tracks, but it was enough to give us light and air in the musty earthy place. Being so close to the ground, my little guy, squatting on his haunches, was pointing to something that caught his attention. I came by his side and peered down, following his finger. A ray of late morning sun hit the spot just right and there in a rather large crevice between two floor boards was a piece of something rose and white in color and vaguely familiar. He tried to loosen it with his finger.

"No, Bobby, it may be sharp. Let me find a tool to loosen it." Always intrigued with a "find" from long ago, I hurried to the room off to the side where Papa kept an array of tools on a pegboard, each hanging meticulously from its own hook. A screw driver was on the worktable and I grabbed it, hoping Bobby did not get into mischief as my back was turned.

Returning, I went on my knees and gingerly pried the object out of its vise. Turning it over in my hand I recognized it as a fragment from my mother's everyday dish set, the pink and white design following the circular rim of a dessert plate. Someone had brought her dish into the barn? Bobby, uninterested in such a thing, scampered off to the ladder leading to the hay mow. Frantic from past experience, I had to stop him from climbing, which started a battle of the wills. I quickly tucked the china fragment into my pocket while luring Bobby away from the ladder with a promise of a ride in his child seat strapped on the back of my bike. The piece of china lay forgotten in my pocket, and the oddity of finding such a thing in that place slipped away as quickly as our day. This was a beautiful Saturday with so many possibilities before us.

~

Nancy sat with Mama and me on the porch while Laura attempted to give Bobby a bath after our supper of creamed beef over mashed potatoes, a very German dish which our guest seemed to thoroughly enjoy.

Nancy asked my mother if it was a hard to talk about her husband, seeing as she was only a widow for a year. Mother said that talking about her memories helped with her loss and Nancy smiled. "That is a very healthy sign that you are able to cope with your grief." Mama nodded, but that far-off look entered her averted eyes. The diminishing evening sun filtered in from behind a huge snowy white cloud bank and reflected in the blue orbs of her eyes.

"What are you remembering?" Nancy asked softly. In return, a slow smile played at the thin lips. I wondered if she would answer, half surprised when she did.

"This time of year, Jacob and I would ride our bikes far into the countryside. Canning was exhausting, and Jacob would be in from haying, a messy, itchy job. There was a little waterfall in Souder's Creek and we'd take off our shoes and go in, clothes and all and just sit under the pelting shower. And we'd laugh! There was nothing like that feeling of the water washing us clean, sending the gritty residue of hay and sweat right down the creek bed. I guess it was more like a babbling brook," she smiled with her recollections. Nancy and I sat quietly, living the memory with her, caught up in the mental vision of the youthful lovers sharing a happy time. No baby Anna added to the mix yet, no moodiness, no sullen Papa. Just two young lovers. When did it all change? A silence followed and we waved at two young girls pedaling past, their blue skirts billowing, young laughter leaving a sweet afterthought of those days of childhood.

"Were you newly married?" asked Nancy.

"Yes, that's when Jake first took me there. We'd pedal out there to Souder's in the spring and summer, too. It was our special spot." She called Papa *Jake!* The nickname struck me like hearing *Lizzy* for the first time. "But then things changed and we did not go there ever again," Mama said wistfully. I looked at her, head down, wisps of hair blowing back and forth with the movement of the porch swing. For some reason I felt an unwelcomed sense of shame.

"What changed?" asked our visitor. Once again I noted how soft and caring her voice came across. This answer, if Mama shared more, could lead to some answers for my questions. Silence. Mama brought her head up and there was a puzzled look causing her brows to draw. Her mouth formed a questioning pout.

"I really can't say... Maybe that is when Anna was born..." Nancy steered the conversation back to neutral ground.

"Were you able to continue riding your bikes while you were pregnant?"

"Oh no! No one saw me during my confinement. No one!" Agitation was building. I think my blood pressure rose. This was not a normal response to a long awaited pregnancy between two young married Mennonites. Nancy calmed the imminent storm. Oh, she was good! Nancy stood and stretched, changing the mood instantly.

"I just love your sunflower patch, Elizabeth. It is like faces of the sun smiling down from tall stalks. Will you walk with me over there?" It took Mama a moment to switch gears in her head, but she managed, and because she enjoyed Nancy's company she was eager to prolong the evening. After two hitches to get herself up, she rose from the swing. "Come with us, Anna. Bobby is sound asleep and you know he won't waken easily. The three of us walked to the garden plot near the outbuilding Papa used for repairing things. The huge sunny heads bent down to greet us from a height of six or maybe even seven feet. Nancy was entranced and reached to touch the nubby centers. "Do they have a scent?" she asked. No, replied Mama, but they don't need one. They are the source of her winter feed for the birds. "Are these the seeds?" Nancy asked, fingering the centers.

"Yes, under there," Mama said, patiently, while pointing toward the centers. Mama explained the seeds would fall or scrape out easily as the pods dried after the petals had fallen.

"Did Jacob plant these sunflowers or don't they come back year after year?"

"Some do, but these sunflowers are annuals. Jacob liked seeing a majestic row of them, and they are a happy looking plant. I started the seeds on the inside porch in April."

Nancy shielded her eyes with a cupped hand and surveyed the acreage, stopping as she faced the barn off in a short distance. "May I see your barn? I am fascinated by them." I held my breath. Mama looked to her as if to say, "What barn?" The graying brown hair shook. "I do not like barns."

"Why is that?" Nancy asked nonchalantly, again reaching up to study a sunflower.

"Awful, dirty places." Mama replied curtly. Nancy and I gave each other a raised eyebrow look before following her lead as she turned and once again fled toward the security of the farmhouse with its brick and stone foundation. A sturdy refuge from whatever storms raged in Mama's subconscious.

After Nancy bade her goodbyes, we remained on the porch, Mama and me. We sat in silence. A week ago Aunt Laura had returned to the family farm for harvest time. I missed her terribly. The two of us sat long enough to watch the sun set, listening to the night sounds of the insects, watching the bats swoop from the treetops. When the last vestige of pinkish red dissolved into the far hills we left the porch and resumed the same position inside the living room. Just two single women biding time and a little boy sleeping in the old pantry.

~

Our Ohio Conference, another name for our group of meetings (or what other folks call churches), was proudly organizing a historic society. We were following the model of a similar group in Pennsylvania called the Franconia Conference, which had built a new wing to house archived materials and family heirlooms, some from the Rhine area in Germany, some from Holland, an eclectic mix that truly identifies our heritage.

A historian, one of our own from Franconia, Pennsylvania, came to our aid as we planned and labored over recording each piece of history, every family Bible, every old five-star, log cabin, bear paw or wedding ring quilt, every colorful *fraktur* that told of family events like births and weddings within the borders of bird's wings and tulip petals. He came armed with his own electric typewriter, fancy Brownie camera, and a small tape recorder to capture voices telling stories and singing songs from the *Ausbund*. This gentleman, Mr. Eli Kulp, became particularly engrossed in our local pow-wow doctoring and in signs on fence posts, what he called the traveling man's hieroglyphics.

Unless you are old order Mennonite, the term pow-wow doctoring would cause all kinds of questions to form. I imagine to those outside our Fellowship this sounded rather primitive and tribal, but our elders defied progress and clung to heritage. This was one the old timers believed in with a vengeance. Pow-wow was our old folk magic system. Oh, every traditional Mennonite relied on God and Christ to be sure, but also incorporated powers of good to overtake powers of evil by making use of religious symbols and prayers. Hex signs on barns and horse shoes nailed above doorways meant to charm away any evils that might fall on the animals. Pow-wow doctors, considered gifted by God, were good people in opposition to the *hexerei*, who were the dark evil powers that caused harm. Quaint, but kinda spooky, even if one was raised in the tradition.

I thought Mother would have nothing to do with Mr. Eli Kulp and his gadgets, so I was near shocked that bright September day when, returning from Miss Arlene's, I opened the screen door and saw Mr. Kulp, leaning across the kitchen table holding up a small microphone to my mother's mouth. As I cautiously tip-toed closer, I heard her speaking her childhood Pennsylvania Dutch German: *In*

Namen Gottes des Vaters und des Sohnes, und des Heiligen Geistes...

I came beside her, forced a smile of greeting at our visitor, and, after Mr. Kulp pressed down on the stop recording button, asked Mother what she was doing.

"I am telling Mr. Kulp about the charm that will keep you safe every day." She was literally beaming. Who *was* this woman??

" A *charm*, Mother?"

"Oh, Anna, you know what I mean... more like a prayer to the Father, Son and the Holy Spirit, for our protection. Whoever is stronger than these three may come and do to me as he pleases," she said as if proudly reciting from a scouting manual. I was speechless. How could my mother, who was not considered an old-timer, still remember enough from her childhood to recite in the language of her ancestors? And had she really called it a charm? We lived in 1969, for Pete's Sake!

"Oh Anna, stop staring at me like that. I learned it from your grandmother who learned it from her mother. To ward off rabid dogs, gunshot wounds, knife cuts, and drowning." She laughed. "You know, things like that. We must strive to keep our traditional ways!" She waved an airy hand. "Mr. Kulp wants to record these things for our history, and since I can still remember, I will share." She turned back to our borrowed historian. "What else do you want to know about?" I shook my head. She was downright chipper! Will this woman never stop surprising me?

I left the two of them, while Mother's words branded in my ears: "We must strive to keep our traditional ways." *So what happened to your prayer caps, Mama? And why am I mulatto?*

When Mr. Kulp in his eagerness pressed to see the signs on our fencepost and barn, Mother scurried inside her room like a rabbit chased by a fox. "You talk to him now, Anna. He wants to go to the barn. Leave Bobby to me." So I did. In fact, I was rather excited to see what the man had to say about our carvings in the fence and barn doors. As we walked past the kitchen garden and on toward father's domain, I asked Mr. Kulp about his work. He had graduated from Eastern Mennonite College in Virginia with a major in history and communications. He was older, maybe by nine or ten years, and his hair was receding. Like Molly's, it was a soft brown and was ruffled gently by the breeze. His light blue button shirt was clean but wrinkled, and he was hot as the wet patches revealed under his arms. Sturdy tie up shoes left an interesting tread in the dry dirt of the worn path. He was focused in anticipation of what was to come and was walking at quite a clip. I showed him the fence marking first, still visible on the unpainted beam.

"Mr. Kulp? When do you think these signs were carved here?" I asked as our scholar wrote feverishly in a spiral notebook, aviator sunglasses covering those rather nice brown eyes. He was not a tall man, not like Papa or Cousin Abram, but stood about three inches taller than me, which put him at around 5'7". He was not married, a fact he nonchalantly revealed on his initial visit. He seemed to exude intellectualism, and, if I were honest, was a trifle boring in his single-minded pursuits. Still, every now and again, a nice, shy smile would appear, surprising all of us.

"Well, vagabond language did not originate until the 1930s, so we can guess it has been here maybe thirty years or less." He traced the markings with his fingertips as the sun was hitting the fence just right, displaying the "language" in all its simple glory.

"Right away I can tell you what these mean. This one," he pointed with a ball point pen to what looked like two crescent moon eyes and a big smile, "means you can sleep in the barn." But that did *not* make sense and I told him so. "Honestly, Mr. Kulp, no hobo ever slept here in our barn."

"Ever? Are you certain?" he pressed. He was moving on to the barn door. I scrambled behind. Actually, did I know for sure? What about before I was born, or when I was little. Maybe men slept here and we did not even know it!

"This one means, umm," he stalled on the rectangle with a dot in the center and fiddled with his pencil before propping it behind his ear. "I better look this one up again because I *thought* it meant "Danger - Beware! Brutal man lives here!" But that cannot be right…" He started writing again and talking softly to himself. I looked at the sign- *Beware*! It told poor homeless men- *Danger... danger from a brutal man*...there was only one man who ever lived here...the unwanted memory of Molly's unbelievable tale about my father flashed neon before me. The word "danger" went over and over in my head until I wanted to yell, "NO!" but something deep inside me countered, "*Well, maybe...*" I felt a little queasy.

TWENTY-FOUR

Nancy sat back in her chair, long brown hair behind her ears, tanned legs propped up on an old upholstered foot stool. We had finished our first month of weekly dinners and chat sessions, and I believe she was insightful enough to piece together a few puzzle pieces of our lives, Mama's and mine. Bobby had a long day playing with a little boy Molly was also watching at her house. The change did him good, my rumble tumble guy, to get away from this quiet one-kid home and explore new places, playing tag and catching bugs in a little net. Now he looked contented and relaxed, paging through the old *Childcraft* books I'd found at a flea market. I watched with a smile as his eyes grew heavy.

"So, Anna, have you made any new discoveries?" Nancy asked in a quiet voice while Mother, just out of ear shot in the kitchen, was pressing grapes for her jam. A conical colander in its stand clanked against the table as she mushed the purple fibers with a long wooden pestle.

I had to think, *what had I learned?* So much had happened. "I met Bobby's father, did I tell you that? Oh sure I did, last summer. I don't think I am over that one," I added with a cynical smirk. "I really wondered if he had a heart change that Sunday when Bishop Clark preached or if he went up because he saw me respond." Ah, said like one who believes the world revolves around self. Nancy fingered a tassel on the worn pillow by her elbow. Her pensive mood made me wonder if she thought less of me.

"I know the power of God. He can change a person in a moment, even take away any urgings from addictions," she said. "I've seen it happen more than once. But I understand your skepticism. Just remember that as a Christ-follower you will be called upon to forgive when you feel you shouldn't have to, and if you don't, your heart will not be at peace." *Ouch.*

I was pretty sure I was not at peace so when she asked, "Are you? At peace, I mean," I dismally shook my head. I had only given Bill Meyers lip service that hot summer Sunday, said what he needed to hear, but it hadn't come from my heart. He had been so…pathetic.

How quickly I had let my guard down from that Sunday morning when I could not wait to rid myself of my sins of hatred, to only two hours later when I told Bill I forgave him for his brutal attack on a me and hadn't really meant it. I thought for months that Robert Malone was Bobby's father. In a short moment the rightful father confessed and the ugly reality, which did not fully sink in until a day later, sent me reeling. I accused one man publically, and though the charges were dropped, he was sent to prison with my testimony against him. No matter all the other charges he had against him, I had said he, Robert Malone, attacked me, and looked on him with such hatred. The hatred eating away at me was not even directed against the right man! Robert Malone had called me a liar. Well, I guess I was. No matter that I had been so sure, it was a lie. So, back to Nancy's question about personal discoveries. I was tired of thinking about myself, and instead thought about newsy happenings in our community. The smell of Concord grapes floated out from the kitchen and Bobby's head started to get heavy.

"Mr. Eli Kulp came to town from the Franconia Conference in Pennsylvania. He's helping our church organize a historical society and museum of sorts in the fellowship wing of our church. He was pretty interested in our music, and our way of life which is similar to his."

"Did you sing some songs for him?" Nancy asked, smiling in her relaxed fashion with her head resting on the back of the chair. She now knew of my secret passion.

"As a matter of fact I did, right into his little microphone," I answered squaring my shoulders and puffing up a little. "I'll be famous now for sure, whether in a positive way or not remains to be seen!" We laughed as Mother came to join us, hands purple, stains over her apron, but happy in her progress.

"I just finished twelve pints of grape jam. I love the smell of concord grapes, don't you?" Mother plopped down and let out a big breath. She had little brownish gray curls around her neck which stuck there by sheer sweat. Nancy went in to see the glass masterpieces cooling on the table. We heard a *pop* as the first one sealed, then another in rapid progression. "I love that sound! I want to hear twelve pops!" laughed Mama. Nancy came back to her chair and we sat counting up to eleven. "Well, no problem if one remains unsealed. That will be for our breakfast table in the morning." Mama was pretty in her happiness and smiles, produced by canning preserves, of all things. Personally, I disliked canning and thought it much easier to buy whatever off the shelf at Snyder's market. But the whole process brought such a feeling of accomplishment into my mother's small world that I could hardly voice my negativity.

Bobby had fallen asleep on top of *Childcraft*, Volume One, his pudgy fair cheek resting over his favorite illustration for Eugene Field's poem,"The Sugar Plum Tree." I excused myself to put him to bed. He was so thoroughly spent he did not rouse enough to fight his bed, not even as I pulled his clothes off and struggled to get the limp body into his cotton pajamas. I fought to keep myself from crushing him in my embrace, so urgent was my ache to never let him go. Just like Mama, I rocked him with my body and sang softly until I felt him go limp again in my arms. I lowered him slowly and carefully into his toddler bed, patting his back until I heard his deep sleep breathing resume. Bobby's bedroom was now upstairs with Mama's and mine, and, as I tiptoed down the steps to return to the living room, I smiled at the animation in Mama's voice drifting up the stairway along with the smell of the grapes.

"I felt very honored to help Mr. Kulp with some of our Pennsylvania Dutch traditions. He really got excited about our pow-wow doctors." I entered the room in time to see Nancy's eye brows go up. "Why, yes," Mother chattered on. "I have remembered every one we've had since I was a girl, but that is not hard because the mantle is passed from parent to child, a real gift from God."

"What exactly is a pow-wow doctor?" Nancy asked with hesitancy as if fearing to hear the answer. "Does it have to do with the indigenous native Indian tribes?" That thought seemed to give her a ray of hopefulness as she cocked her head awaiting the reply.

Mama looked blank, as if to say, "What do Indians have to do with us?" "Not at all," she responded, then proceeded to go into depth about the superstitions of our heritage and how charms were used to ward off certain illnesses and calamities. I heard enough the other day to make me uneasy. I know how important it is to keep the legacies from one generation to the next, but this one left me feeling...cold.

"Elizabeth, may I ask you a personal question?" Nancy ventured. My ears perked up. Chuckling, Mama told her she could ask, but might not receive an answer.

"Do you believe in the Lord Jesus Christ as your Lord and Savior?" Mama was taken aback and straightened in her seat. Her posture showed offense since Mennonites do not give air to such personal convictions. Our beliefs went without saying. Nancy was expectantly waiting so the she-bear in my mama rose to the occasion.

"Of course I do! I am a Mennonite and that means I am a believer in Jesus Christ!" Mama replied staunchly, her words hanging in the air.

"Do you still believe in the power of this pow-wow doctoring?" Now Mother cocked her head, looking like a cornered animal.

"Oh, I see where you are going with this. Nancy, I know who the real power in my life is and in the life of our pow-wow doctor. It is the Father, Son and Holy Spirit. Don't you worry about the state of *my* soul. How about you, Nancy? Are you a believer in Jesus Christ?" That was slick, if I do say so myself. My mother turned the tide of the conversation, venturing where few *Mennischt* dare, and she did it as well as the counselor herself, but my friend did not miss a beat.

"Yes, Elizabeth, I truly am. I had a life-changing experience when I was eighteen, just starting at Eastern

Nazarene College." Nancy sat up as she answered. "I gave my entire life into the hands of the Lord, to use me as he saw fit."

"And how does he see fit, Nancy? What are you doing for him now?" Oh my, how would Nancy respond to that loaded question?

"As you know I am a doctor. But I don't specialize in general health of the body. I mostly help people get past mental and emotional issues." There, it was said and said well. I watched Mama for her response.

"Ah, that must be very, um, difficult," she answered carefully. "I just assumed you were a doctor of the ... body, like you English folks seem to need so often." *Ach, low blow, Mama.*

Nancy smiled, accepting the sparring match. "Oh, I am! The mind is the control source of most of our body. I would love to help everyone find peace of mind, therefore have healthier bodies." Mama was quiet now. I looked at her pale thin face, with its pink wash over her cheeks. What was she thinking? Did she wonder if I had an agenda making friends with Nancy and bringing her into our home once a week? Did she think it was because of ... well, her issues, for lack of a better word?

"Yes, I see," Mama finally replied. "That is a very admirable, what you folks call, umm, a career. And I am sure it must help you focus on things other than your fiancé in Vietnam." With these almost thoughtless words, Nancy's bright smile now looked plastered in place. Her face seemed to fade. She closed her eyes and lowered her head. "Oh dear," murmured Mother. "I did not mean to make you sad..." Nancy shook her head, and once again looked at us with forced enthusiasm. "I pray for him all the time," and we nodded in agreement. War left mars and scars all around us. Even the young boy who had innocently bought Robert Malone's red and white '57 Chevy and ended up in court, had been drafted and fallen shortly after. Twice in his young life he had been at the wrong place at the wrong time.

"By the way," I interjected, "Have you heard from Jerry lately?"

"Yes, about a month ago. It is awful there. There is no one he can trust. Some of his friends are losing their minds to drugs and doing wild, crazy things. I pray for him as often as I think of him." She looked burdened and sad. "And that is very often." It was definitely time to get up and move.

"Mama, would you mind if Nancy and I went for a walk?" I asked. *No, go right ahead. You girls need the exercise.* She was tired and would soon be preparing herself to go to bed. The kitchen would have to wait; she would subdue the mess in the morning.

The fall evening was a beauty. We put on our sweaters and walked the periphery of our land, the part that was still ours. The air had that autumn tanginess, a certain smell of leaves and goldenrod, and the feel of crispness that comes with the inevitable onslaught of winter. A streak of orange ran across the western sky. Our hills were rolling and lovely, graceful black curves of landscape in contrast to the glowing sky. We spoke of our shared concern for my mother, of the surmised mental block that was impeding her forward progress toward healing.

We walked in amicable silence for a while before Nancy asked, "Anna, have you heard the new Simon and Garfunkel song that came out after Christmas last year, *Bridge Over Troubled Water*? I replied that I had and it was a great song, one that I often sang along to. "The words really speak to me," she said as I nodded. "I haven't heard you sing, but I'd like to. Can you sing that song as we walk?" Talk of war had brought a somber edge to the peaceful backdrop of our evening.

It was an awkward moment for me at, but I complied because my friend asked it of me. Nancy started singing along, as if we both knew we would be there for one another when needed, a bridge in times of trouble. Any awkward feelings dissipated as we were cloaked in the covert blind of twilight.

When our song was over, Nancy stopped by the fence and leaned into it. After a minute, she spoke with fervency. "No wonder you have a dream, Anna. You are right to want to pursue your singing as a career." She patted my arm and we started walking again. "And I will be here for you, a bridge over your turbulent water. You may need that bridge sooner than you think." I wondered what she meant but did not ask. Later, though, I would think on her words as I snuggled under my warm blanket.

It was now almost dark; the orange streak had disappeared moments ago. Twigs and leaves snapped under our shoes. A dog barked in the distance. Our house looked warm and cozy with a single light burning in the kitchen and one in Mama's room. "Anna, never let anyone take your song away." I thought about those words long after Nancy had gone. I promised myself I wouldn't let that happen. Because if I did, I would have left a gift box wrapped in lovely paper, my name on the top, with an untied bow, wrapped for all time, the contents forever a secret. I'd be crushed if someone did that to me after I took such love and care to send something so precious. *Unwrap your present, Anna, the time has come for you to sing!*

~

LOOK and *LIFE* magazines for 1970 were always propped on the periodical shelf at the library. *LOOK,* especially, was my favorite. I learned much about the current world outside my Mennonite perimeter, digesting the stories and photos of famous people and faraway places. In the December issue, I learned about a jazz singer named Lena Horne. Miss Horne was of mixed ethnicity, a very beautiful, tan-skinned woman. I stared a long time at her pictures. The path to becoming a star had not been easy, not because of her features so much but because of her background. Having made no secret of her ethnicity, she was boycotted from movie sets and broadcast contracts, yet she fought on to banish black/white stereotypes which also made me very uneasy in my mind. With sadness I remembered the name I was called that fateful day when I was twelve, just a little girl. The locker room experience still stabbed at my heart with Tina DeFranco's taunting words regarding my skin color and certain "ethnic" foods. That part I had not even understood until I was in my twenties. So how did Miss Horne handle her personal life? I was hungry to learn about people like me, and these magazines seemed to give me some insight outside my own little world. The large pages were man-handled, proving I was not the only curious one.

We should have been past all these interracial things as twentieth century people, but they were raw issues even in this new decade of the '70s. I needed to know I was not all that unusual and although I had never been to a movie house, I would have liked to watch the films I had read about like *Show Boat* and *Imitation of Life* because of their mulatto themes. Televisions were becoming commonplace in homes of the worldly. I only had my radio and that was enough.

We were steeped in Christmas Eve children's pageant planning. While in Aunt Laura's sewing room, my radio playing as I fashioned angel wings, I heard a sultry voice purr out *Santa Baby*. Terrible words which meant little to me, but such a saucy, fun melody. I was hooked on that jazzy tune. I was careful to sing it away from the house, and still, every time I did so, I felt my ancestors frowning down on me from the heavenly gates. Along with the unacceptability of singing for entertainment, Mennonites do not follow the German tradition of *Sinterklass,* in our old country tongue. True, my parents shared the story of good St. Nick, but all emphasis of the holy day, Christmas, is on the Biblical birth of the Savior. A mulatto singer and actress named Eartha Kitt performed *Santa Baby* and the song became a hit, played often on the radio stations that year. Miss Kitt was a mulatto from the South who made it big in the entertainment industry singing, dancing, and acting, so I was told by Miss Arlene's customer, Linda Cummings. Linda was very worldly (she bought metallic gold buttons with metallic gold thread), and very *schnooty.*

"*What?*" Linda had blurted with her eyes popping, "You've never seen *Batman* on TV??" From her tone of voice I felt insulted and embarrassed and must have worn a very puzzled look. *Bat what?* "Eartha Kitt is the actress who stars as Catwoman," Linda huffed in disbelief. "I can't believe you've never seen a TV show or a movie." She grabbed her small bag as if we contaminated it. "You people are really living in a time warp!" She looked around for moral support, a silly thing to do in a Mennonite store. As she shoved her paper bag in her massive purse, snapping it shut with vigor, she gave me a look of sympathy. "Poor girl, living such a restricted life. I feel sorry for you." Behind her ringed fingers she whispered to me, "You need to see more of the world." With a shake of her head she was out the door. Miss Arlene muttered '*good riddance*' under her breath. That brought a momentary grin to chase away my chagrin.

Trying to calm myself, I forcefully patted wrinkles from some bolts of Christmas prints as I accessed what just took place. Insulted, that's what I was. Miss Arlene must have felt the same snub, but it was directed at me. *Linda Cummings had attacked me like a cat with bared claws. Time warp? You poor woman. I feel sorry for you because I know better than to say hurtful things. You call me a poor soul… Well, I think you are the poor soul, living such a worldly life that you think Christmas is about Eartha Kitts singing "Santa Baby" and oh so shocked that I have not enjoyed watching someone pretend to be a character called "Catwoman"…* the sound of it struck me as *schtupid*. I was shelving the bolts with such a vengeance Miss Arlene could not help but ask me if I was all right. I was mighty hot for the time of year.

As I made my way to the storage room to grab a box of white thread, I became aware of a pivotal change in the direction of my thinking. At least I lived in the real world and faced real life with all its challenges. I had no desire to slip into a world of make believe on a television set. How did anyone have that time to waste anyway, watching a little box as they just…sat? What little I had seen, mostly on the small set at Widrig's, was alarming even if made up. Adults in private embraces, children showing disrespect to elders, even war shows with blood and agony. Mr. Widrig said it was all acting, all fake, as he laughed at my alarm. Yet, hadn't I so coveted doing just that in the school drama production seven very long years ago? I was a far different Anna Moyer than that girl of fifteen. Now, to occasionally hear the news via the resonant voice of Walter Cronkite and to view the footage of war in Vietnam, all this was enough to take my mind off the supremacy of a caring God and set me into agitation. No wonder the Bible says to keep our minds on Christ and to think on things that are pure, just, right, and true. God already took upon himself the awfulness of a broken world. My own little world seemed broken enough much of the time, but I could face it as I remembered how God had always been with me, and would show me his direction for my life. *Please, God, show me soon.*

I began to consider that God's plans for my voice might *not* revolve around earthly or worldly pursuits. In fact, more and more, I hoped not. Why would I want to be part of a world so foreign and so separated from my upbringing and from the *Gemeinde*, our Fellowship? *Santa Baby* lost its appeal...completely. I was changing.

TWENTY-FIVE

"There is something I wanted to tell you last week, Nancy, but couldn't bring it to mind." We sipped coffee, so full after a meal of chicken and dumplings that we could scarcely move. Mother decided Bobby needed bathing, and his wails penetrated the walls like they were rice paper. Nancy giggled after we covered our ears from a piercing scream that sounded like the poor boy was being drawn and quartered. He hated getting his head wet, unless he was in a pool or creek in the summer. "I better talk fast because this is not one for Mama's ears." She nodded and set her cup down. I had the full attention of her bright brown eyes.

"Remember I told you a church historian came from Pennsylvania to help us get a history museum together?"

She nodded. "Sure. What was his name?"

"Eli Kulp. Well, I took him out to our fence and barn to see the hobo markings so he could record them. That was months ago now. He could read the signs pretty well. One meant "you can sleep in barn," another meant "good food." But the one that bothers me is the one he thought meant "Danger- brutal man."

"Oh, my, how exciting!" Nancy shivered with anticipation, but, seeing my grim face, quickly changed her tune. "No, I guess that is not so good. But this Eli was wrong about it, right?"

"I have a terrible feeling he was not wrong about that. You see, uh, my cousin, Molly, told me a while back that Papa almost killed a man in the barn, that there was blood on his hands."

Nancy shifted in her chair and crossed her legs. Her expression grew very serious. "Oh dear... not something a girl wants to hear, especially about her father." She looked right at me. "Do you believe your father could have hurt someone, Anna?"

"Oh, Nancy, I wish I knew what to think! I saw a side to my father that made you not want to cross him, especially when I was a child, but he was a peaceful man, for the most part."

"So, something could have triggered his anger, and, maybe, just maybe, it had to do with the hobos, since one of them marked the fence with that sign, in secret." I had not thought of that exactly, but yes, if that hobo sign meant what Mr. Eli Kulp thought it did, well, it was easy to draw a conclusion. In the depths of my barn jacket was a piece of china, broken and discolored. Then there was the poor man in the snowstorm; such unwarranted cruelty to turn him away. Pieces were fitting together one by one. Did something happen, maybe a robbery? Or drunken behavior, which my father hated? My mind was sifting and sorting. I think I knew I was onto something but it was not crystalizing.

"Anna," Nancy was treading softly now and she lowered her voice as we brought our heads close, "Could something have happened to your mother, say, in the barn? Remember she did not want to take me out there. Could it have had something to do with a hobo?" I just stared at her. Whatever was piecing together in my mind just became a little clearer, like rock candy as it cools. She went on with her theory. "Could your mother have been attacked and then was defended by your father?" What she said was shocking and my head came up as my eyes widened. At the same time I saw Nancy's eyes focus on something past my left shoulder. She leaned back slightly, sucking in her breath and laying her hands palms down on the table. I turned even as I knew my mother was standing there. She had come down the stairs and we were so engrossed with our heads close together that we did not see or hear her steps. I saw Mama's hands doing that thing she did…rubbing her skirt over and over as she rocked slightly on her heels. *How much had she heard?* She loomed over to us, her eyes large and veins protruded from her thin neck. She had heard enough.

"Mama," I said gently in an attempt to dispel her agitation. "Sit here with us." Maybe she hadn't really heard anything. Or, maybe she would open up if Nancy had struck a nerve. No such luck.

"I do not wish to sit." Her hands rubbed incessantly, fingers tense and spread open. "But I do wish to say something." The rocking stopped. "Doctor Widrig, we invited you into our home as a friend, but you have crossed a line, a very serious line." Mama was shaking and as close to fury as I'd ever seen her. "To put such thoughts, such *trash*," she spat the word, "into my daughter's ears will not be easy for me to forgive." She reached past me, taking my cup and saucer. From the force of her shaking I thought the set would be dropped, broken into pieces like this life of ours. I was not even done with my coffee but I guess that did not matter now. Nancy stood and pushed out her chair. "I am sorry. Eliz…"

Mama turned abruptly, her back to Nancy, her staccato movements threatening to topple her good china as she forcefully piled one on top of the other. She whisked out of the dining room. Nancy was obviously dismissed.

"Thank you so much for the delicious dinner, Mrs. Moyer." Nancy called after her, moving closer to the kitchen. "I count you both as my friends and I would not intentionally hurt either of you." Mama ran the dish water, ignoring Nancy's words. My friend turned to me and shrugged. She came back and put an arm over my shoulder as I sat, dumbstruck. "Anna, thank you for being the wonderful person you are," she whispered in my ear. As she withdrew, she held out her hand. Mama had returned to clean up the table. "Mrs. Moyer, may we finish the evening as friends?" Nancy obviously did not want to leave on these unpleasant terms. Mama for the second time in my recollection refused the hand of fellowship. She scurried to the other side of the table to collect Nancy's cup and saucer as if clearing the table was of vital importance, then took off for the kitchen once more. Surely we'd hear a crash of dishes soon. Their survival was questionable.

    I finally found my legs and stood to see Nancy to the door whispering, "I'm so sorry…" Nancy nodded. I added, "She'll come around," but felt little hope for that.

    Silence pursued evening into night. Mother retired early which was her norm. With the lamp was turned off, I crept upstairs to look in on my sleeping boy. His face appeared so different as it was illuminated by the light of the wintery gibbous moon. Had I really conceived this child seven years ago? My life changed in an hour one afternoon? Well, I could not even think of living without him. I left his door slightly ajar, a beam of light settling on the braided blue rug by his bed. Something, a noise outside, maybe, caught my attention. I froze. What was that sound? An animal? I listened. There it was again, coming from my mother's room. I stepped closer, concerned that she might be ill, but again stopped as the sound assaulted my ears once more. It was a cry, an anguished cry, deep and groaning, muffled by a pillow or blanket. My poor mother…my poor dear little mother. If only she could let out whatever was trapped in her. I tiptoed to my room, saddened beyond description.

TWENTY-SIX

God is a master artisan. I have felt and seen this to be true. He is a master at creating possibilities out of impossible scenarios as he works all things, even evil for good, in the lives of his children. Looking back on it all, I see the Masterhand setting up, moving around, and bringing all our craziness into a sane and lovely pattern of reconciliation and deliverance. God works his hardest to bring us back to him and help us through this troubled life. He is our bridge over life's troubled waters, directing us to a place of refuge. Even though it seems we are the only ones affected by personal woes, we have only to look past ourselves to see the bigger and greater picture. Our lives are more interwoven than we could ever imagine.

~

Thinking back on my twenty-second Christmas which arrived in all its beautiful simplicity to our church, I see where the hearts of our families at Hemlock Creek Mennonite Fellowship were especially warm and open to the new decade. The younger generation of Mennonites was embracing newer ways and trying out its wings.

My cousin Esther was to be married on the Sunday before Christmas, and she asked me to stand with her, which I was honored to do, seeing she had only brothers in her immediate family. Cousin Abram played his guitar, a most unusual addition to our traditional service. Our lovely Esther dressed plainly in her Sabbath best and carried her small Bible. Many relatives filled the family's living room, overflowing into the dining area. All was spotless but no holiday decorations or wedding décor greeted the visitors; it was not done in these functional, humble homes.

Esther was on my Moyer side, Father's niece. Once again, like shades of the Moyer reunion, Mother seemed to retreat into herself and I watched family dynamics at work as they fought against her. She quite honestly did not fit into the Moyer clan at all, whether by choice or by circumstance, I did not know. Oh, relatives were civil to her, but warmth was clearly lacking. My great-grandma Minerva Moyer, always the matriarch, greeted everyone in her brusque fashion, melting mother with a glance. Maybe Jacob's choice of a wife had disappointed the family, or Mother's issues assumedly interfered with her role as a suitable helpmate. Whatever the case, I truly felt pity and compassion for my mother. I knew how it felt to be on the outside.

After the ceremony, I noticed the homemade dandelion wine proudly gracing the center of the serving table, now in a simple decanter surrounded by tiny glasses. Sam and John, Eva and Mariah's husbands, being young and restless in this staid social situation, returned several times to the table, and it wasn't for the cherry crumb *kuchen*. Hopefully, they wouldn't have Minerva to answer to in an hour's time.

I enjoyed the company of my three Clemmens cousins: Eva with her tall Sam, now most congenial; Mariah with her carefree, wild John; and Molly on the arm of her new beau, quiet and studious Eugene Hannings. It was a joyous day for all except poor Mother. The young husbands displayed admirable self-restraint, Bobby played well with most of his cousins, and we sang hymns to Abram's guitar. Ample trays of food were a constant temptation and I felt myself growing sleepy as evening approached. I contemplated gathering Bobby and Mother and calling it a day when John spoke of his friend, and I remained in my wooden folding chair, anchored by curiosity, not wanting to miss the news.

"It's the most absurd thing, you know, but he is going to do it," John was saying.

"Do what again?" asked Sam, attempting to hear above the children's laughter over their board game, *Uncle Wiggley*.

"He's going into the ministry." John replied as if he was losing his best friend to the war effort or the mission field in the Congo. Mariah added, "And he was one of your wild pals!"

"Oh, it was like he changed overnight," John went on, "and he wouldn't touch any drink or have a smoke." I sat wondering and waiting to hear a name, but none was offered.

"Who are you talking about, John?" I slipped innocently into the conversation.

"My friend, Bill Meyers. Did you ever meet him, Anna?" I nodded and let them go on with their conversation which had morphed into which jobs were held in great demand, of which the ministry was not one. So, God had done a work in Bill after all. A real true heart change. Nancy was right to give God the benefit of the doubt. I, on the other hand, had shown little mercy and even less faith.

"He's leaving shortly, after the holiday. Good old Bill…"

"Where's he going?" Abram asked.

"He's taking off for our state college to get his general credits, then his plan is to go on to Goshen College for his pastoral training." John shook his head. "Man, I just can't believe it…Bill…a minister! I'll sure miss our good times…"

"Hey! You still have me – I'm wild!" Everyone grew quiet and looked hard at our conservative hard-working Mariah, then the laughter burst out and Mariah giggled, putting her head down in embarrassment. The crowd laughed to her husband's responses of "Yeah, right... Mariah, the wild child!" A blush spread over her face, unaccustomed as she was to such teasing.

Wild Bill. Oh, if they only knew how wild! But that was the old man. Bill had become a new man in the Lord.

How ludicrous.... ironic... and so like God.

~

In the spring of the year, 1970, a series of events brought a strange combination of joy and sorrow. I turned twenty-two and my three cousins and their guys took me out to dinner at a local smorgasbord. It was very seldom I had ever eaten away from my home. We had a great time and laughed over memories as we sat relaxed and comfortable in one another's company, though I must admit the food was in no way comparable to our wonderful Mennonite fare. Still, I was touched by the thoughtfulness in my honor. I was getting used to being the only single in a group of doubles. It seemed that was my destiny.

Unbeknownst to us as we ate and laughed together, the nation was once again in crisis that seemed to build upon itself until an awful monster threatened to dismember our freedoms. That same day, as we unknowingly celebrated, the radio and television stations blared out the awful news of the Kent State shootings. The Ohio National Guard was called to the campus to squelch a student demonstration against President Nixon's Cambodian Campaign. Many felt this would only prolong the war. Sixty-seven bullets were fired in thirteen seconds. The outcome stunned the country and especially those of us living in Ohio. How could this have happened, our students shot on their own campus, here in America, in our own state? Four university students were killed, some of whom were not even participating in the demonstration, and nine were wounded. Bill Meyers was just an innocent bystander who had been knocked down during the mass confusion that followed. Unable to get up, his legs were trampled and he was left lying in the Commons area, as if crushed in a stampede of cattle. Mariah's John told us Bill had totally embraced our Mennonite stand on pacifism, praying for and writing to several school buddies who were fighting over in a small country we had never even heard of until the early '60s. A student journalism photographer captured some of the tragic moments of what was later called The Kent State Massacre, and his gut-wrenching photos were picked up by newspapers. Sometime later one of the library periodicals published a photo of the male student fallen where he had been shot, with a young girl crying out in horror over his body. I don't know what I would have felt had I seen Bill Meyer's body lying wounded or worse yet, dead... with the academic buildings and an American flag waving in the background. It all seemed too great a contradiction.

Mariah, bringing the news the next day, cried on my shoulder, grieving for their friend's state of health and helpless in the face of her husband's anger at God.

Devastated, John Longenecker was full of angry questions over his buddy having received such needless, senseless injuries.

God... Are you there? Where were you? It would have taken one small movement on your part to have kept him safe. Bill Meyers was on your side, God. He wasn't a militant. How can I believe in a God who allows these things to happen to his own. These were John's questions. He was not of our Fellowship, but a fringe part of the Brethren congregation, and did not have much spiritual support during his time of questioning. Mariah, crying over the chaotic state of our world and the senseless bloodshed, was never aware of the fact that she had just told me my child's father had been seriously injured. I held her and rubbed her back and prayed for God's healing touch on his shattered body, and then I wondered why I prayed that. It wasn't as if I liked the guy... but I did feel something, pity maybe, I just didn't know what. After Mariah left to share her sad news with Cousin Abram, I wanted to cloister myself and my son in our home and leave the world behind, like Mother used to do. Once again I wondered what my poor mama had seen or experienced that caused her to close the door of her mind. In our awful world of war and killing, it was a tempting thing to do.

~

God pursued me, as Nancy Widrig's words hauntingly reminded me that an unforgiving heart brings no peace.

When I looked in Bobby's eyes I saw Bill's. *Forgive him, Anna. Forgive him and mean it!*

John Longenecker gave us the updates on Bill's condition. His legs had been broken in several places. Now a wheelchair was his only mobility for the time being, but there was hope for use of his legs in time. John was encouraged to hear that Bill had been accepted into Goshen College where he was determined to start in the fall despite his physical limitations. Kent State was as marked as the red and white Chevy.

Still, God pursued me. Bobby's eyes, Bill's eyes, the color brown with greenish hue in the light, the shape, the dark upper and lower lashes without a curl, windows into the soul. I prayed for Bill's restored health so he could become a good minister. Before I knew it I had prayed for forgiveness for my unforgiveness! Soon I felt compelled, and I mean urgently driven, to write a letter, which a year ago would have been unthinkable. How selfish I had been! Now I believe God pursued me in the name of forgiveness more for Bill's sake than mine. God called him for a purpose and I needed to free him from my hatred and vindictiveness. *He* needed deliverance.

Mariah provided the address. God would not let me have peace of mind until I had settled the score. I did not write a rough draft, I simply got out a sheet of notebook paper and wrote.

Bill, August 8, 1970

This is Anna Moyer. Bobby is fine and growing tall. He started first grade this fall and is a happy though mischievous boy. He gets along well with others and likes picture books, Lincoln Logs, tractors and playing outside, especially in the barn. I think he will be a good farmer someday.

I was sad to hear the news of shooting at your college and I am sorry about your injuries. John told us that you are getting around again and wanting to continue your education to be a pastor. I think that is a real good thing to want to become.

I am so sorry, Bill. Please forgive me for not really forgiving you. But I do now. I have been praying for you. And I am sincere about this. Hope your life turns out well.

Sincerely,
Anna Mae Moyer

Unwanted and uncalled for, the burning tears trickled from my eyes as I folded the paper and slipped it in its envelope, licking the flap. It had not been easy to give up my need for vengeance and my right to hate, but once done, I wondered how I could have held on to such destructive thoughts for so long. It had been like a poison. That night I slept better than I had in a long time, better than Bobby who had a night terror that, from his screams, raised the hair on my arms as I was preparing for bed. Mama slept through it all, which made me grateful for her sleep aid. I held my shaking little one and sang a succession of gentle songs for twenty minutes until he drifted into a jerky sleep. It had been an emotionally draining day, but thankfully sleep no longer eluded me as I was gently embraced in its dreamless dimension of unconsciousness.

TWENTY-SEVEN

It had been three years since I first met Bishop and Rowena Clark. They now pastored in a new facility in the city of Chicago, funded by the different groups of Mennonites in Indiana, Ohio, Pennsylvania, and the state of New York. Their interracial group had grown significantly to include the homeless and fatherless. Bishop Clark, his advanced years taking their toll on his desired energy and unfulfilled plans, had slowed considerably, though his commanding voice projecting God's message still rang strong and true. How our lives came to intersect once again was through the maneuvering of God's hand.

~

I would turn twenty-three in May of 1971, and I was still at home caring for my son and my mother, though Mama needed decreased amounts of care compared to my younger years. Nancy and I had been careful in our approach with her but were not much closer to any answers about my conception or Mama's suspected trauma, though I had my assumptions. I worked full time and had major responsibilities at Miss Arlene's fabric and home décor shop, as she, herself, was showing signs of age, mostly in forms of back and hip pains. Bobby, firmly established in second grade, would turn eight in July. He was keen on Pee Wee baseball and kickball, and climbing trees. Eva and Sam had their first child, a daughter named Jane, and Mariah and John were expecting their first, also. Cousin Abram and his wife were adding yearly to the church nursery roster. Molly and Eugene decided to marry when he received his job promotion and, thankfully, Molly was able to continue caring for Bobby when school days ended. She was saving every bit she could in anticipation of her big day, and practically coveted a lacey, tea-length dress she had spotted in the window of Henninger's dress shop. I think she made some kind of deal to pay weekly increments, so crazy she was to have that dress for her wedding day.

The invitation that renewed my acquaintance with the Clarks arrived in February. Bishop and Rowena Clark were planning a special dedication service in late April, thankful for their new facility and consecrating the building and the services to the glory of God. I was asked to sing a few special songs, to be their guest. The church would pay my travel expenses and a small honorarium. Would I please consider and respond by month's end. I wasted no time thinking on it. After consulting Mama first, then Miss Arlene and Molly, whom I asked to stay overnight at our home for the duration of my trip, I bought a two-way train ticket and all fit into place. Mama fretted. I was going too far away, states away, alone, but I knew this was something I simply had to do.

I traveled on the B & O passenger line to the city of Chicago. Upon arrival I must say I never expected such an eye-opening experience, though I knew this country girl would have her share of reality shocks. Riding the train was stress in itself, but I managed by putting my shyness behind me, asking for directions and help. I watched as other passengers stuck their tickets in the seat slot ahead of them, and followed their lead, my eyes following the conductor as he walked, swaying with feet apart, grabbing and punching the tickets with a paper punch. I saw how some turned the train seats to face the other way to avoid the sun or to have intimate conversation within families.

I was lulled by the rhythm and sway of the train as it rolled on, mile after mile, and thought about the diesel monsters that made their way daily through my town. Now I knew what it was like, riding in one of these massive hunks of smoke-belching metal. I was pushed by the crowd as we herded off the train car at the huge, dirty station in Chicago, and I stood there, my small suitcase in hand, fighting tears. With great relief I heard my name and there was Rowena Clark's smiling face, her arm waved high. Two young men from her church were by her side, there to greet and help me get to the mission building where she and the bishop had their apartment. We boarded a bus to another section of the city. Chicago stunned me. Dayton, Ohio, where I had traveled several years back with my three Clemmens cousins, possessed none of the vast size or scope as this city had, with its huge ethnic diversity and its major gaps from rich sections to the poorest of poor inner city areas. Strange to say, but physically I fit in without question. I could have passed for Rowena's daughter, and was probably thought to be until proper introductions were made.

I had practiced hard to perfect *His Eye is On the Sparrow*, *I Believe*, and *Through it All*, and was scheduled to sing these three songs for two successive services, including the simple hymn, *Just As I Am*, a standard of every Billy Graham crusade, and Bishop Clark's personal favorite.

That first evening, as I stood and made my way to the old piano, slightly and gratingly out of tune, I felt a keen sense of belonging, of doing what I was made to do. I started my song introduction, aware of many eyes upon me: elderly ones at peace with their station in life; young women with little children in need of baths and clean clothes; down and out black men. Dark arms next to white arms and every skin tone in between. Despite my nervous and clammy fingers, my pounding heart that seemed to clog my throat, I sang for all I was worth, messing up on the piano several times, though that did not register a lasting negativity against the songs overall. I felt like part of something big, something outside myself. I heard a wonderfully inspiring message from the good, aging bishop, shook a gazillion pairs of different colors of hands, smiled into umpteen sets of eyes, but the most rewarding surprise was that Rowena and I became fast friends.

"Tell me about your childhood, Anna," she asked as we sat in their small apartment living room the next afternoon with glasses of iced tea. I looked out the window with its metal blinds, seeing another apartment as high up as we were, with geraniums growing in red profusion from two indoor window boxes. A blue blanket was hanging to air from another window next door to the geraniums. It felt like the Clarks lived in the clouds.

"Where do I begin?" I fumbled, trying to formulate a starting place.

"Start at the beginning," was her response. She smiled and I was disarmed, ready to share my innermost secrets. Along with Dr. Nancy Widrig, Rowena Clark would be the only other person who would know so much about my life up to that time. I started with my confusion about being born with black features. I even shared my suppositions about Mama's trauma, and my wonderings about Papa's attack on a vagabond traveler. I talked about the piece of Mama's dessert plate pried from the barn floor, the hobo sign on the fencepost, Papa's blatant disregard for the freezing, starving hobo's welfare, Mama's refusal - or inability - to talk about her pregnancy, and her admission that she was once in a state similar to mine. Yet, for all my readiness to bare my soul and heart, I checked myself before sharing the details about my brutal attack and

Bobby's birth. It was too personal, too private. I wrapped up the whole package with Papa's statement that I was part of Mama but not him. All this I told Rowena as she sat, sipping, and pondering my life with great interest, as though sifting through evidence to solve a great mystery. I felt I was going through a checklist: first this, then that, then this again…the events of my life, or most of them, since age twelve, just a little over a decade ago.

"You have omitted a very important part, Anna." I knew what she wanted to know, and I nodded, once again focusing on the blood-red geraniums, such a strange thing to see amidst brick, brownstone and metal. I had not mentioned my fifteenth year and the living, breathing result.

"You want to know about Bobby." Suddenly, I felt exhausted and my mind was beginning to shut down. I leaned my head on the white doily gracing the back of the chair. He was part of my present life, but his beginnings were not. I had removed them from me. Eight years seemed ages ago. I really did not want to start up on the whole sordid thing. Would it suffice to say God used evil for good?

I lamely offered, "My son Bobby is going to be eight soon, in July, and in second grade already." I smiled trying to work up the energy to go on, if she insisted.

"You were very young. How old when you gave birth?"

"Sixteen, for two months. I was fifteen when I was...I... was...attacked by some white boys. One became...one is...the father of Bobby."

There, it was said. Did I shock my new friend? Would she act differently toward me? I wanted to take a shower, to clean the stain off my life. I rose to take my empty glass to the small galley kitchen with its eating bar built into the outside wall. The sink already had some cups setting on a sink protector. I rinsed my colored glass and gently added it to the collection.

Suddenly it hit me. I was acting just like my poor mama, trying to forget, trying to tune it all out, trying to pretend all was well, and that awfulness never happened. *Oh, Mama! How much more you must have suffered all alone, at a time when your situation was viewed infinitely worse than mine. Or, did you love my biological father and then fight to forget that love ever existed?* That, too, would have been considered...unacceptable, in blatant disregard for maintaining the right fellowship. But, *Lizzy only ever loved Jacob.* These words from Sheriff Mike's mouth were almost audible. Could my mother have fooled so many people? Was she shielding some kind of lie?

I turned and looked directly into the waiting brown eyes of my hostess. I opened my mouth to say something and nothing came. It was impossible to vanish, just disappear. Like my mother, the only route of escape would have been to go into my mind, thereby shutting off any access to an outside world that questioned, probed, or wanted me to go where I did not wish. But I was not my mother, and I could not go that far into myself. Running my hand over my hair, a habit of which I was all too aware, I returned to the cramped but cozy living room, smoothed the chair's white doily and secured the pins that held it in place. Rowena was one unruffled person as she sat calmly finishing her iced tea and…waiting. Waiting for me to continue, maybe? Or, had she given up on discovering any more about my son's existence. I heard myself returning to the conversation in spite of my attempts to shut down.

"Bobby's father was one of the students at Kent State when the militia shot into the crowd of war protestors. He was injured from a fall trying to run away. He got trampled on and his legs were broken." Rowena's brown eyes widened like two amber tiger-eye marbles. For fear of any misunderstanding I blurted, "But there is absolutely nothing between us. No relationship, I mean. Never will be." My words charged out full force. I heard her sigh deeply, exhaling slowly through circled lips. To my relief her expression was gentle and her eyes were glistening with unfallen tears that conveyed her empathy.

"Oh, Dear, I am sorry. Your life has been quite a series of hardships. But my, how you have pressed onward in the face of it all, and how God uses your lovely voice for his glory. You are an amazing young woman," she said with sincerity. I was floored. *Me, an amazing person?* I shook my head in denial. *Nope, not me, I'm just plain Anna Mae Moyer.* I figured I may as well go on.

"I really don't know much about Bill...uh, Bobby's father. He was one of three boys, but only he..." I could not say the words. I looked at the gentle eyes before me and shook my head. I was done. She nodded with great compassion in those eyes which showed a clear view of understanding and nonjudgmental love. I felt very close to her at that moment, and resisted the urge to go into her arms and cry like a little girl.

Rowena did not ask any more questions. We returned to the mission school where I received a tour. Sitting in on a classroom, I realized how these little lives were changed because of God's workers here in a place that was just as challenging as any foreign mission field. Could I do something like this? Could I leave the beautiful, peaceful land of my family and move to a congested, sardine-packed city like Chicago? What if God "called" me, made it clear he wanted me here and my conscience offered no rest until I obeyed? Could I raise my son in a city?

I was asked to sing with the children and had so much fun that I hated to leave after the wonderful hugs. Small arms clung to every part of me. This prompted a yearning to return to Bobby and feel his strong, young arms around my neck, patting my shoulder and back. It was time to return, but the Chicago experience changed me forever.

TWENTY-EIGHT

I had been dreaming. A girlish Cousin Lydia, who was in reality now a matronly mama of two, and I were playing. Clap, clap...Miss Mary Mack, Mack, Mack, all dressed in black, black, black... Clap, clap. Babies cried all around us, but we kept playing, paying no mind to the din. A touch on my shoulder – *You're it!* Cousin Abram? But how did you find me? I'm hiding in a dark place. I've always hidden here. Run, Anna, run! Run for safety. I run, but tread air, my legs like cast iron moorings. The house is dark, no one is home. Where is Mama? Papa?? Panic rises. I am completely alone. I force myself awake, as I've done with each recurring dream. It takes me a moment to orient myself as my heart rate drops back to normal.

I needed Miss Nancy. *Both* of us did.

No, I was not like my mother. I would not go inside myself and trap the memories that made me who I was. The Chicago trip opened my thinking to all the many roads I could follow. Only God knew what was best for the "me" he created. I hated waiting, though. And waiting was just what was required of me. Wait for God's direction. Wait for opportunities to sing. Wait for my son to become more self-sufficient before uprooting, if that was the best direction for us. But the overreaching question that trumped all others was *what about Mama?* That one detail was like my brick wall...impassable. So I waited through the seasons: another birthday, another summer, and yet another fall. Fall. The time of the year when dormant memories threatened to erupt into consciousness. Was my life going to amount to years in Miss Arlene's fabric shop? I loved her but...*was this what God created me to do?*. Still, with each new morning, I would rise from my crumpled bed to start another day, the same as all previous ones.

~

Mama was a plodder. She was getting along finding comfort in her widowhood by volunteering at The Mennonite Historical Society. Her penchant for organization made her a very suitable archivist, and she punctiliously planned two afternoons a week as if she were going to a paying job. She came home fatigued, but more content than when she holed up in the refuge of the house. Often she came through the door so weary she hardly made it through dinner, but she had found a niche for herself. At the newly dedicated historical building, she only had infrequent contact with strangers - quite to her liking I might add - working closely with one or two relatives and a denominational curator. Mr. Eli Kulp also worked at the conference center. He liked our sleepy little town, and decided to make it his home. He had a way of looking at me that I wasn't supposed to notice, but I caught him studying me more than several times and it made me uncomfortable. Anyway, I was pleased with Mama's gradual strides out of her depression, especially since we all thought Papa's death would really shut her down. True, for months we thought we lost her, but back she came to us, a little every day. My mother was certainly a different Elizabeth Moyer than the one I knew as a child. Bobby became central in both our lives, poor little guy. One woman is usually enough for any boy. But my ten-year-old whippersnapper took things in stride, and the three of us became a family nucleus, completed by a host of orbiting aunts, uncles, and cousins.

The waiting game was starting to wear on me. My best, most productive years were passing by, so it seemed. Aunt Laura, still as unmarried as Sheriff Mike, came over at least once a week, carefully watching her sister to gauge her emotional state. I counted Aunt Laura as my friend, too, and we could talk of many things…to a point. There was always a limit, a line we did not cross. But I needed to cross it. I needed to know certain things. Maybe Mama would open up if Aunt Laura were there for support. Could I try again with my mother? Could she finally remember and share what happened the year I was born?

The anniversary of my very own trauma had passed without any notice except my own. It was a ring-around-the-moon evening. A gaggle of forlorn sounding geese was honking overhead. Such a strange mournful sound. I found myself looking upward and saying, "Good-bye," with sadness in my heart. Winter loomed heavy before us, ready to envelop our world in its oppressive mantle of cold and darkness.

November began with a chill that never left. I had taken my time finishing the nighttime routine with Bobby who now stayed up until 8:30. Thankfully, Aunt Laura was spending an overnight with us to help me sew some new skirts and jumpers. Mama was knitting a blue and green striped pullover sweater for Bobby. I finished reading aloud the last chapter of *Brighty of the Grand Canyon*, which turned out to be a favorite for us both. Bobby shivered as I hustled him into warm flannel pajamas imprinted with footballs, baseballs, and basketballs. Laura and I sewed two pairs to get him through the cold season to come. He made a beeline under the covers and whisked them over his head, giggling with his face down in his pillow. I was surprised how long he had grown. His feet almost reached the footboard. I played a drumroll on his back and he laughed, finally coming up for air. I listened to prayers for his Small Fry Football team to win on Friday, for the fifth grade teacher, Miss Yost, to change her mind about giving homework over the weekend, and for his Aunt Molly's wedding which was in two weeks. He prayed she would not forget him. I reassured him that would not happen, but he seemed to think a baby would come and ruin everything. I smiled and kissed the dark curls. *How could a baby ruin anything,* I thought, as I got up from his bed and turned off the light on his nightstand. A stray goose honked dolefully in the night as if to say, "Hey, wait for me. Don't leave me behind!" *I know how you feel, little goose.*

As I tiptoed down the stairs, I saw Mother, her knitting project in its bag by her chair, with her book on her lap as her head sporadically jerked while she nodded off. She had been at work that afternoon and moved slowly, as if inordinately tired, preparing supper. Laura sat in a straight ladderback chair that matched her posture. Her fingers were always moving. One-third of a granny square afghan was emerging as she joined the squares. I sighed and plopped down into the chair that matched the sofa. The ottoman was out of foot's reach and I debated whether to get up to retrieve it. No, better not get too comfy. Now, the question...should I start the conversation down memory lane?

Aunt Laura saved the day. "So, Anna, how were things at the store today? See any old school friends?"

The moment I sat down I began to relax. I yawned and shook my head to clear away the mental cobwebs. "It was a busy day since ladies are planning the Christmas presents they want to sew. And yes, I did see two familiar faces from high school. Ruth Keyser and Jennie Lukens bought fabric for the harvest supper."

"Ah, that Ruth and Jennie...always up to something..." replied Aunt Laura, absentmindedly.

"Oh, and you'll never believe it, but Nancy Widrig came into the store around 3:00."

Laura looked puzzled, showing she did not recall Nancy, but my mother did. I did not say that I had called to meet with her. My mother must have remembered her final, frosty words to my dear friend and counselor. She was wide awake now, watching me.

"You remember Nancy, Mama. She and I became friends when we met at Carl Widrig's funeral. He was her cousin." Laura nodded and did not miss a stitch. Mama closed the book on her lap. The title was appropriate for the season: *T'was Seeding Time* by John Ruth. Uh-oh…was she going to bolt?

"Mama, please think good thoughts about Nancy. I had asked her to come and help us."

"And why would you think we needed help? I thought she came simply as your friend. I felt deceived and that was not like you, Anna."

I sat straighter and looked directly at my mother. Her eyes darted around the room, as if she were deep in thought and not really seeing anything. I used a soft gentle voice, thinking of Nancy's calm approach.

"Mama, I love you very much and I think you are a wonderful person. Don't you want to get healing from the past?" Laura did skip a stitch. I saw her pull out the yarn and start her row of crocheting over again.

"I have no past to get over, Anna. I don't know what you are…"

"I am talking about my birth, about Papa and the man in the barn…"

Laura's hands stopped instantly. Mama just stared at me, her mouth slightly open. The metal tea kettle began its shrill whistle prompting Laura to practically run to the kitchen. Mama watched her leave, her face a picture of complete childlike vulnerability. A blank look came into her eyes.

"Mama, please…tell me….tell me about what happened in the barn before I was born. I found a piece of your china plate stuck in the floor and there is a sign on the …"

"Enough!" I jumped at my aunt's voice, so uncharacteristically sharp it alarmed me, sending my pulse rate soaring. When had I ever seen Laura with such anger etched on her usually calm and gentle face? She stood very tall with her arms locked by her sides, hands clenched.

"Stop, Anna Mae," she said quietly through a firm mouth. "We will talk in a little while, you and me."

She walked over to the rocker and gently took the book from mother's lap, placing it on the end table with its beige doily covering round glass marks in the wood. Then she took my mother's arm. "Come, Lizzy, time for bed." *Lizzy.* Almost a name of endearment, said with such love and compassion, like I heard from Sheriff Mike. A childhood nickname. But my mother was an adult! I sat back and waited again. Always waiting for something. Was Laura going to tell me all? Or would she demand that I never bring it up again. Did she know anything?? If she did not, I would go to Sheriff Mike and force his hand. Within ten minutes the top step creaked, followed by a soft tread. I did not wish to see my aunt's face with such anger directed at me, and was relieved to see its familiar softness had returned.

Laura did not look at me but went through the living room into the kitchen. I heard the sound of cups placed in saucers, of the tea kettle being returned to the stove top. She returned to the living room and placed a saucer, then the cup for me on the long coffee table, the steam filled with the aroma of apple spice. She returned to her straight chair setting her cup on the adjacent stand. Resignation formed on her soft white face, a sigh escaping as she readied herself for whatever was to come. I was shaken. Facing conflict was not second nature. Would this be the day when I found out all? Or nothing. Would the door to my past again slam in my face? I waited, that much I had learned how to do. After several sips, and I could not imagine how she could sip without scorching her tongue, she set the cup down and clasped her veined hands on her lap, finally looking at me.

"Anna, I guess it is time for you to know it all. Your mother does not remember anything, and probably never will. We do not *want* her to." She shifted in her chair, head down, before going on. I wondered who the "we" referred to. My mental cobwebs disappeared with a rush of adrenaline and I sat up straighter. I had waited fifteen long years to reach this point in time.

"Jacob and Elizabeth were so in love, Anna. Everyone knew how deep the love match went between them. In her mind, there was no one but Jacob." So, I was not the product of forbidden love? Now that the door was opening, I found my mind back-pedaling. I was becoming nervous and timid in the face of the revelation I had waited so long to discover. Did I really want to know? What if I could not live with it? The unknown made me squirm. And Laura's wording puzzled me, "in her mind…"

"Love match?" I seemed stuck on her phrasing. I could only think she meant a flame, which Molly would have likened love with.

"They were a perfectly matched pair who seemed to have no disappointments in their new life together," I nodded my understanding, "except in one area," she went on quietly. "They wanted to start a family so badly. Your mother truly ached for a little one in her arms. But no baby came for several years. Her heart was so tender, so warm. Everyone loved sweet and funny Lizzy." Uh-oh, *what* had she done, so desperate for a baby?

Laura smiled with her recollections. As it was hard to see the young Jacob in the older one, so it was with Mother. I had trouble matching Laura's descriptions of a young Lizzy with the woman I knew as Elizabeth Moyer, my mother.

"Your mother loved to laugh and she loved a good time. When we were children, she would goad us outdoors in all kinds of weather just to run across a field, or ride the old Morgan our Papa used to hitch to the buggy. Lizzy was the life of every gathering." Laura's fond smile faded and grew grim as it disappeared altogether. She had little eye contact with me so far, as she searched for the right words. "While growing up, I remember our Mama responding to the traveling hobos' needs with a metal plate of bread and *lottwaerrick*... applebutter," she corrected herself. "There was always some clean hay for an overnight sojourner. Harmless men who had fallen on hard times or simply chose that life of wandering. Always grateful, thanking Mama with toothless smiles." A pause. My parent's grandmother clock, a family heirloom, ticked its steady rhythm and chimed a single *dong* on the half hour after nine. All was quiet.

"Lizzy was not so different from our mama as a *goot* Christian wife. Only, she felt the poor men must be served with her regular china so for at least one day they would feel like a human being, not one fed from the dog's dish."

I knew where this was going. I saw it all plainly before the words came. The hobo signs, the piece of china…

"Aunt Laura, please don't go any farther into this part." I was trembling because I knew for certain now. Just a few more details were needed to fill in the gaps. "Can you jump to the part where Papa was involved?" She leaned her head slightly and gave me a look as if trying to comprehend what I knew, then, after a deep sigh, she continued.

"It was October of 1947." *October*. I should have known. Over and over life changing things happened in this month. Talk about reoccurring details. "The world outside was involved in a terrible war that the whole world was part of. The nation was suffering. But we Mennonite girls were pretty sheltered. We never lacked a meal, or a place to keep warm, or the security of a close family. It is the way of our people. War did not touch our homes because we did not believe in it. But no one is exempt from war. No one. There was a regiment of colored soldiers who fought for our country. They had been treated unfairly and unjustly for all their efforts. One came home with a leg full of shrapnel and found no work in his home city of Pittsburg, so he was traveling west. No income, no resources, no home or family. Elizabeth was kind to this man. She had a heart of pity. He was young and good looking in his way." This was the part I did NOT want to hear. I thought I told her so…but I was trapped in my own curiosity. Was this the man who gave me my features? Was I at long last going to hear about my biological father?

"He had a wonderful voice. He would sit on the porch and sing. I would hear him as I rode up on my bicycle." A certainty settled over me. A large puzzle piece just found its place, its notches and inserts a perfect fit. I slowly nodded in reconciliation. *My father.*

"It sounds like he was here for more than a day?" I asked, seeing the frame around the puzzle and just needing to fill it in.

"He helped your father on the farm to earn a little before heading west again."

"How long?"

"About three weeks. He ate and slept in the barn. Being early October he was comfortable in there." There was a break in the monologue so we sipped our tea in silence. I did not taste a thing. I felt heavy as a brick. No sounds came from the upstairs where Bobby and Elizabeth Lapp Moyer slept in innocence.

"One day, around late afternoon, your father came home early from plowing up the far fields. This is his story, Anna. Your mother could tell us nothing at all. She went dead in her mind about what happened, and still is, so this is Jacob's story." I nodded, full of so much pain already, but needing to "feel the brush."

"Lizzy was not in the house, or in her gardens. Sometimes she went walking down the tractor path to the far pine trees and back, but she was not seen there in the distance. Jacob said he started walking toward the barn when he heard a commotion, and some noises, not screams but, he said, it sounded like Lizzy was crying out like she was hurt. He ran and slid open the door to find his precious Lizzy indeed very much hurt...very...compromised."

She needed another sip, clearly shaken from the retelling. I felt like a silver elm leaf, just as fragile and trembling in the wake of this violent storm.

"You do not have to go on, Aunt Laura," I whispered. "This is too hard for us both." I truly regretted my curiosity. What healing could come of such knowledge? It was too much, too overpowering a poison to our minds. But she was determined. I saw her set her chin, as I had seen before in my mother.

"You have hounded your poor mother in the past, Anna. You have wanted, no – *demanded* - this knowledge and you are going to listen, before you ask the wrong person to get what you want."

I was sincerely chastised, and wanted nothing more than to erase my selfishness and my demanding tendencies. I regretted thinking of going to Sheriff Mike to get my way.

"Mother truly does not remember *anything*?" I asked, my voice sounding small.

"There are times she seems to have some vague recollection, but it does not come to full light. Maybe she could be *forced* to remember, but why would we do that to her? Why bring such pain back into her life for no reason? Does that sound kind to you?"

"It would help her cope with her deep depression..." I replied with a halting voice because now this sounded so lame.

"Does it seem to you she is suffering in her mood swings? Is she hurting you or Bobby with her depression, as you call it?" I had to admit aloud that mother was not like she used to be. She had progressed back into the real world. A slight sound caused me to put a finger to my mouth, silencing our conversation. We listened. Nothing more. Just an old farmhouse with its creaky wood and the ticking of the old German clock. We sat in silence before Laura went on, and now the words began to tumble over themselves.

"Your father lashed out in his sense of betrayal and rage, as any *goot* husband would. But this man started hitting Jacob, harder and harder even as he fell to the barn floor. Of a sudden, Jacob said he heard a terrible crack at the same time his abuser fell backwards. Elizabeth stood with the heavy manure shovel still in her hands, eyes large as plates." My aunt, in the retelling, was the image of misery itself. "Blood," Laura murmured into her lap, "so much blood. How could one man have so much blood?" she shuddered. "His head was cracked open, Anna, wide open." Laura's hands started shaking with the telling of her memories. "Lizzy shook so violently we could do nothing with her except clean her up and put her to bed."

For all I know the clock may as well have stopped ticking. It was a good thing I did not have my tea cup in my hand. It would have shattered in a million pieces, just like I felt at that moment. Imagination had never led me down this path. I gasped as I began to process the picture of this massive puzzle. My fragile pale mother…and that man had been my "father." Where had such strength come from to even heft that shovel in the air?

"What happened then?" I asked in a breathy whisper. I had visions of a police car and ambulance out by the barn.

"Two days later we buried him in the back field."

Dear God! My heart skipped and lodged itself somewhere in my esophagus. "You did not tell *anyone*…?" Laura bent low shaking her head side to side. "Not at the time…" Now I felt crushed. It took a couple seconds to realize the impact of what had been done. I whispered, "He was … My mother kil…" but Laura cut me off with anger in her blazing blue eyes.

"You heard me, Anna. Now you know it all and that is all I will ever say on the sad subject, and you are never to bring it up. Tell your son whatever you deem best when his questions come, but don't tell him all. *Just don't tell him all."*

I could not move. The story that Molly told me was what the family believed, and it ended there. My father had not, but my mother had…and Jacob took the blame. *She only ever loved Jacob.*

I jumped as a series of loud thumps caused my aunt's cup to fall to the floor. We heard a scream from the top of the stairs, a piercing thing, followed by a series of violent bangs against the wall.

"Oh *Gott*, no," Laura pleaded as she quickly rose from her chair, sending it crashing to the floor. The guttural moan was now amplified by Mama repeatedly banging her head against the staircase wall as she sat slumped in her nightgown on the top step. Added to this now were the cries of a frightened child. Once again, Laura was by her older sister's side, kneeling on the stair step, wrapping her in love as if she were a child. Over her shoulder she directed me to get the pill bottle hidden in an upper kitchen cabinet. I did not know any remained. After slipping one into Laura's hand along with the remainder of my tea to wash it down, I left my mama in her sister's care and went to calm my son, whose screams had escalated. It was hours before the house was quiet once more, but the screams and cries echoed in my head. Sleep was not to come to me or my poor aunt. We spoke no more on the subject. The door was closed.

Actions can affect so many for so long a time. God forgives and forgets but we are not God, and forgetting is nigh-on impossible. Who would help us with this massive clean-up? I did not waken Bobby for school the next morning. All was quiet in the house during those long morning hours. I telephoned Miss Arlene and said I would come into work in the afternoon. She asked no questions and I offered no explanations. Now I *did* want to be like my mother. I *did* want to forget the truth I craved for so long. It was not worth the fallout.

~

The blood on her hands had never had opportunity to be wiped clean. My mama had burned, cleaned, and replaced so much in her little world in an effort to remove the stain that tainted her deepest conscience. She had been permitted, or enabled, to sleep through the time after she delivered the blow that killed my "father." All those little hidden bottles on the upper shelf in the right corner kitchen cabinet, those empty reminders of illness that were defying time in the family dump site located at the corner of our property, all aided in keeping Mama from remembering and facing the horrible truth in her life. Had she truly believed she had never been with another man? That I was Jacob's daughter? How strong the mind can be when selecting what to recall.

Dr. Nancy Widrig was our mental and emotional savior. Mama shut down for a solid week after her head-banging epiphany. Maybe those little pills were to blame, maybe not. Whatever the cause, it gave me time to sort through a myriad of feelings, and decide what to do next. I talked often with Nancy to get her professional advice and to lean on her as a friend. As she had said, I needed her as my bridge over troubled waters. I knew nothing about post-traumatic stress syndrome, or bipolar disorder. Even serious depression was not something I knew how to combat, especially in someone as dear and close as my mother. Nancy loved me like a sister and cared for my mother like a daughter, and, gradually, Mama responded. God indeed washes whiter than snow.

Papa, the only man I will ever call Papa, was true to his heritage and had taken care of his own. His line of defense had been to bar the door and let sleeping dogs lie. If he had lived, would we have been able to reach this point of healing, not only for my mother, but for myself and for Aunt Laura?

And what of Laura Lapp? She bore a very weighty secret for over twenty-four years, defending the bubble around her sister's life as protectively as the presidential bodyguard. Would my mother survive this brutal reality attack now that she knew the truth? There again, Great-Grandmother Moyer's words played over in my mind, a reverberating echo that repeated … "Take care of our own…*my* own," and I resolved to daily put on the mantle of caregiver for my little family.

As far as I can tell, only one other person knew my parent's secret and now my secret: the man who called my mother *Lizzy* and protected my family from the very system he was sworn to enforce and defend. Well, that must have cost Sheriff Mike many a sleepless night. Such is the price of love, I guess. Maybe he and Laura had more in common than they realized, but a shared confidence does not a relationship make. Too bad, for they would have made a *goot* couple.

~

As time passed, my mother grew inordinately tired. In fact, she would return home bone-weary after only several hours of volunteer work at her beloved historical society. She was not an old woman and my alarm became more justified when, one evening in August, I hid my head in my pillow to keep her from hearing my uncontainable sobs. She had just shown me a large mass that protruded from her nightgown, her thin body only serving to emphasize the growth which resembled a melon that had lodged in her intestines. I might not know much, but I knew that was not right.

TWENTY-NINE

We tore down the main part of the barn in 1972, leaving the milk house and the granary standing. A group of Amish men dismantled the barn and took the wood away, even the metal roof disappeared. They salvaged all they could with our blessing. Bobby was not going to be a farmer, that became apparent. His interests lay in other areas, like car and engine repairs.

The upper lot was someone else's now, yet I walked to the top corner purposefully that May morning of my twenty-fifth birthday, winded from the uneven ground and the distance. Despite the spring sun warming my back, I felt a rush of melancholy when I found the large flat stone that covered the grave of the man who shared my features and my musical ability. The strangest thing met my eyes: the amazing wild, blue forget-me-nots were growing profusely, weaving their stems past smaller stones and clods of dirt. This once very alive man - was his song my song? The song of a cry for the world to validate his worth as a human?

I raised my face to the sky before turning quickly from this past part of me. Then I turned away from that stone and gathered momentum as I returned to my home, the place where as a child I played with my cousins and hid in the springhouse. Jacob Moyer was my father, for all his "warts and wrinkles," and he held my heart for being the only man in the world I would or could ever call "Father."

Mother passed on, only fifty-one years old, from a female cancer, and at twenty-eight I became the sole owner of the farmhouse and two adjoining acres. Years passed, eight more to be exact, when Bobby left for a life of his own, finishing high school in 1982 and joining the Air Force so he could further his schooling later on. Once again, his dreams were like mine, so non-Mennonite. My life felt torn in two when he boarded that flight for Texas, but as was typical, family gathered around, and I was not left alone to face the occurrences of everyday life that I had shared with my boy for eighteen years. We Mennonites take care of our own, I remember and smile.

I stayed in the family house with a "new" used piano, a tall imposing upright Steinway from the Victorian era, and a cabinet full of sheet music. All kinds and styles from hymns to blues to folk and Broadway tunes. I offered voice and piano lessons for $4 a half hour, but most of my students received about forty-five minutes worth. I had one third-grader exactly like Tommy Heckler who, the minute the clock chimed, popped off the piano stool as if it had zapped his hind side, and off he ran, often leaving something behind like his jacket, but he was not the norm. There was my precious little Melinda, of Amerasian descent, who was adopted by a large family in my church. Ah, the purity of her voice would bring tears if I was not careful. She was assigned the role of the young daughter of Emile in our Rogers & Hammerstein's *South Pacific* production, and she proved the perfect charmer in this, our one and only outdoor production. Recitals were the highlight of my life twice a year and I put my all into them.

One spring all the music performed was from Rogers and Hammerstein's *Oklahoma*, though I toned down the character of Ado Annie quite a bit. The next year featured favorites from *The Sound of Music*. We dressed in period style with each theme, keeping Aunt Laura busy on her new Kenmore cabinet sewing machine. A large scrapbook chronicles the years through photos from parents and an array of local newspaper features. My church also started a drama and musical group, and I was called upon as a resource person. What a progressive change for our fellowship group!

So, over the years, my "children" and I have become quite the celebrities in our own little world of Hemlock Creek, Ohio. I view them all as my own when I smile at the framed Rockwell print of a family tree centered over my piano, a gift from Miss Arlene when she sold her store. My "tree" has reached out to a full and imposing height with its graphed branches leafing in glorious colors of red, orange and yellow. In the Book of Revelation in the *Holy Bible*, the Apostle John writes about the tree of life bearing fruit and its leaves "are for the healing of the nations." I like to think I have helped people of every age to have emotional healing through the power of music.

Sheriff Mike finally married a widow from a neighboring town, and Laura resigned herself to her spinsterhood, as did I. An amusing event occurred when Mr. Eli Kulp, in a moment of bumbling compassion, asked me to marry him. But I knew that was not to be. I was quite content with my life as it was, and told him so ending with a *thank you for your consideration of me*. Silly thing to say. It was an awkward moment for both of us, to say the least.

Bill Meyers stayed true to his word and did not contact Bobby until years later. As a minister in the Mennonite conference in Pennsylvania, he asked my permission to make a connection with his now adult son and I agreed, as it seemed only right. God had truly transported that young man from a cruel, drug-filled lifestyle to one of a moral, upstanding leader. He had recovered from his college injury and walked well with a slight limp, and seven years ago married a faithful Mennonite girl he had met at Goshen College. The name Robert Malone was never heard again.

God must really enjoy orchestrating transformations in human's lives, so clearly evident when I think of myself as a young girl full of hurt and hatred. How my parents' lives had also changed. And Mama? Yes, she lived a rather normal life in her last decade, much to our surprise. She lived her last years well.

It was a joyous day when I received a letter from my dear friend, Nancy Widrig, telling about the wonderful and tearful homecoming of her precious fiancé, Jerry. With her area of expertise she was, indeed, qualified to help with the mental issues he faced as he started his slow assimilation back into society after the atrocities he faced in Vietnam.

We are all in need of a Savior who can change the heart from the inside out. Maybe the life lessons I learned were through the pain of the brush cleaning the wounds. It seems no one is exempt.

Gone were the girlish days when I pined for notoriety as a singer, long since content within myself to sing in my own little world and share the pleasure music brings to the soul. And so, I sang as decade followed decade. Almost every spring until their heavenly admittance, I traveled to Chicago where I sang at the Mission and allowed the Clarks to love me like a daughter.

In the bigger picture, the Reverend Billy Graham carried the good news of Christ to millions of souls. As I write he has celebrated his ninety-fifth birthday, still speaking about Jesus and the love that leads to salvation and eternal life. Wars ended and were replaced with new wars, as were the presidencies. Family reunions came each summer like a well-timed clock. Smiling faces grew older, children continually surprised us as they shot up and became adults under our very noses, as if this were something new. Weddings, births, deaths - all the cycles of life showed up at the reunions. And we shared them.

Life is not meant to be a solo act. Mennonites know this better than anyone. My cousins and I are still close, living not too far apart. Dear cousin Molly and schoolteacher husband Eugene, who live the farthest away, visited last month with their four children in tow. I looked down to see the two incredibly blue eyes of their youngest daughter carefully studying my face. I knew the inevitable questions would come on the ride home. In my mind I could almost hear Molly say in reply, "Oh, that's just Cousin Anna." I smile to myself.

~

EPILOGUE

Fifty years have passed since Martin Luther King Jr. stood before our nation and gave hope for a united equality and a dream of seeing black and white children walk side by side. There have been seven presidents in office since 1970, and after the war in Vietnam my son and I lived through two successive wars and an equal number of military "conflicts," which in my mind is just another name for war. The Mennonites maintained their pacifist stance through it all. The country needed its young farmers, though we were persecuted verbally and monetarily for our unbending stand.

At my writing, we have a black president, bringing to fruition Doctor King's dream of white arms and dark arms side by side on a conference table, at an ice cream counter, on a bus, at a lunch table. My son, Bobby, grew up quickly the first time he heard someone call his mama the *N* word. I did not share too much of our background, but at ten years old he could understand love and acceptance verses hatred, bullying and belittling. I fumbled and stumbled in attempts to plead my case before my ten-year-old boy who never thought I was any different from his classmates' mothers. After all, I was just his mama.

It took years for my story to come to light. By the time Mother started failing, I finally had a story, but I didn't share it. Let the relatives continue to hypothesize. Just last year at one of our final Lapp reunions I overheard a blond, blue-eyed preteen incredulously ask her older sister, "Is that relative a black lady?" The response was "Sshh!" with a swat on the arm. So, it was all mine, this story, *my* story. I carefully preserved it in a box and placed it out of sight. Oh, some of it had to come out for Bobby's sake - but not until later. Later inevitably came when he was sixteen and heartsick over a girl who refused his attentions because of the color of his mama's skin. That got me thinking that maybe my story, actually the Jacob Moyer family story, has some great lessons for others to learn. It is a story of changing times against the backdrop of the unchangeable nature of humans, how good and bad rains down on all alike, and God somehow uses all of it for our good when we allow him his rightful place in our lives. We all need deliverance.

I just wish I had my Papa a while longer so I could tell him I understood now. What I could not fathom as a ten-year-old girl, all the silence, the lack of closeness, and the anger that sometimes came from his quiet mouth, all those things changed after my attack. What he could not do for his wife, he did for me. He would have been a very *goot* father figure for my boy who grew so quickly that he reached adulthood before I did, so it seemed. I am saddened that Bobby does not have many memories of his grandpa. So I have told him stories, and his childhood perception of his grandpa will have to suffice.

~

So, you have stuck with me through my story. Door B has been opened. We must be careful how we judge any of the people in our lives. Don't we all have a story that others could easily criticize? And if our story changes another's perception of us for the worst, what do we do? Do we hide and mold away in a dried-up cocoon of our own making? Where does that get us if we are to view this life as our greatest gift to open and use for good?

I truly hope my story has not brought on pity or, even worse, made me out to be some kind of martyr. Please don't do either of those things to me. God has filled my life with so much good. If the telling of my story has brought some healing or was of some encouragement to you, then I have fulfilled my goal.

Yours truly, *Anna*

In loving memory of three beautiful Sisters, forever in our hearts.